Praise for *Ghost*

"An absorbing and exciting story full of science, sex, and intriguing plot twists."   —*Publishers Weekly*

"Fisher offers a pitch-perfect balance of a cohesive scientific vision with poignant, naked emotion."

—*RT Book Reviews*

"I have a winner! This is a really fun sci-fi romance—with a very cool setup and characters—that I couldn't put down. . . . I loved it!"   —Felicia Day, actress, blogger, and geek

"A won't-let-you-go story . . . Hooked me right up front and kept on twisting and turning all the way to the satisfying end. Fantastic! A wonderful read!"

—Kat Richardson, national bestselling author
of the Greywalker paranormal detective novels

"A heartfelt science-fiction romance with an intriguing mystery, an accessible what-if concept, and a whole lotta chemistry."
—*Heroes and Heartbreakers*

"Grabs you right from the start and doesn't let go. An entrancing, addicting read, it keeps you on the edge of your seat with a fresh and fascinating take on the human/alien problem, while at the same time it seduces you with a poignant love story. It's a psychological thriller, a science-fiction adventure, and an endearing romance all rolled up in one. Highly recommended!"

—Linnea Sinclair, award-winning
author of the Dock Five Universe series

TOR BOOKS BY SHARON LYNN FISHER

Ghost Planet
The Ophelia Prophecy

THE
OPHELIA
PROPHECY

SHARON LYNN FISHER

TOR®

A TOM DOHERTY ASSOCIATES BOOK
NEW YORK

THE OPHELIA PROPHECY

Copyright © 2014 by Sharon Lynn Fisher

A Tor Book
Published by Tom Doherty Associates, LLC
175 Fifth Avenue
New York, NY 10010

www.tor-forge.com

Tor® is a registered trademark of Tom Doherty Associates, LLC.

Library of Congress Cataloging-in-Publication Data

Fisher, Sharon Lynn.
  The Ophelia Prophecy / Sharon Lynn Fisher.—1st Ed.
    p. cm.
  "A Tom Doherty Associates Book."
  ISBN 978-0-7653-7418-9 (trade paperback)
  ISBN 978-1-4299-6055-7 (e-book)
  1. Science fiction.   I. Title.
PS3606.I7769O64 2014
813'.6—dc23

                                        2013025944

Tor books may be purchased for educational, business, or promotional use. For information on bulk purchases, please contact Macmillan Corporate and Premium Sales Department at 1-800-221-7945, extension 5442, or write specialmarkets@macmillan.com.

First Edition: April 2014

Printed in the United States of America

0 9 8 7 6 5 4 3 2 1

For Debbi and Laurie:
indispensible betas, devoted fans, dear friends

ACKNOWLEDGMENTS

The second book is harder than the first. There are expectations to live up to—your own and everyone else's. There's the fact that while you're writing the second, you're still working on copyedits and galleys for the first (and later on there's the release and blog tour, ongoing promotional activities, and so on ad infinitum . . .).

I guess what I'm saying is you need a lot of help. Or at least I did.

But before I get to that, a few technical notes and acknowledgments . . .

This book twisted my brain in all sorts of cool new directions. For themes in the book, I'm grateful for inspiration from Mary Shelley and her dark tale of a man-made creature spurned by his creator. I'm grateful to Emily Anthes and *her* book, also inspired by Shelley (at least in title), *Frankenstein's Cat: Cuddling Up to Biotech's Brave New Beasts*. Though it would have greatly simplified my research had this book been released before I wrote mine, I'm really glad it came out in time to help me do some tweaking. Also, in the early writing stages I attended an informative seminar held by ScienceOnlineSeattle— I was probably the only person in the room whose eyes lit up when they started talking about the perceived potential for Open Science to go horribly wrong. It was my first exposure to terms like "garage bio" and "DIY bio."

Regarding locations in my book . . . Though I stuck as close to the real world as I could in describing them, I had my way with geography and landmarks (at least to some extent) in Letterfrack, County Galway, Ireland; Moab, Utah; Arches National Park (Utah); and Granada, Spain. I have fond memories of visiting all these places, mean them no disrespect, and hope they shall forgive me.

On a final research note, many thanks to Michel Navedo for fielding random questions about Spanish.

And now for the beautiful people in my life who helped make this book possible . . .

At Writers House . . . My agent, Robin Rue, who always listens, gives great advice, and once called me "very well-mannered." I think I laughed about that for three days. Also Beth Miller, who is a lightning-fast e-mail responder and does her best to answer even the oddest questions.

At Tor . . . My editor, Whitney Ross, who is unfailingly kind and supportive. Thank you for going to bat for me, and for making my books better. My publicist, Leah Withers, another expert at fielding odd questions—thank you for holding my hand during my first blog tour.

Debbi Murray and Laurie Green . . . for eagerness and enthusiasm that keep me going on the hard days. For making my books better.

MaryEllen DiGennaro and Lisa Polec, for hand-holding and support during scary times this year, and for helping take care of me, body and mind.

For generous moral support and love during the writing of this book: Melissa Watkins, Donna Frelick, Mark Gleave, Vanessa Barnveld, Dominic Groves, and Rick and Kathy Cissna. For distraction when I needed it: Buco e Beppo and Terris Patterson.

For tremendous support of my first Tor book, *Ghost Planet*: authors Heather Massey and Willa Blair.

For keeping me limber in body, heart, and mind: yoga instructors Tracy Hodgeman and Morgan Kellock, and also the Kadampa Meditation Center Washington.

For going above and beyond to support me in meeting my deadlines, for being a Faraday shield in my lightning storms, and for love—always for love: Jason Knox.

And finally, my darling Selah, who never lets me forget, "If you don't believe in things, you'll never look for them." When she goes to live with the fairies, I hope she'll always remember how much her mamma loves her.

I ought to be thy Adam,
but I am rather the fallen angel.

—Mary Shelley, *Frankenstein*

THE
OPHELIA
PROPHECY

ENEMY HANDS

Water pooled around Asha's hips, soaking her thin cotton dress.
She studied the glimmering surface of the lake, and the rocky
hillside looming on the opposite side.

The reservoir. How did I get here?

Closing her eyes, she pressed her fingers to her temples. The
last thing she remembered was climbing to the roof of the Archive with her father. It was a beautiful fall evening, and they'd
planned to picnic and watch the sunset. She'd stepped off the
ladder onto the corrugated, whitewashed metal, and then . . .

Sleep, Ophelia.

She grasped at the words as they breezed across her consciousness. They had the ring of command, yet she had no
memory of who had spoken them, or why.

A masculine moan sounded, so close she rolled into a crouch
and skittered into the shallow water. The lithe movement of
her own body surprised her almost as much as the unexpected
voice.

Just beyond the depression she'd left on the beach, a naked form stirred. A stranger. His gaze riveted on her. He sat up straight, fists digging into the sand. No, *not* sand. His body rested on a bed of some soft, fibrous material.

She remembered the flimsy dress—now wet and clinging to her body—and hugged her bent legs, concealing herself as best she could. Her heart pounded against her thighs.

"Who are you?" they both demanded.

So the confusion was mutual.

"You first," he said. A command, not a courtesy.

She hesitated. The man now seemed familiar—something about the eyes. They curved down at the inside corners, making them appear to slant under his dark, arched eyebrows. But she couldn't place him.

He rose to a crouch, eyes moving over her like an extension of his arms, prying at the locked arms that concealed her body from him.

She reached up to release the clip that held her coiled hair to the back of her head, thinking she would cover herself with it. She gasped to discover her heavy tresses were gone.

Tears of confusion welled in her eyes. Fear knotted her stomach.

"What's your name?" the stranger insisted.

"Asha," she whispered, uncertain. There'd been another name a moment ago. A name that had seemed to mean something. Her throat tightened, strangling her words, as she said, "I don't understand."

"What are you doing here?"

She raised her eyes to his face, shrinking from the heat of his gaze. "I don't know."

His eyes bored into hers, probing for the thoughts behind them. He frowned, brow furrowing with doubt. *He doesn't believe me.*

"Who are *you*?" she repeated, indignation nudging past the fear that gripped her.

He slid his hands up his shoulders to rub his neck, baring the hard lines of his stomach, revealing pale marks under either side of his rib cage. *Scars.*

"Paxton," he said. One hand moved to the back of his head, and he winced. He probed the sore spot with his fingers.

"Why are you here?"

He raised an eyebrow. "I don't know."

She glanced again at the fibrous nest. "What's that?"

"Carapace."

She blinked at him, no more enlightened than before. Before she could question him further, he rose to his feet, scanning the horizon. Her eyes lingered on the marks below his ribs. She glanced away before her gaze could slip lower.

He stood so long—motionless and studying the edge of the sky—she began to think he'd forgotten her. His composure was troubling. There was a shared mystery here, clearly, but they were not equal participants.

"How can you be so calm?" she asked, voice lifting with anxiety. "Do you know something I don't? Has this kind of thing happened to you before?"

Paxton glanced down at the nest. "Yes."

She waited for him to explain, but the low whine of an approaching ship changed the subject. Panic jolted her as the black beetle hummed into view, dragging its own reflection across the surface of the lake.

She sprang to her feet. "That's an enemy ship!"

The war was over, but the Manti ruled the air, still keeping tabs on the last dregs of humanity. Citizens of Sanctuary were forbidden to wander away from the city—and the reservoir marked the boundary.

"We need to go!" she cried.

Again his eyes skewered her to the spot. "No need. That's my ship."

"Your ship? I don't . . ."

And then suddenly she *did*. She sidestepped a couple meters down the beach, gaze flitting between ship and enemy.

Overhead, the beetle whirred to rest, cupped wings lifting to allow a controlled vertical landing. With a series of loud clicks it nestled into the sand, hover gear lowering and locking back against the hull. The skin of the vessel was lusterless and black—a secreted resin that looked like rubber. She watched the hull lighten from jet to blond, until it was almost invisible against the sand.

"Pax, you okay?" The feminine voice came from the ship.

"I'm okay," called Asha's companion. "Drop the ramp."

"Who's that with you?" the voice asked.

Paxton frowned, glancing at Asha. "I was hoping you could tell me."

Pax could see the woman was ready to bolt. He could *feel* it.

She was a wisp of a girl. Narrow shoulders. Graceful limbs. Cropped brown hair—unruly except where it was tucked behind her ears—and round eyes the color of coffee beans. Despite her fair complexion, sun exposure had stained her arms and shoulders a light copper. His eyes explored the curve and swell of flesh exposed by the threadbare dress. His fingers twitched at his hips.

"Whoever she is," his pilot continued over the com, "I can smell from here she's scared half to death."

"I know, Iris. Drop the ramp."

"Lord of the goddamn *flies*, Pax, you're not thinking of bringing her on board."

"Why wouldn't I?"

"Because obviously it's a trap. Your carapace was activated. Something went wrong down there."

"Obviously," he said, rubbing at the knot on the back of his head. He stared at the woman, and she took another step back. "But short of exploding, I'm not sure what she can do to us."

"Well, for starters, *explode*."

He gave a groan of impatience. "*Banshee* can scan her for internal com or explosive devices. Besides that, she might have the answers I don't, so drop the fucking ramp, Iris, because this is no place to be arguing about this."

The ship's boarding ramp opened with a thunk and lowered to the sand.

He took a step toward Asha and held out his hand. "I'm not going to hurt you."

She stared like he was a snake. Her gaze drifted for the third time to the scars on his abdomen. Something prickly and unpleasant rolled in his stomach.

"Come with me," he ordered.

Like hell, was the reply conveyed by her expression.

No time for this. Pax lunged for her.

A moment later he was flat on his back, staring at blue sky, trying to reactivate his diaphragm. *What the fuck?*

He turned his head, watching the woman run along the water's edge.

"Want me to catch her for you, Brother?" Iris taunted over Banshee's com.

Growling in irritation, he jumped up and bolted after her.

What Pax lacked in the more exotic of his family's genetic advantages, he made up for in strength. The woman was stronger and faster than she looked, but he caught her in less than a minute. She shrieked as he hoisted her over his shoulder.

"Hurt me and I'll hurt you back," he menaced, curving his arm over her hips.

Her teeth sank into the soft skin just below his ribs.

Pax seized her around the waist and dumped her onto the sand, falling on top of her. Blood smeared her lips—*his* blood. He caged her between his legs, gripping her wrists in his hands. He wouldn't underestimate her again.

"I warned you."

Pax dropped his face to her neck, breathing deeply. He'd only meant to confirm she wasn't transgenic—modified DNA didn't always manifest in obvious ways—but instead he got a nose full of something else. His Manti senses told him that mating with her now would very likely produce offspring.

His nose grazed her cheek without any conscious impulse of his own. Her chest rose and fell with her panicked breathing, her breasts moving against him, making everything worse. He pressed against the leg she'd raised between them, hardening so fast it hurt.

She gave a horrified cry and writhed against him, waking him from the trance of arousal.

You're not an animal! Pax strained for control. He understood the biology. He knew that pheromones were to blame, and the inherited mutation that enhanced his sensitivity to them. But his understanding did nothing to decrease his drive.

Through no fault of his own—through the fault of humans, in fact—he *was* an animal. At least part of him was, and sometimes his preternatural urges and abilities flared beyond his control.

He sucked in ragged breaths as he fought his body, fought his instincts. But god, the *smell* of her . . . He released her wrists and rolled her onto her stomach, ducking his head to inhale the scent at the nape of her slender neck, just below the hairline.

She was human, no question. And that was unfortunate. Because through the red haze of arousal he could feel his body *tuning* to her in a way that it should not. The shock of this discovery weakened him—for only a moment, but it was a moment too long.

The woman braced her arms and legs against the ground and heaved her body upward. The unanticipated movement toppled him, and she scooted away and scrambled across the sand.

But she made it no farther than the pair of black boots that planted themselves in her path.

Pax followed the line of the new arrival's long and lean body, his eyes meeting hers. Iris frowned.

"Aren't you the one who told me agitation makes a female more likely to chew off the male's head?"

Sighing, he let his head fall back in the sand. "She's human, Iris."

"I wasn't talking about *her*."

The impulse to run fired impotently. Asha's limbs had frozen with shock.

She suddenly understood the resurrection of archaic terminology like "changeling" and "fae." For those who didn't know, didn't understand, or chose not to believe what these beings really were—next-generation byproducts of unsanctioned but well-funded biohacker projects—it probably seemed the only plausible explanation.

The inhabitants of Sanctuary lived a cloistered life. As an archivist, Asha had seen hundreds of images, but images were easily enhanced. Exaggerated.

But Iris was . . . devastatingly real.

Her exquisite face—small and pointed, dominated by large, pearlescent green eyes—was framed by a rigid, shield-shaped hood as brightly green as summer grass. The hood merged with her shoulders, and what was below, Asha had thought at first to be part of her costume—a set of elongated wings, the same color and texture as the hood. They lifted and settled, adjusting slightly with every movement she made.

As Iris strode toward Paxton, Asha noticed the Manti woman's arms, slender and tapered like any woman's—except for the row of spikes running from elbow to pinky finger.

Humanity referred to its enemy generically as Manti, though genetic experimentation had involved DNA from a variety of species. But Iris *was* mantis. Darkly alien—darkly *other*— with a beauty born of nightmares.

According to legend, a single creature like this one had triggered the fall of humanity. And yet at the moment it was the male Asha feared most.

Asha shifted her body slowly, crouching as she considered her next move. Paxton detected the motion, and his gaze cut her direction. She noted the rise and fall of his chest, his still-labored breathing. She had no idea why her body was suddenly capable of amazing feats, but she didn't dare run from him again. She wouldn't give him another excuse to grab her.

The Manti woman knelt beside him. "You'd better rethink this, Brother. God knows I hate them, but I don't want to see you . . ."

As Iris hesitated, Pax's gaze slipped from Asha.

"Think of your mother," Iris urged him.

His eyes flashed. "Do I ever *stop* thinking of her? I'm not Father."

"I know." Iris's hand crept up, fingers combing through his short, dark hair. Some of the tension in his face released. "I know you don't want it. But if she's on the ship with us . . . Can you control it?"

His features grayed in the bright sunlight, but he said, "I can control it."

The sister frowned. "I don't like this. Your head is still clouded with *mating*."

Asha's heart took flight over the sand, wondering why the rest of her didn't follow. She remained frozen, hoping her new talents included blending against the beach like the ship.

Iris rose, wings nestling close against her clothespin form. She held out a hand and pulled Paxton to his feet. The siblings were nearly the same height, and both taller than Asha.

"I need to find out what she knows."

Iris started for the ship, resigned. "What are we going to do with her?"

"I want you to lock her in your quarters."

Iris stopped, turning slowly. "You better be joking."

"Just *do* it, Iris," he grumbled.

Her frown deepened and she gave a curt nod. "My lord."

He rolled his eyes at her servile tone and glanced at Asha. "Go with Iris," he ordered.

"Don't do this," Asha pleaded, her voice choked with fear. "I don't know *anything*."

But she did know something. She knew if she got on that ship she'd never see her home again.

BANSHEE

When Iris turned her scowl Asha's direction, Asha rose to her feet before anyone else could lay hands on her. She was no match for Paxton alone, and she was certainly no match for the pair of them.

She started toward the loading ramp, her enemies trailing behind her, and ascended into the mouth of the monster. The Manti had learned from and quickly surpassed their human creators, using extreme biomimicry techniques to develop technologies that were both functional and fantastic. The ship was a perfect example.

Inside it was cool and dark, like a cave in the desert. Chillbumps rose on her arms, creeping up between her shoulder blades to her neck.

After a few steps she stopped, forward momentum arrested by her instincts shouting that she should not be here.

"Keep moving," called Paxton from the ramp.

"She needs more light," muttered Iris. "Banshee?"

A pair of luminescent bursts brightened the corridor on either side of Asha, startling her. The light gave her skin a greenish cast, like Iris's.

Paxton drew up even with his sister. "Give her some clothes and confine her. I'll get us out of here."

Iris lifted an eyebrow. "You're suggesting she should wear mine?" Her form-hugging crepe dress was completely open at the back to accommodate the unique aspects of her physique.

Paxton simply frowned and motioned for them to follow.

Asha kept close to Iris as they continued down the corridor, ship vibrating rhythmically beneath her feet like a contented cat. The light circles traveled alongside her, revealing the green, veined pattern of the membrane that covered every surface.

Paxton stopped in front of a more rigid-looking plate, running his palm along the surface. A watery pulse sounded, and the plate swung in an upward arc away from a doorway.

Asha hovered just inside while he crossed the room to a trunk at the foot of what seemed an overlarge bed for such a small ship. She marveled at how unruffled he seemed by the fact he was naked. She felt completely exposed even in the flimsy white dress.

He rummaged a pair of dark, form-fitting pants from the trunk and pulled them over his hips, then tugged a green mesh shirt over his head. The fabric of the shirt had a pattern of alternating solid and transparent leaves that revealed ribbons of chest and abdomen—and somehow managed to be more suggestive than his nakedness.

He finished by shoving his feet into boots and sticking his fingers in his eyes.

"I hate these damn things," he grumbled, pitching something into a bin on the floor.

Paxton looked up at Iris, and Asha gasped. His eyes were

no longer brown, but the same pearlescent green of his sister's, though more human-sized and deeply set. The light eyes—contrasted against olive flesh and heavy, dark brows—blended an alien quality with his intense good looks.

It occurred to Asha that he'd gone to some trouble to pass as human—the colored lenses, the symmetrical scarring on his torso hinting at the possibility some part of him had been removed. But why?

Paxton ran a hand through his hair. "How long was I gone?"

"Let's talk later," Iris replied. She crossed her arms and studied his face. "I was worried."

The softness in the look he gave his sister was hard to reconcile with the dark, desperate hunger of the man who'd attacked Asha. Even as the thought crossed her mind his gaze shifted to her, and the predatory intensity returned. She pressed her back against the wall, hoping Iris's maternal attitude toward her brother would continue to shield her as well.

"Take what you need," Paxton said, waving at the trunk. "Secure her out of my sight and meet me on the bridge."

He started for the door, and Asha slid along the wall, out of his path.

"Last chance, Pax," called Iris, and he stopped and turned. "This decision has consequences."

Paxton fixed his eyes on Asha. "I know it does. But it's too late to second-guess now."

Asha shivered and pressed harder against the wall, preparing to spring to Iris's side. Another watery pulse sounded, very near her ear, and she did just that. But Iris—startled by the sudden movement—gave a sharp hiss, and her wings rose perpendicular from her body.

Asha hung between the siblings. She clenched her fists at her sides, bemoaning the lack of defensive positions in this house of horrors. Noticing Paxton's attention focused on the wall, she followed his gaze and saw several lines of text had materialized where her body had rested.

INJURY ANALYSIS
Left wrist: Stress fracture with contusion
ALERTS: Elevated adrenaline and progesterone levels

Asha touched her throbbing wrist—the pain had been no more than a peripheral distraction until now. A pale blue smudge spread over the flesh at her pulse point.

Hurt me and I'll hurt you back—a flag for the file her brain was compiling on Paxton. He didn't make idle threats.

Though the Manti's grip could certainly have caused the bruising, the break had probably happened when she levered his much larger form off her back. How had she managed *that*? Probably had something to do with "elevated adrenaline."

Paxton's frown deepened. "Do you think you could—?"

"I'll look at it," Iris sighed. "You know you're bleeding, Brother?"

"And someone's taken a hammer to the back of my skull." He rubbed the spot again as he turned for the door. "I'll be on the bridge."

When he was gone, Iris reached for a clasp at her neck, and Asha watched her lift the rigid hood from her shoulders, placing it on the bed. Then she removed two leather sleeves from her belt, and she fitted one to each forearm, strapping them into place to cover the spikes. The fact that the spikes *were* part of her physiology erased any relief Asha felt about the hood.

Iris knelt next to the chest, sifting through Pax's clothing with her long, delicate hands. She was an amalgamation of two vastly different life-forms, and yet her movements were controlled and graceful. Harmonious. It was easier to imagine her a displaced member of some ancient, highly advanced civilization—only Asha was the one who had been displaced.

Maybe the damage was all inside. Many had speculated about the long-term psychological effects of transgenic experimentation, but there'd been no new research since the Bio Holocaust. There was no one left to *do* the research.

If there was such a thing as a Manti expert, Asha was it—the only archivist who focused almost exclusively on the genesis of the Manti, and the Bio Holocaust that eventually wiped out their creators.

"This will have to do," said Iris, handing Asha a shirt and pants.

The shirt was made of a stretchy black fabric and fit well enough. The pants were lightweight and loose, barely clinging to her pelvic bones. She cinched them tighter with the drawstring, groaning at the pain the effort caused her, and rolled the legs to keep from walking on them. She breathed a little easier now that she wasn't so exposed.

Iris picked up a box from the nightstand, examining rows of amber jars before plucking one out. She motioned for Asha to sit down on the bed.

Asha hung back. Iris had given Asha little reason to fear her. But there was a disturbing lack of emotion in those alien eyes, and she looked like she could be lethal if she chose.

"I don't need to trick you to hurt you," said the bug woman.

That was true enough. Asha moved to the bed and sat down, sucking in a breath as Iris took hold of her left hand.

"Ah, Pax," Iris murmured, running a fingertip over the bruise.

Iris dabbed ointment from the jar and gently smeared it over Asha's wrist.

"There are microorganisms in this salve. They'll penetrate your skin and heal the bone faster. There's a numbing agent as well."

Asha stared at her, thinking about humanity's most recent brush with Manti microorganisms.

"It—" Asha swallowed, giving her wrist an involuntary tug. "Will it work on me?"

Iris smiled dryly. "We're not as different as you like to believe."

Next Iris drew a roll of gauze from the box and wrapped her wrist and hand. The wrapping felt cold and damp, and soothed the ache. Moments later it had dried and hardened to a flesh-colored, protective cast.

"Thank you," said Asha, flexing her fingers. She heard the scrape of the lid closing back over the jar, and glanced at Iris. "And thank you for trying to—to help me, earlier."

Iris replaced the box on the nightstand. "I did that for Pax." Her tone flung cold water over Asha's gratitude. "My brother was not himself."

Asha closed her mouth in time to stop the retort on her lips: Then what exactly *was* he? She recalled her earlier thought: *Maybe the damage is all inside.* The exchange between the siblings on the beach had indicated the brother was at least to some degree in conflict with his impulses.

"Come with me." Iris crossed to the door. "Pax wants you to wait in my quarters until he's ready to question you."

Unfortunately he'd not been conflicted about his decision to take her from Sanctuary. There appeared to be no likelihood of escape through Iris. And no sign of her missing memories. All of which left her feeling close to hopeless about the final outcome of this encounter with her enemy.

"Banshee," said Pax, sinking against the back of his chair with a hard sigh, "search your image database for the woman on board. Report any matches."

"Yes, Captain," trilled the ship.

While Banshee scanned image banks, Pax squeezed his eyes closed against the images in his own brain. The lithe, athletic body exposed by the gauzy wet dress. The full lips and warm, round eyes. The way she carried herself—like she was both frightened of him and not.

He shook his head. Iris had been right; what he was doing was dangerous. His body was effective at countering most kinds of attack, but like his father he was vulnerable to this one. Unlike his father, he'd root that part out of himself if he could.

"Banshee."

"Yes, Captain."

How to make all this understandable to a machine? A partly *alive* machine, granted, but hardly sophisticated enough to accurately process the command he was about to give.

"Banshee, I want you to protect the human woman from attack while she is on board."

Seconds ticked by as the ship conducted its version of thinking.

"Does this order include yourself, Captain?"

Pax understood the AI's confusion. If he didn't want Asha attacked, why not refrain from attacking her?

"Yes, especially me, Banshee. The chemicals in my body, and the ones in hers . . . they may cause me to . . ."

He groaned, rubbing his temples. Would he really do it? If his senses were flooded with her, would he be blind to her resistance? Deaf to pleas for mercy? He thought of his mother. How frightened she must have been, attacked by her enemy. Bearing his child in a strange city.

"You don't wish to mate with the human woman," replied Banshee, understanding the situation more accurately than Pax had expected.

"That's right, I don't." *If only that were true.* "But I may try.

I want you to prevent it. Do you understand? If that happens, Iris is in charge. Until I'm . . . myself again."

"Yes, Captain."

It was the best he could do for now. And it would get easier. He'd caught the woman at an unfortunate time of her cycle. Her body was firing all sorts of signals she most likely wasn't even aware of—it was a difference between human and Manti women. In a day or so she'd be safe from him.

But would he be safe from *her*? He tried not to think about what else had happened on the beach. Something more than his mating drive, which he'd felt before. The new sensation had taken him over completely, increasing his desire to mate with her, yet also arousing his empathy. Triggering a protective instinct. Other Manti had experienced this type of connection—it had come to be referred to as tuning. Pax had always viewed it as a romanticizing of complicated hybrid mating drives. Now he understood that it was very real.

But he was pragmatic, and she was his enemy.

"No matches, Captain," said Banshee.

"What?"

"No matches for the woman in the image database."

If the ship couldn't give him answers, he'd have to get them from *her*.

He leaned against the console, pressing his hands to his forehead.

"Try to think about something else." Iris joined him in the cockpit.

He wasn't sure whether she referred to his headache or Asha. But he wasn't likely to forget either anytime soon.

"Get us out of here," he grumbled. "I can't even see straight."

Iris pressed her hands against the console, fingers sinking into the pliable, living resin, and the ship hummed to wakefulness. "Home?" she asked.

Good question. He hadn't thought at all beyond his decision to bring Asha on board.

"Not yet," he said. "I don't want to see Father until I have some answers. I need to know whether we've been exposed." He rose to his feet. "Let's get closer to home and find a place to park for a while. Check in with the fleet and find a spot where we're not likely to encounter other ships."

Iris studied him. "Where are you going?"

"To do something about my headache."

Iris's eyes followed him as he left the cockpit. He headed for the Scarab's small galley, where they stored medical supplies. He knew he should have the ship's AI check him out and make a treatment recommendation. Instead he fished out a bottle of painkillers and swallowed one of the green tabs dry. Then he swiped an antiseptic pad over the bite wound.

He left the galley and found himself turning toward the crew quarters rather than back to the bridge.

The mystery of the situation gnawed at him. A hole in his memory—caused by an unexplained knot on his head—after a visit to Sanctuary was dangerous. And he didn't like not knowing how the human woman was involved. No theory he had formed came even close to answering his questions.

He stopped outside his sister's quarters, pausing only a moment before sliding his hand over the door panel to open it. But the panel didn't respond.

"Open the door, Banshee," he ordered.

"Iris ordered me to secure the door, Captain," replied the ship. "Shall I request her authorization to override?"

His heart pounded, and he wiped his palms on his pants. Even from the other side of the door he felt the pull of her biology—the ripeness of her body, compounded by an inexplicable need to keep her close—as it twined around him like a vine.

Which is exactly why I ordered Iris to lock her away.

"Emergency override, Banshee."

The long pause that followed—along with his second-guessing of his own judgment—triggered impatience. "Banshee, I gave you an order."

"My systems detect no threats to ship or occupants, Captain."

"Bloody hell," muttered Pax. He turned and called down the corridor, "Iris! Meet me outside your quarters."

"On my way," she replied over the com.

He heard the cockpit door slide open, and she greeted him with a deep frown. "What are you doing?"

"Open the door, Iris. I'm going to question her."

She shook her head in frustration. "Haven't we been through this? Why do this to yourself right now?"

"I told you I can handle it," he said, the continued contradiction hardening his resolve. "I'm not *asking*, Iris. Open the door."

The dark tips of her brows knitted together, but she said, "Open the door, Banshee."

Before he could step inside she added, "I won't be a part of this. When you regret it, don't come to me for comforting." She turned sharply and headed back to the galley.

Asha hadn't been in Iris's quarters more than five minutes when she heard Paxton shout in the corridor. She cast about her, looking for something she could use as a weapon. The chamber was much the same as Paxton's—sparse furnishings, ornately carved, with rich, bright fabrics adorning the bed.

She fled through a doorway into a bathroom, eyes moving over the horizontal surfaces. Snatching up a comb with a pointed handle, she jumped into the shower stall.

"Lights out, Banshee," she murmured, crouching in a corner. To her surprise the ship complied.

"Asha?" Paxton's voice rang in the chamber. Heavy footsteps crossed the floor, pausing near the bathroom.

She squeezed the comb and raised it.

"Put that down," he said firmly. "I'm not going to hurt you."

She gave a silent groan. The low light had only disadvantaged *her*.

"Stay away from me," she warned.

"I need to ask you some questions, and it's best for both of us that it doesn't happen in this tiny dark room. I'll ask you once more to drop that and come out."

She rose unsteadily. She believed he didn't want to hurt her, but she didn't trust him not to. When she heard him moving closer, she launched out of the shower stall, stabbing with her makeshift weapon.

Paxton caught her wrist, easily twisting the comb free as his arm snaked around her waist.

"Stop it!" she cried, shoving at him with her free hand. She yelped as pain shot up her injured wrist.

Suddenly the lights came up, and steam plumed out of the wall right next to her head. Pax jumped back with a shout, and a jet of hot water struck him square in the chest, knocking him to the floor.

Asha shrank back, even as she willed her legs to move the other direction. Before they could respond, she felt a crawling sensation at her middle.

A thin membrane spread over her hips and abdomen. She gave a cry of horror and jerked forward. But in the space of three heartbeats the same material that covered every surface of the ship had sheathed her body from shoulders to knees, confining her against the wall of the ship.

"Iris!" cried Asha, for whatever good it might do. From the

exchange she'd overheard at the door, it was clear enough the sister had washed her hands of the situation.

"Release her, Banshee," barked Pax, rising to his feet.

"Negative, Captain."

Asha loosed a strangled sob as the reply pulsed through the wall, waterlogged and echoing. Panic surged through her as she fought the living sheath.

"You're frightening her, Banshee," said Pax.

"I have been ordered to protect her from attack, Captain."

Paxton's eyes widened, and he muttered an oath. "She attacked *me*, you mutinous lump of—"

"I've inferred that it is your wish not to hurt her, Captain."

"You *inferred*?"

Silence from Banshee.

The captain's fists clenched at his sides. He spoke through tight lips. "Release her as soon as I'm gone, and seal the door to Iris's quarters. Then wait for my orders. Understood, Banshee?"

"Yes, Captain."

INTERROGATION

"You can't really fault Banshee."

Pax stared at Iris in disbelief. "Is that supposed to be a joke?"

"No, it's not."

"It doesn't concern you at all that Banshee's *inferring*?"

Iris frowned. "I didn't say that. But you gave her permission to think for herself in protecting that girl. What did you expect?"

Pax closed his eyes, sighing in frustration. Iris was right. His decision-making skills had deteriorated markedly over the last couple of hours.

"Look," continued Iris, "I'm sure we can sort her out when we get home."

"Banshee or Asha?"

"Both. But I mean the ship."

"And until then?"

"Until then I guess you better play nice with your pet."

He scowled at the mischief in his sister's eyes.

"Pax," said Iris, sobering, "you know what I think about you bringing her on board. The order you gave Banshee was justified. I don't get why you're upset that she followed it. You should be relieved."

The creeping awareness that all three females were getting the better of him deepened his scowl. "Excuse me if I'm not relieved by the fact this casing stuffed with tissue and circuitry has sided with our enemy against me."

Iris gave a smug smile. "You at least have to appreciate the irony."

He eyed her, baffled.

"It's just what they did to *us*, right? Played god because they could, then cried foul when their creations turned on them."

She had a point. The Manti, not their creators, had been responsible for merging insect and plant DNA with artificial intelligence. The Scarab fleet had made the Manti masters of the skies. And now this particular serial number had gone sentient over a barely there, sylph of a human woman who'd all but forgotten her own name.

"Your philosophical strain is diverting enough in the palace, Sister, but at the moment I think we'd benefit from a little pragmatism."

His reply had the desired effect—dampening the fun Iris was having at his expense. She rose to her feet and glared down at him.

"All right. Question her. If she's a spy, she goes out the hatch. If she's not, she goes out the hatch. Pragmatic enough?"

Banshee released Asha and she stumbled to the floor. Rising on hands and knees she scrambled out of the bathroom.

Her heart beat like the devil's own drum as she sat panting, trying to think.

Though instinct still screamed that the inside of a living, breathing, *reasoning* Manti ship was the very last place she should be, it was a circumstance she could not change. And for the moment it appeared Banshee was her only ally. She returned to the shower stall and sat with her arms folded over her knees. She felt safer there, found it easier to think. Her gaze fell on Iris's comb. She picked it up, gripping the toothed end in her fist. Her hand trembled.

"Where is the captain, Banshee?" she asked.

"The captain is on the flight deck." Banshee's voice had no direction. It seemed to come from everywhere at once. She felt like Jonah in the belly of the whale.

"Can you notify me if the captain leaves the bridge?"

"Yes, Asha."

She shivered. It knew her name.

"Can you tell me where we're going?"

"Navigation information is restricted to crew members."

"Can you tell me the names of the crew members?"

"Augustus Paxton, captain. Iris Paxton, pilot."

"There's no one else on board?"

"Passenger Asha. Surname unknown."

"Right. Am I the first human to board this ship?"

"Ship logs are restricted—"

"Okay, Banshee." She thought for a moment and asked, "Are you happy?"

The pause was more significant than the answer, as the answer was pretty much what she'd expected: "I do not experience emotional response."

"I see. Well I do, Banshee, and I want you to know I'm grateful that you protected me."

"I was acting on the captain's orders."

"The captain didn't seem to think so. What *were* the captain's orders?"

"I have been ordered to protect you from attack."

Asha took a deep breath, relaxing her grip on the comb. "I'm glad to hear it."

Time to clear her mind of the encounter with Paxton. She had other pressing concerns.

Whatever else was going on with Banshee, she was presumably mostly machine, and therefore a huge repository of data. The ship might be able to help Asha find some possible explanations for the holes in her memory. But she would have to assume any exchanges with Banshee would be shared with the captain.

Do I have a choice? No. She needed answers.

"Banshee, list causes of amnesia."

"The most common causes of amnesia are injury, shock, post-traumatic stress, psychological conditions, and drug or alcohol use."

Common sense had suggested most of these already. She was convinced her memory loss had something to do with Paxton.

"What types of psychological conditions?"

"Repression and hypnosis are two examples of psychological causes of amnesia."

"Hypnosis?" Was it possible someone had *deliberately* tampered with her memory?

"A state that resembles sleep but differs in being induced by the suggestions of—"

"Yes, Banshee. Thank you."

So why would anyone want to tamper with her memory? The fact that she knew more about the Manti than most humans and had somehow ended up in the company of one of them seemed important. But this wasn't something she could discuss with Banshee.

Could it be that something traumatic had happened to her?

Considering Paxton's behavior toward her—and the fact she'd been practically naked on the beach—she could easily imagine traumatic events that might have taken place. But there'd been no signs of assault. And his memories appeared to be missing as well. It didn't add up.

Finally out of sheer desperation she asked, "Banshee, can you tell me what the captain was doing so close to Sanctuary?"

This question was met with silence, which she'd expected, but she'd had to try.

"That information is restricted to crew members," Banshee finally replied.

"Naturally."

"Asha?"

"Yes?"

"The captain has ordered me not to interact with you independently."

She glanced up at the ceiling, frowning. "Since when?"

"Twelve seconds ago. The captain also asked me to inform you that he intends to question you in eight hours. He suggests you use the time to sleep."

Sighing, Asha rose to her feet. Exhausted as she was, sleep wasn't likely to bring back her missing memories. She needed to jog her brain somehow. If she could tell Paxton what had happened to them—reassure him she wasn't some kind of spy—maybe he would consider releasing her.

"Can I have a shower, Banshee, or is that on restricted access too?"

Not recognizing the second part of her question as sarcasm, Banshee responded a moment later, "The captain has approved your request for a shower."

"Terrific," she muttered. "Thanks."

* * *

"Asha."

She sat up straight, gasping. It took a moment for the unfamiliar surroundings to register. Iris's bed was huge in comparison to her own back at the Archive.

So it hadn't been a nightmare. Well, it had been. But the awake kind.

"What is it, Banshee?" she asked, voice gravelly from sleep.

"The captain has left the bridge."

She jumped up and crossed to the bathroom to splash cold water over her face—and retrieve her weapon, such as it was.

"I thought you weren't supposed to talk to me," she murmured, drying her face and hands.

"Your request for notification was made before the captain's order."

Sounded a little too much like rationalization for a machine, but like Banshee's earlier intervention, it was in her favor and she wasn't about to argue.

She ran her fingers through her hair to smooth the ends, which seemed to have a life of their own. She judged by the growling of her stomach that it was approximately morning.

Except for Iris stopping by with a dinner of thin soup and some kind of sweet flatbread, Asha had spent the night alone with her thoughts. None of her missing memories had returned, and she'd lain in the bed trying to make sense of everything until she'd dozed off.

Her first thoughts on waking were of her mother, who served on Sanctuary's governing council. If anyone could help her it was Miriam St. John, who was a lioness when it came to her only daughter. By now she'd probably turned the city upside down searching for Asha. But even her mother's political powers would not be enough to find and pluck Asha from the innards of a Manti ship.

As for her father . . . He'd be frantic at her disappearance. Just the thought of it made her feel sick—Asha and the Archive were all he cared about. But unlike her mother, he wouldn't have the solace of action. He found it hard to face the world outside his office. He would do nothing—*could* do nothing—for her.

The idea of her parents ever having generated enough intimacy between them to produce a child was mysterious and baffling. But in the aftermath of the Bio Holocaust, perhaps instinct had driven some beyond reason.

"Banshee, open the door."

Asha glanced up at the sound of the captain's voice. She tucked the comb into a back pocket, slipping the handle under her shirt, and walked out to the bedroom.

His luminous eyes locked with hers, and she shrank against the wall.

"Come with me," he ordered.

"Where are we going?"

He stepped toward her. "To the bridge."

Her fingers pressed the wall behind her, and she felt the tips sink in. She jumped as the wall at her back gently vibrated. Impossible to say whether the motion was intended as reassurance, but it served to remind Asha that Banshee had orders to protect her—and had demonstrated she would do so regardless of any contradictory order.

Asha pushed away from the wall, following Paxton into the corridor.

They made their way to the bridge, where Iris swiveled in the pilot's chair to watch them. As Asha's gaze moved beyond Iris to the window, her jaw dropped.

To Asha—who until the previous day had never been beyond the landscape of what was once Arches National Park—it seemed like Banshee must have lighted on the most colorful, most alive spot on Earth. The ship perched atop some precipice—a rocky outcrop surrounded by a carpet of golden grass. Beyond that, snow-dusted mountaintops in one direction, the sea in another, and rolling green hills filling out the rest of the view. Far below she caught the reflection from a lake, with a picturesque ruin beside it.

She'd seen images from all over the world—all the most dramatic scenery—in the Archive. Her father made a point of teaching her about mankind's treasures, as he called them. Something they couldn't afford to forget.

She guessed they were somewhere in northern Europe, maybe the British Isles. But just like the first time Asha saw Iris, the real thing could not be compared to photos. She was the first of her generation to see something like this close up.

She was the first of her generation to see the ocean.

"Is this where you live?" she asked in a voice subdued with awe.

"No," he replied, his tone softening from earlier. "The climate is much too cold."

Of course. It was a foolish question. It was part of the reason Sanctuary had been established in Arches, near the ghost town of Moab, Utah. The bugs—both human-sized and microscopic—liked heat, but the desert was cold at night, and far too dry. It was thought to be the reason Sanctuary's founders had survived. Many had speculated there were other pockets of humanity preserved in the least habitable parts of the Earth. Maybe Asha was going to find out if that was true.

"Why have we stopped here?" she ventured, glancing at Paxton.

The captain just looked at her. Studied her, like *she* was the anomaly.

His gaze shifted to Iris. "Leave us. You need sleep."

She eyed him archly, but answered, "That's true."

Iris rose and moved toward the door. She drew up even with Asha and turned.

"Weather eye, Brother," she warned.

"Always. You know that."

"Inside the ship as well as out."

"*Iris*."

The mantis woman shrugged, and she left them.

Paxton motioned Asha to sit in her place.

"You haven't answered my question," she said.

Paxton crossed his arms over his chest, his expression tightening with impatience. She moved to the pilot's chair and sat down.

"We've stopped here because I can't take you into our city until I understand who you are, and what you're after."

A hard, desperate laugh pushed past Asha's lips. "Then we can end this right now. My name is Asha St. John. I'm an archivist. I don't want to go to your city. All I want is to go home."

Some of the tightness in his expression gave way to a sort of surprised . . . curiosity. "What do you archive?"

She hesitated, wondering whether she'd made a mistake in letting this slip.

"Don't lie to me, Asha," he warned. "I'll know."

She swallowed and sat up straighter. "If you can read my thoughts, what's the point of interrogating me?"

Paxton moved to the control panel—or to the slanted membranous surface that would have been the control panel on a regular ship—and leaned forward to gaze at the ocean.

"I can't read your thoughts. But unless you're suffering from some yet-to-be-detected psychological disorder, Banshee will know if you're lying."

That she could easily believe.

Paxton turned from the window, resting against the console. "What do you archive?"

"Images and video. News articles. Anything digital."

"About . . . ?"

She bit her lip. "You. Your people, I mean. Your genesis and rise to power." He lifted his eyebrows in surprise, and she added, "Mine is only a small part of the Archive. It's mostly our own history and culture."

"Know thyself, know thy enemy."

She didn't know the source of the quotation, but she knew what it meant, and he was right—but only partly. The Archive's mission statement was "preserving the past for the future." They envisioned a future without their enemies in it. When it came, they intended to use the Archive to recover all they had lost.

She flailed for a way to change the subject, but he saved her the trouble.

"What were you doing at the reservoir?"

She lifted her chin, meeting his gaze. "I don't know. Maybe you can tell *me*."

"Banshee," said Paxton, eyes fixed on her face, "are you with us?"

"Yes, Captain. Elevated heart rate and respiration, consistent with her fear response upon arrival."

Paxton scooted toward her, leaning close. "Someone hit me hard enough to knock me out. The blow activated a defensive carapace—a sort of hard cocoon that protected me from further harm. I remember nothing except a dream about a yammering old woman."

Asha shrugged, a gesture far more relaxed than she felt. "I was almost outside bounds. Maybe you tried to take me and someone tried to stop you."

Paxton shook his head. "Why would someone stop me from taking you and then leave you behind?"

"Do you have a better explanation?"

"Yes. You were planted for some purpose. I was supposed to take you."

He could be right, she knew. It made no less sense than her explanation. And it was more appealing than believing she'd gone crazy and wandered into the desert, though she would not have been the first to do so. But if she was to have any hope of going home, she had to convince him she wasn't a threat.

"If someone in Sanctuary wanted you to pick me up, why would they knock you unconscious?"

"Something went wrong, maybe. I don't know. But it would also explain why someone has gone to the trouble of teaching an archivist self-defense. An archivist who just happens to specialize in my culture."

She dug her fingers into the armrests. She could tell by his expression he'd made up his mind. Without access to her own memory, she had no grounds for argument. Or maybe her memories would only confirm his explanation.

"I am *not* a spy," she snapped, eyes burning with tears of frustration. "I don't *care* why you were at the reservoir. I don't *care* what happens to you or your ship, or what you believe about me. All I want is to go back *home*."

In the space of a heartbeat he'd plucked her from the pilot's chair and dumped her onto the console.

"Banshee!" she cried, wriggling away.

But he leaned in, caging her between his arms, his body, and the windshield. The end of his nose was no more than an inch from hers.

"Banshee and I understand each other better now," he warned. "Don't expect her to help you."

Asha pressed her lips together, her heart racing.

The captain raised an eyebrow. "You *need* to care what I believe. In fact right now I'd say that's your biggest concern."

An angry sob burst from her throat. "You think so? How about the fact I might be going crazy? That every passing moment takes me farther away from my family than I've ever been? That I'm a passenger on a ship that's more than half alive, and its captain keeps attacking me?"

The angry hue drained from Paxton's face. He eased back from the console.

She righted herself, and he watched her struggle to rein in her emotions—to hold on to her dignity. He knew beyond a doubt she was afraid of him, but she refused to let it master her. The respect he felt for her ticked dangerously upward.

"It was never my desire to attack you," he said. "I'm ashamed of it."

Asha met his gaze, unblinking.

"That doesn't surprise you?"

"Not what you've said. Only that you said it."

Clever girl.

"Why can't you control it?" she asked.

Pax stepped back and crossed his arms, studying her. She perched like a butterfly on the edge of the console—light and fragile, trembling softly. *Light, yes. Fragile, no.* He had a stinging ache in his side to remind him of that.

"One difference between humans and animals," he said, "is humans have the desire and the ability to control their impulses. I'm part human, part animal. I have the desire but not always the ability."

"But you're . . . okay now."

He nodded. "It's triggered by a female's reproductive cycle." This was an oversimplification, but he wasn't about to discuss the *tuning* with her. He didn't have a handle on that yet himself. "Unfortunately receptivity is not a factor."

"You mean it doesn't matter if I don't want to."

"Not to my subconscious impulses." She swallowed audibly, and shifted on her perch.

He added, "It does matter to *me*."

Her shoulders dropped a fraction with the release of tension. "This is a result of your insect DNA?"

"Not directly. I think it's specific to transgenic organisms." More oversimplification. Most members of the youngest Manti generation were transgenic, chimeric, *and* hybrid. "Transgenic" was the commonly accepted shorthand.

"Even in the insect world there are courtships," he continued. "My lack of control . . . I think it's the result of human impulses and instincts being out of balance with the increased aggression and enhanced hormone receptivity introduced by mantis DNA."

Her brow furrowed. "You sound like my father. He's an archivist too, and a scholar. Did you go to school?"

"Of course."

She flushed, and for reasons he could not have explained, it fired a tiny arrow into him.

"We have a school in Sanctuary," she said. "But I'm sure it's nothing compared to the ones you have."

"I haven't noticed any obvious deficiencies," he said softly. "You understand me well enough."

Her fear of him didn't prevent her targeting him with a look of vexation. "I'm not saying I'm stupid."

"No." He fought the grin pulling at his lips. "Neither am I.

I've studied beyond my formal education. Possibly in areas that would not have been . . . useful to you."

Biology, physiology, psychology. Philosophy, sociology, political science. Hardly practical subjects for a species just trying to survive.

He watched her, curious whether she'd take offense. If he was honest, he was curious about everything she did, down to the way she kept crossing and uncrossing her ankles. The way she rubbed her lips together while she was thinking.

"Did you have something removed?" she asked suddenly, eyes grazing his midsection.

His amusement withered. His lower rib cage tingled, just as it always did when he tried to flex the appendages that had been surgically removed every year between birth and age seventeen, when finally they stopped growing back.

"Why?" she continued, taking his silence as confirmation.

"Asha," he said, ignoring her question, "when we leave here, I'm taking you home with us, to Granada. For the time being, I have no choice but to consider you a potential threat to myself, my family, and our interests. You'll be closely watched, and I'll continue asking questions until we have answers."

He watched the color drain from her face. Watched the questions flashing in her eyes. Waited to see which of them she'd ask.

"Who *are* you?"

She'd chosen the question that was easiest to answer. But doing so would ensure she'd never go home.

That was a foregone conclusion now, though. She'd interacted with his ship. Both he and Iris had let details slip that Asha's confused brain might examine more closely once she was away from them—once her memory returned. She was an archivist, after all, who had specialized in his culture.

This decision has consequences. Iris had been right to say so. And his city was no place for someone like Asha.

"Who do you think I am?"

Asha had thought she *knew* who he was. The menace in the sky over Sanctuary. The ship that watched the borders, ensuring containment of the human survivors. She'd been warned since she was a child that the border was guarded, and anyone caught beyond it was taken back to Granada. The Manti capital was an ancient symbol of ruling conquerors near Spain's southern coast. Warm, humid climate. Appropriately exotic setting. She could easily picture Iris standing before the oblong reflection pool of the Alhambra, framed by the arched portico.

As she studied the Manti captain, a name bubbled up from her internal database.

"One of your generals had the name Paxton—*Emile* Paxton, I think. Are you related to him?"

Paxton gave a slow nod. "I'm his son. He's the amir now. Our highest ranking military and civil official."

She stared at him, astonished. So that made him what? A *prince*?

"Why does an amir need to send his son to watch over the defenseless remains of his conquered enemies?"

Paxton hesitated, studying her. But then his focus shifted to the windshield behind her. He stood blinking at the landscape outside the ship. She slipped off the console and turned, following his gaze.

He touched the windshield, and an image of the countryside appeared on the console below, overlaid with a grid. He tapped a square labeled "C25."

The grid was replaced with an enlarged section from the original image.

At first she saw a low rock ledge in a sea of scrubby grass, but on closer inspection the rock took the form of a camouflaged ship, identical to Banshee. It tipped at an odd angle—part of it seemed to have sunk into the ground.

"Bring Iris to the bridge, Banshee," murmured Paxton.

"Friends of yours?" asked Asha.

Paxton frowned at the image, drumming his index finger on the console.

The cockpit entry panel slid open, and Iris joined them. "Who is that?"

"I don't know."

Iris bent over the image. "Banshee, do you recognize that ship?"

"Yes, Iris. SC-011, Nefertiti."

The brother and sister shared a look of surprise.

"Can you get any readings? Is anyone on board?"

"I'm sorry, Captain. Nefertiti is unresponsive, and I can't take an accurate life-form reading from this distance."

"I don't like this," said Iris. "Let's get out of here. We can report it when we get back."

"What if the crew's still on board?"

"It's been weeks. If they're still on board they're dead."

Paxton continued to study the enlarged image, and somehow Asha knew what he would say.

"Regardless, we need to recover that ship if we can. Engines online, Banshee."

"What's the ground like around that ship?" asked Iris as Banshee moved into position. "It looks soggy."

"Yes, Iris. The raised area is solid, but the area around it is blanket bog."

Pax knew by the stiffness in Iris's tone she was not pleased about his decision. But he also knew she wouldn't defy him.

"It looks like we might be able to squeeze in beside her. Can you confirm, Banshee?"

"There is room for both ships, Iris."

"Okay. I'm only going to be in the way on this one. Take the landing, Banshee, slowly. And let us see the ground."

The static image on the ship's console switched to video of the landing target.

"No room for error," murmured Pax. "Banshee, notify us if anything starts moving inside that ship."

"Yes, Captain."

He wondered about the fate of the missing crew. Had they managed to cross the bog? Were they awaiting rescue on some nearby patch of solid ground? Hard to imagine this forbidding landscape had aided their survival. There was a tumbledown cottage maybe a hundred meters away, and a crescent of dense, shrubby woods beyond that. They'd check both places once they'd secured the other ship.

Banshee set down gently next to the listing Nefertiti.

"Stay with Banshee," Pax said to Iris, rising.

"No chance," replied Iris, spinning around in the pilot's chair. "No one's going to sneak up on us here. The only potential for danger is *inside* that ship. I'm going with you."

She was right, and he didn't argue. "I suspect it's empty, but we'll see."

He turned to Asha. She watched them closely, quiet and guarded. He could almost hear her thoughts—she was trying to decide whether this diversion presented any opportunity for her to escape.

"Banshee, keep Asha on the bridge. No interaction while we're gone."

"What if something is waiting for you in there?" Asha asked.

He frowned. "Then I suspect you'll be pleased. Be careful what you wish for, Asha. If Banshee returns to Granada without us, you'll have a lot to explain, and no one to protect you."

"That's exactly what I'm worried about," was the terse reply.

He had underestimated her. *Again.*

"Let's finish this, Pax," said Iris.

Asha's first thought—*this is my chance*—was immediately followed by a second: *There's no way in hell.* She understood enough about bogs to know that even if she managed to get off the ship, she'd be going nowhere in a hurry. And what if she did escape the Manti? She was a *very* long way from home.

She watched from the cockpit window as her captors moved, slow and watchful, toward the other ship. Both carried firearms—small handguns with long, narrow barrels. She knew nothing about recent Manti technology—she'd learned more from observing and interacting with Banshee than she had in all her years at the Archive. Almost all the information she worked with was historical—data collected before the Bio Holocaust. She was left with plenty of time to expand her knowledge in other areas, and to help with her father's research on geopolitics, a concept she didn't pretend to fully grasp.

Nefertiti's ramp was down, and the brother and sister ascended and disappeared. Asha couldn't help being curious about what they'd find. It didn't look like the ship had crash-landed, so presumably the crew was alive. Iris had said the ship disappeared weeks ago—unlikely the crew would have remained so long in such a barren spot.

"Banshee." Asha jumped as Paxton's voice sounded over the com. "Nefertiti is offline. Must have been a power surge. Release your umbilical and we'll see if you can wake her."

"What about the crew?" asked Asha.

"No sign of them."

Paxton returned to Banshee, ducking under the nose to retrieve the released cable.

Something moved in Asha's peripheral field, and she glanced up. At first her eyes could make no sense of what she was seeing. A section of bog beside Nefertiti was *rising*.

Earthquake crossed her mind, but she quickly dismissed the idea. Nothing had moved but that perfect rectangle of turf. When it had risen about a meter, it shifted to one side.

She gave a cry of surprise as a dozen men came pouring out of a hole that had been concealed underneath.

THE HONEYTRAP

Six grubby men launched at Paxton just as he spun around. They wrestled him to the ground, wrenching his gun away from him, and a blast fired over the bog.

Asha gasped, heart racing. *Humans?*

"Iris!" Paxton shouted. One of the men bashed the hilt of a knife against his head, and they shoved his face into the mud.

Asha jumped from her seat and sprinted for the corridor. The panel over the cockpit exit swiveled down, and she dove and wriggled under.

"Asha, please return to the bridge," said the ship.

"Sorry, Banshee," she muttered as she pounded down the boarding ramp, which was already closing. She scrambled over the edge and hit the ground hard, cradling her injured wrist against her chest.

"Freeze, love!" one of the newcomers yelled, raising a knife in the air at her.

She raised her hands. "Wait! I'm a prisoner on this ship!"

The threat in the man's eyes yielded to interest. "Human?"

"Yes."

He motioned her closer.

Her right knee protested as she got up and strode toward the speaker. Paxton's eyes rolled to follow her.

Before she'd closed the distance between them, a pulse of energy struck the ground in front of her, creating a hollow-sounding impact and a sizable crater. She froze as soil rained down over her.

"Release my crew or I'll be forced to fire on you," Banshee threatened.

"Stand down, you beast," the man shouted in contempt, "and we'll consider not killing your crew!"

A shrill cry knifed through the air, and Iris burst out of Nefertiti, propelled along by four more of the newcomers.

"Watch those stabbers, lads!" cried one of them. "She's got a wicked bite, too." An oval of red beads marked the forearm of the woman who'd spoken.

"Hold your weapons on her!" shouted the man who'd spoken to Asha, as they struggled to control their livid captive. "Their ship is making threats."

"What's going on?" demanded Asha. "Who *are* you?"

The man winked at her. His blond hair was closely cropped. He had a trace of a beard and eyes that laughed.

"Humanity's last stand, love. Out checking our honeytrap for flies."

Pax's cheek ground into the dirt as he wrenched his chin so he could see the rectangle of false ground that had sheltered his enemy. A frame made of wood and some kind of mesh, with blocks of turf fixed to it. The turf on the frame was dryer and lighter in color than the turf on the surrounding ground—it was subtle, but something he should have noticed.

How had the patrols missed these people? The Scarab detail was responsible for containing the known human survivors. Sanctuary was the largest group, and the only one that still possessed anything close to a pre-holocaust level of technology. The rest of them were mudgrubbers like these. The British Isles had succumbed to the microbial onslaught faster than other regions due in part to the densely populated urban centers, but there *were* isolated rural areas in Wales and Scotland—and here in Ireland.

The Scarabs had documented—or in the early days, destroyed—all known pockets of survivors. This one had obviously escaped notice.

"How many of you are there?" Asha asked their leader—a broad-chested man with a deep voice and penetrating gaze.

"Questions all around, I'll wager," he replied, glancing at the low clouds. "Morning's gone chill. Our base is not far from here. We can talk there."

The man held out his hand to Asha. "Welcome to Connemara, love. I'm Beck."

Her small hand disappeared in his. "Asha."

"Yank, by the sound of it." He shook his head grimly. "Long way from home."

Beck approached Pax, and one of the men pinning him down jerked his head back by the hair. The leader stooped to look into his face.

"That female important to you?"

Pax's jaw fell open—not the question he'd been expecting. "Listen, there's still time for you to stay alive. Let us go now, and—"

"Don't waste my time, bugman. Answer the fucking question."

Pax grunted with pain as his hair was yanked again. "I don't know her. We picked her up yesterday."

Beck snorted. "Not *that* female. I mean the one that came out of somebody's bloody nightmare."

Pax pressed his lips together and glared.

"I take that as a yes. Here's the situation. I'm going to slice her open right in front of you if you don't order that beast to camouflage itself like the other one, and power all the way down. Full stop, all systems. Understand?"

Nothing in Beck's demeanor suggested he was bluffing. In fact, every bit of information Pax's senses had gathered about the man confirmed he had it in him to do it.

"It won't help you," replied Pax. "Banshee's already sent out a distress call."

"Bring her," Beck shouted over his shoulder. "Captain, we don't know each other at all, and I can excuse you once for assuming I'm an idiot. There's no satellite reception here. That thing could send out a hundred distress calls and it will make no difference if there's no one in range to receive it."

Apparently Pax's *mudgrubber* assessment had been premature.

Beck stood up and walked over to Iris. He reached down and took hold of one of her wings, gently extending the veined, leaf-like appendage while Iris strained against her captors, jets of fury shooting from her eyes.

"Shall we start here?" He positioned the blade of his knife at the point where wing joined frame.

"Beck, stop!" cried Asha.

The leader's head pivoted her direction.

"Please don't." Her eyes moved between Iris and Pax. "It's cruel."

"So are *they*," he grunted. "But there's no need for it, if our captain will do as I've asked."

"Just *do* it," Asha urged, fixing her gaze on Pax.

He had no intention of letting them dissect his sister; he needed to get a better understanding of his enemy. He'd gotten that, and then some, but this round had gone about as far as it could.

"All right. Take your hands off her."

"Order your ship to camouflage and power down completely—no more words than that if you want me to put away the knife."

Pax complied, and Banshee acknowledged and powered down. He took back everything he'd said about Banshee's recent autonomous impulses and prayed the ship would watch for an opportunity and take initiative.

"Bind their hands," ordered Beck, "and let's get going."

A man with a ragged scar down one cheek took hold of Asha's arm, and Pax felt a sudden and confusing urge to hurt him. He bit back an angry challenge that made no sense even to him, and fixed a black look on the leader.

"Hey!" protested Asha.

Beck, who was helping to bind Iris, glanced up. "No, Finn, leave her be. She's one of us."

The scarred man eyed Asha doubtfully. "You sure?"

"Don't be an idiot. You see any bug parts?"

"No, sir, I don't. But I don't see any on *him*, neither."

Tugging another length of cord from his belt, Beck took a couple steps toward Pax. "True enough, but some don't have them."

Finn released Asha. By the frowning and head scratching that followed, Pax knew the man had picked up on the circular logic. "If that's so, how do you know she—"

"Stop thinking and get over here and help me," grumbled

Beck. "You too, Father. Why are you watching the rest of us work?"

"Sorry," muttered a tall man with shoulder-length, dark hair. His gaze moved from Iris to the leader.

"Not like you is all," said Beck.

The man was too young to be Beck's father—no more than forty—and Pax deduced "father" meant holy man.

He and Finn strode over and jerked Pax's arms into position while another man looped the cord in a figure eight. When his wrists were tightly bound, they dragged him over next to Iris, whose face was flushed with rage. She was afraid, too, but no one but Pax would know it.

Beck and the priest conferred in low voices, while Finn aimed an awkward smile at Asha. Cleary uncomfortable, she glanced away, and the man took the opportunity to rake her body with his eyes. Pax's blood warmed from simmer to boil.

In Sanctuary Asha would have led a relatively sheltered and civilized existence. She would have had instilled in her from birth all her notions of friends and enemies, and in fleeing Banshee she had made a choice consistent with those lessons.

She probably had only academic knowledge of what men could become when they had to struggle for survival—when every day was life or death. The education she might be in for sucked the anger right out of him, replacing it with a cold, creeping dread.

The initial relief Asha felt at escaping the Manti—and especially at the discovery of other human survivors—had been churned into apprehension by the violent threats against Iris. What kind of men were these? She eyed the one woman in their company, and found her even harder looking than the others.

Feeling the burn of Finn's gaze on her, Asha moved closer to Beck and the dark-haired man. Fierce as he looked with his almost-black eyes and corded, ax-wielding forearms, the leader had called him "father," and she thought he might be a priest. He'd be the first she'd ever met.

"Where are you taking us?" she asked, interrupting their low conversation.

"We've a shelter nearby," replied Beck. "Kylemore Abbey, not much more than a kilometer away by the old road. It's an easy walk."

Asha glanced down at the flimsy slippers she'd borrowed from Iris.

Following her gaze, Beck laughed. "Not quite proper footwear for the bog. No worries, love. You're a tiny thing—I'll take you on my back."

Her eyes widened, and she took a step back.

"No need to be afraid of me. But as you like." He winked and returned his attention to the priest.

She contemplated the rough-looking plants that carpeted the ground around the ship. The numerous pools of still, opaque water—very likely cold and heaven knew how deep. A fat raindrop pelted the tip of her nose, and she hugged her arms around her chest, gazing at the leaden sky.

"Ready to set out, then?" Beck asked as the priest moved away.

She took a deep breath and nodded.

The big man knelt with his back to her. She climbed on like a child, and he rose with her easily, like she weighed no more than one.

She gripped his shoulders, feeling the hard muscles working beneath a shirt that had been mended in at least a dozen places. Her nostrils registered his strongly male presence. Not unwashed, exactly, but there was the sharp, oniony scent of sweat, combined with an herbal smell that she recognized from required rotations in the greenhouse back home.

His arms tucked under her legs, Beck hoisted her higher and walked—not onto the bog as she'd expected—but into the hole that had concealed his party.

"Hey—wait—"

As he splashed into knee-deep water she saw it wasn't a hole, but a tunnel. Light streamed into the opening at the opposite end. He waded toward it, and the others began dropping into the tunnel behind them.

"How did you tunnel under all this wet ground?" she asked, squinting into the darkness of the tight enclosure.

"It's not an honest tunnel. More like a ditch." He waved at one wall. "This is an old turf cutting—the peat bricks for our fires come from here. It was started generations ago. We just connected it up to this dry stretch, and covered it so it wouldn't be visible from the air."

"Looks like it was a huge amount of work."

"That it was."

"Why did you do it? You couldn't have known the Manti were coming."

"Ah, but we did. When the first ship came down we figured eventually someone would come along looking for it. Did you notice that old cottage at the edge of the bog, next to the thicket?"

"Yes, I saw it."

"We've had rotating watches there for weeks, keeping an eye on this ship."

"Do you know what happened? Why it came down, I mean?"

"Mmm. She came down in a storm. We picked up her crew the next morning, trying to cross the bog."

This was an interesting new concept for Asha—the idea of luring and ambushing the enemy. In Sanctuary they tried to ignore the enemy flyovers, and hoped the enemy would return the favor.

"Where is the crew?"

Beck's body stiffened under her. "Dead."

She stiffened too, thinking about Iris and the knife. "Did you kill them?"

She yelped as Beck lost his footing, and water splashed up her legs and back. But he managed to right himself before they slid into the water.

"We gave them a choice," he replied, bumping her back into position. She clutched at his shoulders to keep her balance. "They could have taught us to fly that ship."

"What did you want with the ship?"

"To find other survivors. We have to band together if we're going to fight them."

Asha lifted her eyebrows. "You're serious?"

He chuckled. "Why wouldn't I be?"

"Well, it's just that—" Indeed, *why*?

She considered a moment and continued, "Where I come from, we talk about that all the time. But I've never heard of anyone doing anything *but* talk. Not since right after the war. I never knew there were other survivors."

He glanced over his shoulder. "Where *do* you come from, love?"

"Sanctuary. It's in Utah, in the desert."

"How many there?"

"Nearly a thousand."

Beck whistled. "That's very good news."

"There are many more of *them* though," she pointed out. "I mean we assume so, based on their numbers before the war."

Multiple births were common among the Manti, and reproduction was almost a religion for them at the time negotiations collapsed. Just like it was a civic obligation back home.

"What you're telling me is you don't think one ship will be enough for a resistance." She could hear the grin in Beck's voice.

"Pretty much, yeah."

"Good thing we have two, then." He laughed, and his laughter was contagious.

"Serious now though," he continued, "that's a useful bit of information. You have more like that?"

She bit her lip. "Quite a lot, actually."

He gave a decisive nod. "Let's get you someplace warm and dry. Then the two of us will have a long chat."

Though still wary of Finn and the others, Asha was beginning to trust their leader. Gradually she was distancing herself mentally from the pair who'd brought her here. Paxton was her enemy. Beck and the others were her *people*. Until now she'd believed the whole of humanity consisted of the thousand souls at Sanctuary.

Yet she was also conscious of a sense of uneasiness about Paxton—uneasiness that had nothing to do with the threat he represented. She had flinched at the rough way they'd treated him and Iris, and the information about the other crew made her worry about what Beck had in mind for them.

"Do you know anything about the bugman who captured you?" asked Beck. "Or the woman?"

Asha had all but forgotten what she'd learned about Paxton in the moments before they'd discovered the Nefertiti. It now dawned on her that, considering what Beck had told her about his plans, it was a very powerful piece of information.

Wait, a voice inside her warned. *Not yet.*

"I know they're brother and sister," she said. "And their

ship is familiar to everyone in Sanctuary. The Manti have watched our city since the end of the war."

Nodding, Beck said, "The ships pass over here as well. We assume they're looking for survivors. As far as I know, we've kept off their radar."

Moment by moment, a new world was opening up to her. A world where other landscapes existed. A world where there were pockets of humanity who hadn't submitted to their enemy.

"The existence of this city of yours perplexes me," he continued. "But we'll save that for later."

They'd reached the end of the ditch, where light streamed through a slightly askew, final section of roof.

Beck reached up and grasped the wire, his shoulders hardening as he shifted the section to one side. Then he stepped onto a ledge cut into the turf, grunting as he hoisted them both out of the hole.

He eased her down onto hard-packed earth. "Stay on the path here and you won't get wet—it's bog all around. The path will take us to the road. Pavement's a bit broken up, but I think you'll manage."

The others seeped out of the bog around them, and Beck motioned to the priest. "You take the lead, and I'll bring up the rear. Finn . . . ?" The greasy little man strode over to join them. "You and Alice are in charge of the prisoners. Don't let your guard down for a second."

"Will do, boss," replied Finn, managing another lewd smile her direction before he turned to his charges.

Pax remained on alert, watching and waiting. He knew the best strategy was to keep quiet and cooperate until his captors began to relax their vigilance—as much as it went against his nature. He also knew better than to underestimate them, despite the unlikelihood any of them had military training. But it was only a matter of time until their inexperience loosed an opportunity.

As they made their way along the ribbon of broken road, he tried to view this cold, damp place through Asha's eyes. Her departure from Sanctuary had been equivalent to stepping onto an alien world. She was wet and muddy and must have been cold, but she hugged herself for warmth and kept moving, gaze constantly shifting to take in everything. Budding oak trees, moss-covered stones, early spring blossoms . . . it must seem a riot of growth to a child of the desert.

When they reached the turnoff for the abbey—clearly marked by rusty but still intact signs in both English and Gaelic—Beck and his people stopped to confer. Iris cast Pax a warning glance as he took a couple slow steps toward Asha. He was risking refreshing his captors' watchfulness, but this was important. And it could be the only chance he would get.

Alarm flashed in her eyes as he approached, and he watched her gaze scan toward the leader.

"Don't trust him," he said in a low voice.

Her gaze snapped back to his face.

"Get away from her," ordered Finn, waving a blade as he returned his attention to the prisoners.

Pax stepped back toward Iris, whose scorching gaze was eloquent: *What the hell are you doing?*

He'd followed his instincts. Iris didn't know he'd told Asha who they were, which made an alliance between Asha and Beck dangerous. If he could insert a sliver of doubt, it might stop her from telling the man everything.

That much made sense to him. What *didn't* make sense was the fact he also felt a real concern for her safety—concern that served neither him nor his sister.

But these people would not have survived on squeamishness. Beck's charm was calculated to relax Asha's guard. To earn her trust. No doubt his next move would be to assess how they could best exploit her.

It might not mean they would hurt her. But then again it might. And enemy or not he wasn't okay with that.

But as she'd chided him on Banshee, she wasn't stupid. He'd paid close attention to her conversation with Beck. Beck had asked her a direct question about Pax's identity, and she had evaded. This would make it much harder for her to tell the truth later. It suggested she had doubts of her own.

They followed the road through a series of car parks, over a footbridge, and onto a paved walk that rounded a lake en route to the abbey. The building was picturesque, designed to look like a castle though clearly built in more recent times. The gray granite façade included crenellations and little towers, but there was nothing defensive about the rows of large ground-floor windows.

The setting was romantic in the extreme, with the abbey reflected in the still, dark surface of the lake. Trees lined the path, twisting to bow at water's edge, and hills loomed on all sides like silent sentries.

Visible signs of human habitation were subtle. An empty bucket left beside the path. A shirt caught in the branches of a tree. A dozen peat bricks left in a jumble on the overgrown lawn. Nothing that would have attracted attention from a Scarab. They were more concerned with actual activity on the ground. Smoke, or signs of agriculture.

As they approached the arched entry doors, propped open with stones, the cry of an infant pealed forth, stamping the silence irrevocably—*here is life*.

"Take the prisoners and secure them with the other one," Beck said to the priest. "I want you to keep watch on them personally." The priest nodded. "We'll question them later."

"What about the human woman?" asked Finn.

Pax noticed Asha moving subtly closer to the leader. Beck fixed the scarred man with a look so severe it made him shuffle back a step. "She's not a prisoner, and she's not your concern."

"Let's go," the priest said to Finn.

Beck started across the section of pavement in front of the abbey, motioning Asha to follow. Her gaze flickered to Pax before she turned, and he didn't miss the flash of uncertainty.

Good. It'll make her careful.

Asha followed Beck around the end of a wall dividing the abbey from the lake, and they scrambled down a short, grassy slope to the main path. The asphalt walkway had been riven by time and tree roots, and rough-edged hillocks made it impossible to walk without watching the ground.

At the path's end was a small chapel tucked in the shadow of a rocky, near-vertical slope. Constructed of stone, the structure was neat and perfectly preserved, down to its pretty arched window.

"What's this building used for?" asked Asha.

"My quarters. No one will disturb us here."

Beck held the door for her, but she hesitated. One corner of his lips crooked up. "You haven't gotten over being afraid of me."

She leveled her gaze at him. "I know almost nothing about you."

"True enough," he agreed with a nod. "We can talk outside if it'd make you more easy. But the weather's taking a turn."

Beck moved into the chapel and picked up a couple of oblong, earthy-looking bricks.

"If you come in I'll get the fire going. It's against the rules before dark, but with the wind and rain picking up I think we're safe enough."

He tossed the bricks into a stove that looked to be a recent addition. It rested next to a window, its rusted pipe fed through a broken pane, with cloth stuffed around it to keep out the draft. The stove door was missing.

As he worked on the fire, Asha hovered near the doorway, scanning the compact building's mostly empty interior. Where the congregation would have sat there was now a long table and two remaining pews. A mattress rested on the dais, and next to it was a nightstand constructed of books. Three stubby candles had been placed on the top volume, and Asha winced to see wax had pooled and run over onto the spines of a half-dozen others.

More boxes of books had been shoved against the back wall, under the biggest window. The glass panes were clear rather than stained, and would let in the morning light. She had no experience with preservation of physical books, but she knew it was not an appropriate place for storing them.

"Now then, we'll soon have you warm." Beck stood up as fingers of orange flame caressed around the straight edges of the peat bricks. The space filled with a pleasant, earthy aroma.

He dragged one of the pews closer to the fire.

Her heart beat faster with each step she took into the room. But the damp cold was a more powerful influence for the moment, and finally she sank into the pew.

As Beck moved onto the dais, she stretched her arms and legs toward the stove, rubbing her forearms while she kept one eye on her host.

Turning his back to her, he removed the Manti guns from his waistband and began to undress. Her eyes jerked back to the fire, heart in her throat. She'd half risen from her seat before she realized he was changing his wet clothes.

Her gaze moved furtively over his shoulders and back, and she thought of Paxton. Like him, Beck was tall, broad, muscular . . . and scarred. Below one shoulder blade was an irregular patch of shiny, pink skin.

"What happened to your back?" she asked without thinking—he'd know now that she'd been looking at him.

He glanced over his shoulder, and her cheeks flamed.

"Burned," he replied. "The bugmen torched our refugee camp. Only a handful of us survived."

Asha had never known anyone who'd experienced direct conflict with the enemy. The virus had done most of their work for them. "I'm so sorry."

"It was a long time ago."

She went back to staring into the fire, and a few minutes later he joined her on the pew, leaving a gentlemanly gap of about an arm's length between them. Still, she fidgeted in her seat.

He leaned his elbows on his knees, spreading his long fingers in front of the fire. "I want to hear *your* story, Asha. How did you come to be taken by those two?" He kept his gaze on the crackling peat instead of her, and she sank against the back of the pew, breathing a little easier.

"I don't know exactly."

He frowned into the flames. "I don't understand."

She collected the pieces together in her head, assembling them into the most coherent explanation she could, considering the gaping holes in her memory.

When she finished, he studied her with furrowed brow. "Have you ever lost your memory before?"

"No. I mean—not as far as I know."

"Do you think someone's tampered with it intentionally?"

The tension from her shoulders eased down to settle as weariness in the center of her chest. "Maybe. I don't know.

I've all but given up trying to figure it out." Tears stung her eyes, but the heat dried them before they could fall. "I just want to find a way to go home."

"Tell me about home," Beck prompted in a low voice.

She studied his softened features, and the sympathy she felt from him warmed her inside as the fire had warmed her out, loosening her reserve. But as she told him about Sanctuary, he looked increasingly confused.

Finally he shook his head. "I don't understand it, love. I can't think of why the bugmen would leave you alone like they have."

"They're superstitious about the rock formations—the arches and pinnacles. The Manti have a sort of reverence for . . . for naturally formed anomalies."

He eyed her skeptically. "But you were picked up there by this captain."

She nodded. "Near the border. I didn't know they ever came that close. But I don't think he was supposed to be there."

Beck's lips parted, and his gaze distanced as he thought about what she'd said. She could see that something didn't sit right.

"You have web access in Sanctuary, and working computers?"

"Working computers, and our own network. But there is no more web, as far as we know."

He leaned forward. "So how did you come by the information in your Archive?"

"The data was all collected and preserved by the woman who founded our city, Ophelia Engle. It was just a refugee camp back then. She'd been preparing for global apocalypse for thirty years."

The name "Ophelia" tickled at Asha's memory for some reason, but before she could chase the thought down its hole, Beck said, "Thirty years?"

Asha nodded. "She had a crawler that downloaded and dumped data onto storage drives. She put some thought into what to collect, but none into how to organize or tag it. We're still sorting out the mess."

"Is she still alive?"

"No. About fifteen years ago she suddenly went crazy. Or craz*ier*. Drowned herself in the Colorado River. That's when everyone started calling her 'Ophelia.' But a small group of people who were close to her took the whole thing very seriously—believed she was a prophet, and kept records of all the crazy stuff she'd said." Until their leader disappeared a year later. Along with his data drive.

"Sounds like a woman worth knowing," replied Beck, smiling in an attempt at lightness.

Asha returned the smile. "I don't remember her very well. But I wouldn't have a job without her."

Sitting back from the fire, Beck said, "So the information in your Archive is all dated."

"Yes, purely historical. Older than the war now—more than twenty-five years."

"And you have no interaction with the Manti?"

His expression had sobered, and she began to feel uneasy. "No. Why do you ask?"

"Because it doesn't add up, love. I can accept that they're spooked by your city. I know far less about them than you do. But I don't imagine they'd have to set foot in it to destroy it. I've seen what they can do. They must have a reason for leaving you alone so long."

Coldness spread out from her belly as she remembered a question she'd asked Paxton back on Banshee. A question he'd never answered.

Why does an amir need to send his son to watch over the defenseless remains of his conquered enemies?

* * *

Impervious to the ages as the abbey appeared from the outside, the inside told a different story. All those signs of human habitation Pax had watched for on their approach were contained within the building itself. Lines for drying laundry, stacks of fuel for their fires, piles of animal bones and other refuse. The opulence suggested by the building's exterior had been rubbed out completely. Furnishings were spare and battered. Smoke had blackened the walls.

The people themselves—mostly women and children—were raggedly clothed. Pinched, soiled, and watchful. Children clung to their mothers' legs, wide-eyed. One woman rested against a wall bouncing a fussy infant. As her gaze shifted to the doorway, where he and Iris waited with the others, she cried out and hurried from the room.

There was one man present, sharpening a knife by a window, and he rose to meet them.

"Father Carrick." He greeted the priest with respect, but he eyed Pax and Iris with open hostility.

"Where are the others?" asked Carrick.

The man tested the edge of his knife with his thumb, his eyes never leaving the Manti. "Here and there. Hunting. Stacking peat. Taking the air in the garden." His mouth twisted into a gap-toothed smile as his gaze shifted to Carrick.

The priest smiled mildly at the man's attempt at a joke. "All right, John. Round up any that you can and keep them inside. We need to keep a watch for enemy ships."

"Looks like we've already found one," John observed.

"So we have. Will you fetch me some rope, if we've any left?"

"All right, Father," he said with a nod. Then he turned and headed for a hallway that led off the large foyer.

As he exited the room, silence enveloped them, and Pax noticed everyone else had slipped out during the exchange.

A few moments later John returned with a thick coil of rope. "Are you putting them in with that other one, then?"

"I am."

The man shot a dark look Iris's direction. "This one might just be a match for it."

Pax and Iris exchanged a wordless, *What other one?* Beck had told Asha the other crew was dead.

When Pax glanced again at Carrick he noticed the priest's dark eyes had fixed on his sister. Pax's body tightened with wariness. But as Carrick directed them away from the doorway, he realized it wasn't anything he'd sensed that had set him on his guard—it was what he *hadn't* sensed. He couldn't get a read on the man at all.

Carrick led them around one end of the building to a small wood, where there were about a dozen women and children washing bedding—in large, old-fashioned freestanding bathtubs—concealed beneath the tangled oak branches.

"Go on inside," the priest called to them. "You can finish this later."

As their curious gazes settled on Carrick's prisoners, they cleared the area without argument, filing back around to the abbey's entrance.

Carrick led the party into the deeper shadows of the wood, to an outbuilding that was a hybrid of old stone foundation and corrugated metal siding.

"Let's go," ordered Carrick, opening the askew wooden door with a loud creak.

Rough hands shoved them inside, and Pax strained to see in the gloom. While his day vision was sharper than his human captors', mantises were daytime predators and he lacked this advantage in the low light. His other heightened senses helped him navigate in darkness, as well as detect other creatures' movements, but seeing into dark corners was not one of his talents.

The information his eyes failed to provide now came in the form of a low, humming hiss that issued from the back of the partially collapsed building.

"What's in here?" he demanded.

"Cousin of yours," growled Finn, holding a knife to Pax's throat while the others hoisted his arms overhead.

Pax glanced at Iris. Her night vision was no better than his, but her sense of smell was more sophisticated.

"Some kind of wasp," she murmured. "Advanced mutation."

"Both of you hush up," snapped the red-haired woman Beck had called Alice, holding her knife on Iris.

Their captors bound them tightly to an overhead beam, about three meters apart.

When Carrick and the others started for the door, Iris called, "What are you going to do with us?"

"Stick a knife in you if it's up to me," replied Finn. "You start any trouble and that's exactly what I'll do."

"Just keep quiet for a while," said the priest in a more moderate tone. His gaze rested on Iris, the whites of his eyes oddly bright in the gloom. "Beck will be in to talk to you later."

He followed the others out, and the door slapped closed. Someone secured it with a chain, dull light streaming around its ill-fitting edges.

Given some time alone together their chances of figuring a way out of this were better than fair—though it didn't bode well that the other crew had not escaped. But the whole situation was complicated by the fact Pax had no intention of leaving without Asha.

"Who are you?" Iris called toward the back of the shed.

A dark shape stirred in the straw. Iris was answered by another vibrating hiss. Hairs lifted along the back of Pax's neck.

The genetically modified came in all shapes and sizes. Fantastic as Iris appeared to the "pure" DNA humans, she was still a reasoning, sentient being. This was not by accident. Pax's father had founded Sustainable Transgenics, with its reproductive advisors and in vitro labs, for the sole purpose of preserving the Manti as a humanoid species.

Instead of feeling kinship with the beast they couldn't quite see, he felt revulsion. None of the Manti liked to be reminded of what they could become if they weren't careful about their breeding behavior. He was keenly aware of his own hypocrisy, embracing the mutations that made him stronger, faster, and more sensually perceptive, while reviling those that caused distasteful psychological and physical traits.

The Manti hated their parent race. They also wanted to remain as like them as they could without casting off their own identity. From a historical perspective, it was not unprecedented. But that didn't make it easier to live with.

Iris twisted her slender neck from one side to the other, trying to get a better perspective on that living, rustling corner of the shed.

"Forget it," he said. "Let's concentrate on getting out of here."

"It might be dangerous, Pax."

"That's my *point*. Now *help* me." He tugged at the cords that bound his wrists to the beam above, and it creaked in protest.

"Stop doing that. You'll pull it down around our ears. I'll try to work loose. I don't suppose you have a plan for after that?"

"You go for the ship. I'll go for Asha."

A prickly silence permeated the air around him, and he glanced at her.

She stared at him. "Have you lost your mind? We haven't had enough trouble from her?"

"More than enough."

"Then leave her. We'll come back later and deal with them all at once."

He shook his head, knowing he deserved every particle of scorn firing at him from her large irises.

"What *is* it with you and this woman?"

I have no fucking idea was not an answer likely to gain him any ground, so he didn't bother. "Come on," he said, giving his restraints another tug. "Let's get these off."

A sudden bang at the back of the shed jerked them both to attention.

"Lord of the—"

A dark shape shot up from the straw, rushing forward and hurtling between them. Iris gave a startled cry, and Pax gripped the beam and raised himself, kicking at the creature with his legs. But it kept right on charging at the door, scrambling close to the ground like it was wounded. Brown cellophane wings cloaked its back—most likely not functional. Human transgenics were far too heavy for flight.

The chain held, but the hinges didn't. A shriek sounded in the garden as the creature scuttled out the doorway. A few meters into the yard it halted, seeming to shrink and draw itself inward. Wings lifted from the hard, dark shell of its torso and began to vibrate.

The wasp lifted from the ground.

"Not good," snapped Iris.

About that much they were in agreement. "Watch your head," he warned.

TRANSGENIC

Before Iris could protest, Pax had thrown all his weight into the rope that bound his wrists to the overhead timber. The beam held, but the rope loosened enough to allow him to slide to the end and yank the beam free from the supporting timber. Iris swore as the beam dropped, bringing down half the roof with it. Pax waded through thatch to Iris, using her arm spikes to sever the remaining rope. Then he freed her wrists and they exited the rubble.

Father Carrick intercepted them outside, ax held aloft. A hunched old woman hovered behind him, watching them with wide eyes. Finn and Alice stood a few meters away, looking significantly less threatening now that their captives were at large.

"You don't have time to waste on us," Pax warned them.

Iris stepped between Pax and the priest, raising her arms and wings in warning. Carrick tossed his head to clear dark waves of hair from his eyes.

The resemblance between the two—both slender and ropey, light skin contrasting with dark hair and brows—created a pleasing symmetry. The priest was no match for Iris, but it would be a fight worth watching—*if* they didn't desperately need to vacate the camp.

"Where did you find that thing?" asked Iris, holding her position as the priest shifted his stance.

Carrick's eyes glittered, and Pax got the sense that—holy man or not—he was in his element, squaring off with an enemy.

"Found it scavenging in the refuse heap. Wounded. Unable to fly. Or so it seemed."

Iris raised an eyebrow. "So you decided to make a pet of it?"

Carrick's lips twisted up at one corner. "We chained it up and left it to die. Beck had the notion we could make use of its parts. The creature's body is like armor."

The old woman suddenly stepped out from behind the priest and approached Iris, a stream of animated but unintelligible sounds issuing from her papery lips.

"Keep back, Mother!" called Carrick. The ax lowered a fraction as he flung out his arm to catch her. He muttered more words of command in the same language she'd spoken.

She stopped with her wide eyes fixed on Iris. Pax caught one word she repeated several times: *shee, shee, shee.*

"She's not a fairy woman," the priest explained in his low, growling voice. "She's a mu—" *Mutant.* But Carrick hesitated, finally finishing with more of what Pax assumed was Gaelic.

The old woman's lips parted again, and she regarded Iris with more awe than fear. Noting that her reply to her son continued use of the word "shee"—and that she tugged insistently at his jacket—Pax determined the priest's explanation had been rejected.

The biohacker who'd engineered Iris's mother admittedly had a whimsical flair. While ostensibly working on a U.S. Defense Department contract to incorporate predator insect traits into human physiology, Dr. Gregoire had been more interested in playing god. Using ancient stories—and the more modern illustrations inspired by them—Gregoire had brought mythological races to life.

In a way the old woman was right; Iris was more fairy woman than any woman ever *had* been.

Pax took hold of his sister's arm. "We have to go. *Now*." Glancing at Carrick he said, "Your captive has most likely gone back to her hive, reeking of attack pheromone because you've made her angry. It's only a matter of time before they come down on top of you. On top of *us*. Unless you want to watch all these people die"—his gaze flitted to the old woman—"you need to take me to Beck."

Asha felt Beck's eyes on her as she turned over the questions he'd raised in her mind.

His brow creased as he said, "I don't mean to trouble you, love. We may be able to get some answers from the two that came with you. The other crew started talking in the end, though what they told us wasn't of much use."

A shudder ran through her. "You tortured them?"

He watched her a moment before replying. "We're in agreement that these are our enemies?"

"Yes. But *torture* . . ." Loyalty was one thing; inhumanity was another. Especially when it came to an enemy who was no longer faceless. "Neither of these two is old enough to have had anything to do with the Bio Holocaust," she reminded him.

Beck leaned closer, and she saw a glint of something she

hadn't seen before—something that reminded her of Paxton's warning.

"If you'd watched those bug ships burn your parents alive," he said, "you might feel differently."

She swallowed. "I might."

Releasing her from his gaze, he sank against the back of the pew with a sigh. "Let's hope we'll find them more cooperative than the others."

She sat processing what he'd said—and contrasting his surface charm with the dark current she'd just felt. She'd just begun to examine her own complicated feelings about the Manti prince and his sister when Beck spoke again.

"There's something else I want to say to you." He angled toward her, and she held her breath. "I think there's a chance you'll see your home again, especially now you've fallen in with us. Until that happens, I want you to know you're welcome here."

She thought about her father back at the Archive. Imagined him shuffling from his terminal to hers. Scrolling distractedly through files. Her hands began to shake.

Beck reached for the hand with the uninjured wrist, holding it between his. His palms felt dry and hot. "I know it's not what you're used to, but you'll be safe here." He gave her hand a squeeze. "And you can trust me to watch out for you."

Her fingers tensed. "What do you mean?"

"We've a hard life here, and not all of the men have a mate. If you're with me, they'll leave you alone."

She pulled her hand free, eying him with alarm. "What do you want from me?"

Beck crossed his arms over his chest and gave her a wan smile. "Not a thing." He shook his head, chuckling. "Well, that's not the honest truth. But I wouldn't touch you unless you wanted it. I can't make any promises about the others."

Ice water trickled down Asha's spine. Yet her heart beat so fast she felt hot. "What kind of place is this?"

"A place where men are surviving, love, and just barely that. It's no Sanctuary. We've no archive beyond what you see here," he waved at the boxes of books, "nor time to spend on such things. Surviving means toiling to feed hungry bellies. Staying one step ahead of our enemy. And it means making babies, so they don't wipe us off the face of the Earth."

She stared at him, her mind running through a comparison of the two men who had been steering her fate for the last twenty-four hours. One had fought to protect her from an instinct he found abhorrent. This one was telling her the same instinct was a fact of life.

But it occurred to her there might be more behind this than a desire to protect her. An excuse, perhaps, to keep her close. *He doesn't trust me either.* And why should he? She'd already lied to him.

Someone rapped on the chapel door, and Beck rose from the pew. "Come," he called.

Asha stood as the priest stepped into the chapel. She gasped to see Paxton move into the doorway behind him.

"What's going on?" demanded Beck, hand reaching to his waist for a weapon that wasn't there.

"The wasp got free," replied the priest. "The Manti captain says the whole hive could be on top of us soon."

"Wasp?" asked Asha.

"This is a trick, Carrick!" barked Beck, his face red with anger. "To get you to release them."

"I didn't release them," the man replied darkly.

"No trick," Paxton asserted, gaze flickering at Asha. "You've got trouble coming. Probably soon. No way of knowing how many."

Beck's gaze moved between the two men, his taut form still on high alert. He clearly didn't know what to believe.

"You should start moving your people out of here," said Paxton. "We're going."

"You're not going anywhere, and neither are we," replied Beck, stepping toward him. "Why should we believe you?"

"I don't care what you believe. But don't make the mistake of thinking you can stop us." Paxton held out a hand to Asha. "Let's go."

Beck moved between Asha and Paxton, and fury burned in his reply. "Go on then, bugman. But she stays with us."

Suddenly Iris burst into the chapel. "We have to *go*, Pax."

Asha moved without planning it, motivated by an aversion to the idea of being forced back into Manti custody. She darted onto the dais, scooping up a gun and leveling it at Paxton.

"No, love!" shouted Beck. The command terminated in an exasperated grumble.

Paxton was already in motion—she had to make a split-second decision. She dropped the barrel slightly, aiming for his lower body without pausing to think about why she didn't want to kill him.

His hand closed over the barrel and she squeezed the trigger.

Nothing happened.

Paxton yanked the weapon free and spun around in time to jam it against Beck's chest.

"Step *back*," ordered Paxton, and the leader moved off the dais. "Asha," Paxton continued, "if you don't want me to shoot him, hand me the other gun."

Asha hesitated, confused.

"Those guns don't work for us," explained Carrick. "Better do as he says."

Damn. Now what?

"Asha." Paxton thrust out his hand. She snatched the other weapon off the bed and handed it to him. He tossed it to Iris.

"Now come on." He reached for her, but she dodged again.

"Wait!" she cried. "What's going to happen to these people once we're gone?"

"They'll move on if they want to live."

He lunged for her and caught her by the wrist. As he dragged her off the dais she shot a panicked glance at Carrick. "How many of you are there?"

"About eighty."

"*Stop*." She yanked her arm, wincing at the pull in her shoulder. "You have two ships now," she pleaded with Paxton. "You could move them somewhere safe. You could take them back to Sanctuary."

"We'll not go anywhere with *them*," growled Beck.

"Don't be a fool," snapped Asha. She looked at Paxton. "I'll do whatever you want. Don't leave them here to die."

There was something wild in Paxton's look. Her heart thumped in warning. *He is half wild. He told you himself. Don't trust him.*

"This is madness, Pax," Iris hissed at her brother. "Let's go!"

"*Please*," urged Asha.

He towed her toward the door.

"No!" she cried, prying at his fingers.

"When we have our ships we'll come back," Paxton told the priest. "Anyone who wants to leave needs to be ready. You can come with us, but we won't take you to Sanctuary."

Outside the chapel the cloud cover had lowered, hanging heavy over the dark surface of the lake. But the rain continued no heavier than an intermittent sprinkle.

"It's too late," muttered Iris.

Asha followed her gaze to a smoke-like smudge low in the sky above the trees on the opposite side of the lake.

"What's coming?" she asked.

The door to the chapel swung open, and Beck and Carrick came out. Beck directed his glower toward the horizon.

"Some kind of transgenic wasp," said Paxton. "Aggressive."

"So we fight?" asked the priest.

"We fight," agreed Iris.

"We need to seal off the entrances to the abbey," said Paxton, glancing at Beck. "Do you have the other crew's weapons?"

"In the chapel," replied the leader. He glanced at Carrick. "Get back to the abbey and warn the others. Keep them all inside."

Beck ran back into the building, and Iris said, "I'll go with the priest."

Paxton shot her a questioning look, but he handed her his gun. "Go up to the roof. Pick as many of them off as you can. We'll be there soon."

Iris nodded, and she followed Carrick down the path toward the abbey.

Paxton's gaze locked on Asha. "Stay close to me. If we get separated, I want you to run. Hide in the woods until it's over. Understand?"

She stared at him, surprised by his concern for her safety—especially considering their last interaction had included her trying to shoot him.

"Okay," she agreed.

Beck burst out of the chapel with the other guns. He tossed one to Pax, and they started down the path after the others. Beck took the lead and Asha followed, Paxton bringing up the rear.

"Do you have other weapons in the abbey?" Paxton called to Beck.

"Knives and spears. Axes. We have a crate of rifles, but no ammo. Not for years."

Pax made no answer, which was answer enough. They were in trouble.

The enemy was close now. The air vibrated with angry humming. Asha picked up her pace to keep close to Beck, and she could hear Paxton's boots scraping the broken pavement behind her.

She fought to steady her mind against terror, knowing this new threat could open an opportunity at any moment. Paxton himself had pointed out that it might be possible to slip away in the confusion of the attack.

But as she ran, panting hard as sweat trickled down her neck, she knew it was time to reassess. Threats surrounded her. She'd woken up to a world that required alliances for survival. Paxton, enemy or no, seemed determined to keep her whole and alive. And he was the only one who could take her home.

A buzzing cry ripped through the air just above her, and something grazed the top of her head. She yelped and Pax fired a shot. Glancing up, she saw a dark insect the size of a man dropping toward her—gleaming black torso like armor and eyes like gold pearls, oblong and soulless. Huge mandibles clicked with menace as a pair of too-human arms extended from the wasp's midsection, grasping her shoulders and dragging her off her feet.

She smacked against the pavement but managed to get her hands and knees under her and roll away from her attacker.

Two more shots rang out, and she scooted away as the wasp slammed onto the path beside her. The buzzing pitched higher and louder as the creature struggled to right itself.

"Go!" Paxton shouted, firing once more.

She ran for the abbey without looking back, but she could hear Paxton's footfalls—and the shots he fired at regular intervals.

Dozens of wasps descended on the abbey, alighting on the crenellated towers and flying at windows. Iris and Carrick perched atop a front tower, *both* weapons sounding as they defended the rooftop and arched entryway. Asha joined Beck and Paxton in scrambling up the hillside toward the abbey, and saved the question for later.

At one end of the stone wall between the abbey and the lake, they crouched together in a stand of low trees. Peering around the wall they could see wasp carcasses scattered around the building's entrance—Iris picked them off from the tower as they rushed the arched wooden doors, while Carrick protected her from attack from above.

Asha could see this plan wouldn't hold for long. One of the wasps made it past Carrick's bullets, landing on the tower next to Iris. Paxton aimed and fired, knocking it from the wall, and the priest shot another that landed behind it.

"How's he firing that gun?" demanded Beck.

Paxton took the other gun from Beck, holding it still until Asha saw a green light pulse against his wrist. There was a dark mark there she hadn't noticed before—a spiral pattern made up of lines and dots. Paxton flicked his thumb against the underside of the grip and handed the weapon to Beck.

"Safety's off. Don't put it down—I'll have to override it again."

"Don't intend to," grunted Beck, turning to fire into the swarm above the abbey.

An uneasy alliance, but for the moment a necessary one.

Asha heard a crash and a shrill scream, and she scanned the front of the building. At the far end a wasp forced its way through the frame of a broken ground-floor window. In seconds the wasps on the ground had regrouped around the alternate entrance, where Iris's and Carrick's fire couldn't reach.

"They're getting in!" she cried.

"Come on," said Beck, jumping up.

Keeping close to the wall, they ran to the opposite end. Beck and Paxton pushed their way through a clump of shrubs and began firing into the swarm.

"How long will these work?" asked Beck, continuing to aim and fire.

"They're micro-projectile," said Paxton. "About fifty shots each." He paused, surveying the building and grounds. "We'll kill half of them if we're lucky."

"What then?" asked Asha.

"Hand-to-hand," muttered Beck. The barrel of the pistol kicked up as he fired again.

Asha swallowed, and her gut knotted at the thought of fighting their way through the seething mass. She'd gotten as close to one of those things as she ever wanted to get.

We need a better plan. She thought about the ambush on the bog.

"What about Banshee?" she asked, remembering the warning shot the ship had fired.

Another scream erupted from the abbey, and Iris shouted her brother's name.

"We have to help them," said Beck, backing out of the bushes.

"No time to go for the ship," said Paxton.

He reached out and snatched a knife from Beck's side before the other man could even flinch. He fixed his eyes on Asha, placing the knife hilt in her hand and closing her fingers over it. "Remember what I said. Stay hidden."

For a moment it paralyzed her—this second, disconcerting piece of evidence that he wanted to save her. But she shook her head. "I'm not going to hide in the woods and watch them kill everyone. *I'll* go for Banshee."

Paxton glanced at the abbey, impatient to be gone. "She won't wake for you."

"What if I tell her you gave the order?"

"She's powered down. She needs my biosignature to wake."

She grabbed his arm, forcing him to look at her. "Is it possible she *didn't* power down?"

She watched his face change as what she'd said sank in. They'd both witnessed Banshee acting on her own interpretation of Paxton's orders. "Yes," he agreed, his expression grim.

"Tell me what to do," she said.

Stepping closer, he gave her a hard look. "Put your hands on the hull so she can read you. Make a lot of noise."

"Okay."

She started to go, but he caught her elbow. "Stay in the trees as long as you can. If you're attacked . . . aim for the legs."

She squeezed the hilt of the knife, shivering.

"Run all the way," he said. "Don't look back."

She nodded, and she took off along the wall, back the way they'd come.

Asha jogged along the path toward the car park, and the road beyond. Every pebble she ground beneath the sole of a thin slipper sent a jolt of pain up her leg. Her lungs burned, raw from the cold, damp air pumping in and out of her.

She was frightened for the people back in the abbey, but she was also relieved to be putting distance between herself and those creatures. She knew some of the DNA experiments before the war had led to advanced mutations—there were videos in the Archive. But she'd seen nothing like this. Alive and fully functioning. And this was no ordinary wasp. Much of the recombinant DNA work had been done for the military, and species were often selected based on traits like size, strength, and aggressiveness.

The fact these creatures existed did not surprise her, but the fact Paxton considered them enemies *did*. Every moment she spent outside her sheltered world pointed to some new error or deficit in her education. Paxton—and even Iris, with her more obvious genetic differences—was essentially human. More human than *not* human. How was it possible to draw a hard line between friend and foe?

The Manti had practically wiped out humanity. Yet the Manti themselves were a result of humanity's quest for more effective methods of wiping out *each other*. As was the type of highly targeted plague that had delivered the Manti victory.

Asha stopped at the car park to catch her breath. She was about to leave the cover of trees for asphalt and open ground.

Paxton was right; she'd lose her nerve if she hesitated. She sucked in a lungful of air and set off again, trying not to hear the shouts of the people trapped in the abbey. By now Paxton was probably among them. She might very well return only to find them all dead.

"Not likely to see her again, are we?" Beck muttered as they circled around to the back windows of the abbey.

Pax wasn't sure whether the leader referred to the likelihood of Asha being killed by the wasps, or the possibility that she'd run and not look back. It had entered Pax's mind that if she managed to wake Banshee she might try to persuade the ship to return her to Sanctuary. It *shouldn't* be possible. It also shouldn't be possible that he and his sister were fighting other transgenics, with humans for their allies. Or that his strange fixation on one of those humans was interfering with his ability to think.

Forget her. It was the one thing he *was* sure of: he had to get her out of his head. Even hoping she really would make it back with the ship was more of a distraction than he could afford right now.

The back rooms of the abbey pressed right up against the steep hillside. Beck kicked in a window and climbed through, and Pax followed.

Inside he smelled apples and smoke. Barrels of fruit and potatoes lined the walls. Half a dozen small children stood near the door, clutching each other in terror. The smoke was coming through the crack under the storeroom door.

"Outside!" Beck ordered the children, pointing at the window. "Hide in the trees on the hillside."

They stared at him, wide-eyed and unresponsive.

"Go on!" he barked, and they untangled themselves like spiders and scrambled toward the window.

Pax tugged open the door, pulling the collar of his shirt up over his nose to filter out the smoke as he moved into the corridor.

"Do we have a plan?" asked Beck.

"Shoot until you're empty," replied Pax.

Dodging the abbey's fleeing inhabitants, they ran toward the front of the building and found the source of the smoke—a pile of burning debris near the entrance and main stairway. Someone had been thinking, but it had been panicked thinking. The fire was driving out the wasps, but also the people. Once they were out in the courtyard there'd be nowhere to hide.

A woman carrying a wailing infant darted in front of Pax, toward the entrance. Her face bent low over her baby, she didn't seem to see the knot of wasps clogging the arched doorway. He caught the back of her dress and gave it a yank.

She fought him senselessly until finally he grabbed her by the shoulders.

"Go out the back!" he shouted, giving her a shove the opposite direction.

"Pax!"

Iris's shout jerked his attention to the front of the room in time to see her bounding down the stairs, the priest and another man on her heels, with at least three wasps in pursuit. Flames licked along both railings, and the lowest section of steps was engulfed in flame as well.

Beck fired steadily into the wasps fighting their way out the entry doors, and Pax shifted position to target the ones crawling after his sister. Four bullets felled the first two, but as Iris and Carrick hopped the burning steps to the ground floor, the man at the rear let out a scream.

"Shoot it!" yelled Iris, as Pax targeted the black globe of the third wasp's head.

But even as he squeezed the trigger, sharp mandibles pierced through the man's chest, stopping his screaming. A second shot finished the wasp, and the two bodies slid together to the foot of the stairs, thudding to a stop against a wall.

"The fire has spread upstairs," panted Iris, joining him.

"Is everyone out?" called Beck.

"All that we could get to," muttered the priest, his expression grim. A bloody gash stretched from chin to ear. Iris's uncharacteristic expression of empathy was something Pax would have to puzzle out later.

A piercing, angry hum drew their attention to the entryway, where an injured wasp buzzed its broken body in a circle, trying to right itself. Finally its abdominal section smacked against one of the heavy wood doors, half torn from the hinges. With a growl Beck aimed and fired, knocking off the pointed section of abdomen along with the arm-length stinger.

"Wasted shot," Pax protested.

Beck strode over and retrieved the stinger, holding it by the oozing piece of hard wasp shell.

Frowning, Pax took aim at the nearest ebony carcass and

followed Beck's example. The bullets wouldn't last much longer—they needed a backup plan.

A shriek sounded out in the courtyard, and Beck called, "Let's go!"

Pax shot off two more stingers and glanced at Iris.

Narrowing her eyes, she said, "I'm not going out like this."

With a bark of mirthless laughter he handed her a stinger. "Glad to hear it."

As they exited the abbey he tried not to think beyond the battle they were walking into. He tried not to think about how he was going to explain all this to his father, or the fact he might not get the chance.

Mostly he tried not to think about Asha.

Asha picked up her pace, veering out of the parking lot and onto the road. She hugged the inside curve, hoping the line of vegetation crowding the asphalt would help to conceal her movement.

As the paved road joined up with the coastline, she broke left onto the earthen track that would take her back to the bog. She could see the ships now, and weighed the risks of shouting to make her presence known.

She had only seconds of buzzed warning before she was struck from above.

The moment she splayed onto the ground she launched forward, trying to keep the thing off her back. But a second blow sent her sprawling again.

Rolling to face her attacker, she gave a cry of horror and revulsion as the wasp dropped down over her, caging her between the spiny legs on either side of its black-armored torso. She thrashed from side to side, kicking at the hard abdomen with all her strength. Human arms extended from the beast's thorax, talon-like hands grasping and pinning her arms to the ground. Translucent, dark amber wings extended in the air behind the massive body.

She held her breath, heart pounding, and tightened her grip on Beck's knife. Her panicked fighting was just wearing her out—she was no match for the beast physically. She studied the blank, alien features, searching for something intelligent in its expression. Would it understand a plea for mercy?

Staring at her own ghostly reflection in the orbs that dominated its face, Asha noticed a focal point, like a pupil, behind the gold, translucent shell. The wasp was studying her as well.

"Please don't hurt me," she breathed.

Dark antennae protruded from the spot where a nose should have been. They hooked outward, like a curling mustache. Her gaze dropped a fraction, and she swallowed a scream as the long mandibles—also hooked, but hooked inward to form a ring—opened wide.

The creature's head lowered slowly, and the mandibles closed around Asha's neck. She jumped as the sharp tips scraped along her skin. Blood pulsed in a panic beneath the flesh at her throat. She was sure the wasp could feel it too.

The creature's face tilted minutely, and Asha heard . . .

Not stronger than us. No. Not smarter. Not better.

A voice. A rasping vibration. A ghastly feminine murmur that she wasn't sure hadn't come from inside her own head.

"*Please*," she choked past the tightening in her throat.

The mandibles clicked open and shut at the nape of her neck. The beast's torso arched, and its abdomen—which carried its deadliest weapon—bent toward her lower body.

This will sting, continued the thing.

She realized with shock the creature was laughing at her. The note of amusement was undeniable. And horrifying.

In a final, desperate attempt, she wrenched to one side and

managed to maneuver away from the descending stinger. As her knees connected with one of the wasp's legs it faltered, and its grip on her arms loosened. With a growl of effort she drove the knife upward against its thorax.

The tip glanced harmlessly off the hard black shell and she cried out in frustration.

But stillness was death, and she continued to thrash against the beast's legs. The mandible ring broke open, gouging her neck as the wasp freed its head from hers. Taking advantage of the space that opened between them, she swung the knife to one side, connecting with something solid.

The wasp lurched and she drew up her legs, shoving its torso away from her. She rolled free and vaulted to her feet.

The stick-like legs were sturdier than they looked, but she'd managed to knock off the lower section of one. The creature moved to attack again.

Spinning out of the path of its off-balance lunge, she brought the blade down on a fragile wing, knocking loose a section the size of her forearm.

Run!

Not pausing to question why her brain had registered this command in Paxton's voice rather than her own, she shot away from her foundering attacker, closing the distance between her and the bog.

She scanned the ground, searching for the entrance to the trench. When she spotted the narrow gap between dry earth and concealing turf, she tugged a section free and dove into the wet tunnel.

Scrambling through the muck, slipping or stumbling every few steps, she remembered nightmares she'd had where she'd run and run but never seemed to make any progress. She could never see what was chasing her in those dreams, but it was difficult to imagine any nightmare could be worse than this reality.

"Banshee!" she shouted when she finally crawled out the other end.

She dashed to the hull, slapping at it with her hands. "Banshee, wake up! The captain needs your help!"

The air stilled to silence in the wake of her shouting. She glanced from one ship to the other. Two hibernating beasts.

Her gaze shifted back the way she'd come, toward the abbey. She couldn't see the building, but its location was marked clearly enough by a column of smoke, and the mass of dark bodies swarming to one side.

Again she slapped the hull. "Banshee, you have to wake *up*! The captain and Iris will die!"

She slid a hand along the resinous membrane. "Come *on*," she pleaded. "You *know* me."

"How do you know she made it to the ship?" demanded Iris as she swung a spiked forearm, punching through the wing of the wasp writhing at her feet. The creature spun toward her and she raised a booted foot, bashing it against the alien face.

The truth was Pax *didn't* know. It was just a feeling. But he couldn't say that to his sister.

"Even if she did," Iris continued, scanning for the next assailant, "Banshee's powered down."

Their ammunition exhausted, they were fighting hand-to-hand with the enemy, just as Beck had predicted. Beck's people with their soft bodies and limited weaponry were no match—casualties littered the strip of asphalt between the abbey and the wall. And it was clear by the darkening of the sky above the abbey that reinforcements had just arrived.

"I know it doesn't look good," admitted Pax.

"Understatement," Iris grumbled.

Their conversation was cut short by two wasps alighting on

the asphalt in front of them. Pax moved quickly, jamming a harvested stinger into the face of one of them. He managed to penetrate one of the gold orbs, which were softer than the armored bodies. As the wasp faltered, he raised his foot and jammed the spike deeper.

Iris finished off the second wasp and they hurried to join Beck, who had a thigh caught in a set of mandibles. Before they could help him, Carrick dove in and knocked the wasp's head loose with a powerful swing of his shovel.

"Can they swim?" shouted the priest.

Pax exchanged glances with Iris. "Good idea," said Iris. It might buy them some time.

"The lake?" asked Beck, gripping the bleeding puncture in his leg.

A shrill cry sounded, drawing their attention a few meters away to a fair-haired woman with a stinger plunged in her hip. Iris was the closest, and she snatched an ax from the hands of a dead man and knocked the stinger free from the wasp's body. Pax finished the beast while Carrick knelt at the woman's side. She was already dead.

"Get in the lake!" Pax shouted to the people closest to him. They stared at him, confused. "Go on! They won't go in the water!"

A boy ran past, and Beck grabbed him. "Thomas, listen! Go around the wall and get in the lake! Tell everyone you see!"

The boy nodded and took off. "Get in the water!" he cried.

A wasp dropped toward him, and Pax targeted and flung another stinger. It sailed through a wing and the wasp plummeted, slamming onto the asphalt, where another man with a shovel waited to finish it.

Pax cast a glance to the sky.

"Forget her," snapped Iris, coming up behind him. "She ran like hell the opposite direction. It's what I would do."

"Get in the lake!" cried a man, as the order made its way among the survivors. "Get in the—"

A wasp snatched him off his feet, clamping mouthparts onto his neck as it dragged him four or five meters along the ground, lifted him over the wall, and then dropped him on the other side.

"Bloody hell!" cried Iris. "This is madness!"

"Listen," interrupted Pax, glancing skyward again.

Banshee swooped in and lowered over the abbey, guns descending from her underside.

"Get out of there!" Pax ordered the handful of people lingering near the smoking abbey.

As he and Iris took shelter against the courtyard wall, bullets sprayed into the swarm of wasps overhead. A carcass plummeted to the pavement no more than a meter away, and others rained down around it, like a giant was swatting flies.

The dozen of them that managed to elude the guns regrouped in the air above Banshee for a suicide run. The sturdy little Scarab simply held position, allowing them to break their bodies against her hull before they joined their companions on the ground.

The handful of surviving wasps retreated as Banshee repositioned over the lake, her gear dropping for a water landing.

"Let's get to the ship," murmured Iris, stepping away from the wall.

"Agreed." Now that the common foe was defeated, the uneasy alliance wasn't likely to hold long.

They rounded the wall and approached the ship as the boarding ramp extended, lowering onto the lakeshore.

As they stepped onto the ramp, Carrick waded out of the lake carrying a small child. The girl's arms clung tightly around his neck, face buried against his broad chest.

"Good fight," said Iris, as he drew up even with the ramp. "And I'm sorry."

The priest acknowledged this with a nod and continued toward the abbey.

Before Pax could ask what she was talking about, Asha appeared on the ramp. She took a few steps toward him, and their gazes locked. Her lips parted, and the color drained from her face. Had she expected to find him dead? *Hoped* to?

His eyes moved to the rivulet of blood seeping down from her neck into her shirt. *His* shirt.

What the hell was he supposed to do now? His amnesiac prisoner, whom he had pledged to interrogate and drag before his father, had just saved his and his sister's lives.

"Nicely done," said Iris, passing Asha as she boarded the ship. "Let's get the hell out of here."

Pax joined Asha on the ramp, conflict and confusion swarming his brain. Why couldn't he speak? Because nothing he wanted to say made any sense.

Finally she saved him the trouble. "Where's Beck?"

It was a natural-enough question. Beck had rescued her from the Manti, and of course she would think of him. Why it made him feel like he'd swallowed a glowing hot stone was a question he couldn't afford to ask himself right now.

ENEMIES AND ALLIES

Asha hadn't realized how anxious she felt until the moment she saw him, when she all but staggered from relief. She lowered her gaze so he wouldn't see how tangled up her loyalties were.

"Where's Beck?" she asked.

"I'm here," called the man himself, striding over to join them on the ramp. Paxton's expression tightened.

The leader's shirt hung in tatters, revealing a long gash across his chest. A piece of bloody cloth bound one of his legs. No trace of his cocky, joking manner remained.

The two men shifted on the ramp, uncomfortable in such close proximity. She knew the hostility they felt toward each other was not far below the surface. What would happen now?

"How many have you lost?" she asked Beck.

The leader frowned. "Many. But it would have been worse if you hadn't come back. Would have been hard to blame you for running."

Beck's gaze flickered at Paxton, and it occurred to her they were both surprised to see her again. Had they believed her capable of leaving them all to die?

"You were right about the ship," said Paxton. "It was a good call."

Beck reached out and took hold of her chin, lifting and tilting her face. The skin on the side of her neck stung as it stretched.

"That's an angry cut," he said.

She pulled her chin free. "I'm alive." Scanning the ground in front of the wall, she counted at least eight bodies—two of them very small. She closed her eyes, heart aching. Surviving against all odds, only to die like this.

"Were you attacked?" Paxton asked her.

Her eyes found his face again. "On the bog road."

He nodded, jaw clenching.

"No doubt they'll be back," said Beck, scanning the sky above the abbey, following the path of approach and retreat.

"No doubt," agreed Paxton.

"You still offering a ride?"

Asha studied the leader, surprised by his change of heart. Though perhaps *not* surprising, considering what had happened since then.

The Manti captain hesitated. "We can destroy the hive. Shouldn't be hard for Banshee to trace them back."

"But is it the only one?"

Paxton nodded. "No way to be sure."

Carrick joined them on the ramp.

"How bad?" Beck asked him.

The priest's dark gray eyes and heavy brows would have given him an intense countenance in any situation, but especially so now. "We lost twenty-six," he replied.

Asha moaned softly. A staggering number for the nearly

extinct. The fact she hadn't known they existed until today didn't make it any easier to hear.

"We've got eight gravely injured," Carrick continued. "One is stung—I doubt she will make it. The others might with proper care."

Asha remembered how the Manti ship had diagnosed her on board. "Maybe Banshee could help them," she said to Paxton.

He studied her a moment, and glanced at Beck. "I can get you someplace safe, and look at your wounded, if that's what you want."

"Aye." Beck nodded. "We'd be grateful."

"I intend to lock you in the hold for the journey," warned Paxton. "When we let you out, you get off the ship. No discussion."

Beck nodded. "Agreed. Carrick, tell the others. Tell them to pack up quickly."

The priest hesitated, dark gaze shifting between the two men. Then he turned and walked down the ramp.

"We can't take you all on Banshee," said Paxton. "We'll have to go for the other ship first. But you can board your wounded now, and we'll see what the ship can do for them. Make it quick."

"Thank you," said Asha.

He moved past her on the ramp without replying, and boarded his ship.

She was still staring after him when Beck spoke to her in a low voice. "I'm going to trust I know where your loyalties lie and tell you I intend to take over those ships. But I need your help to do it."

She turned, startled.

"He doesn't trust me," Beck continued, "and he's protective

of you. He'll keep us both with him. That means we can work together. And his sister will have to fly the other ship."

Her eyes darted from him to Banshee's open entry door. "What is it you want me to do?" she whispered.

"I gather from what you and the bugman were saying about this ship that it's intelligent, and that it responds to you."

It was easy enough to see where he was going. Take over Banshee. Maybe hold Paxton hostage to get Iris to give up the other ship. But Beck didn't really understand. What he proposed was a lot more complicated—and a lot riskier—than triggering the ship's protective impulses. She found it hard to imagine the ship would stand by while she threatened either Paxton or his sister.

But she needed time to think it through. "I don't know that it's possible," she admitted.

Beck grinned at her. "Sure it is, love. You brought it here without the captain's order." He leaned closer. "This bugman has become attached to you, and that's putting it politely. You've mixed up his thinking, and that's going to work to our advantage. You can't afford to be squeamish about using that. Not if you want to go home."

"Tell me we're bringing them aboard for genetic testing." Iris crossed her arms, glaring at Pax. "That's the only way I won't think you've lost your mind."

He blew out a sigh. "Sure. Let's test them."

The fact they, or their parents, had survived the virus that targeted pure DNA was strong evidence they were contaminated.

"And if they're clean?" Iris persisted.

"They go home with us. Of course." If they were clean, he'd

have no choice. It was Granada or Sanctuary. And relocating them to Sanctuary was problematic. He had to assume Asha had been talking to Beck.

"If they're transgenic, we leave them here," Iris said firmly. "Anything else would . . . create complications." The statement was unhelpfully vague. And yet absolutely true.

Pax turned to the window. He watched Asha walking with Beck toward the wall, where the wounded had been assembled. From the back—dressed in his clothes, muddied, and with her tousled cropped hair—she might have been a teenage boy. His thinking would be a lot clearer right now if she were.

"We'd just be leaving them to die," he murmured.

"I need you to explain to me why that has become our problem."

He looked at her. "I don't think you're any more keen on that idea than I am." *Except for fucking Beck. He can go to the devil.*

Iris flushed and let her gaze drift to the window. He had to think whether he'd ever seen her flush for any reason other than anger. But she didn't give him time to resolve that.

"Promise me this is not about that girl," she said.

He couldn't promise her, because it wasn't true. Asha wanted him to help these people, and it mattered to him what she would think about him going back on his word. More than that, in viewing the whole situation through Asha's eyes, he couldn't bring himself to leave them to the wasps. Especially not after what they'd all been through.

Iris turned to study him, forehead creased in concern.

"Doesn't it ever seem to you we've drawn some arbitrary lines in this conflict?" he asked her. "If these people *are* contaminated, they're not the enemy. They're just like us. What right do we have to make decisions about how they live?"

"By that logic those winged monstrosities are just like us."

Pax refrained from pointing out that most humans would just as readily categorize her as "winged monstrosity."

The wings in question began to vibrate. Her back and shoulders had tensed up because she was frustrated—he recognized it from long experience. Pax knew he overanalyzed. It was his worst failing. He sensed she was about to remind him of this.

Instead, she said, "It's not really about the conflict anymore, you know that. It's about preserving our species and our way of life."

Pax laughed, but he wasn't amused. She was parroting their father.

"We *have* no species without them," he reminded her. "We're artificial constructs. Without our enemies, we're not sustainable."

"Not true, Pax. Synthetic DNA is—"

"Untested on that scale. Unreliable and potentially catastrophic."

Iris groaned. "You're starting to sound like those religious idiots. None of this matters right now. The thing I'm most worried about is that *girl*, and the spell she seems to have cast over you and our ship." She rose from her seat at the console. "I want her on Nefertiti with me."

Good call. But no way.

"I'm not finished questioning her," he said. Iris opened her mouth to protest, but Pax stood up and headed out of the cockpit. "I need to keep an eye on her, Iris."

"Who's going to keep an eye on *you*?" she shouted after him.

Once the wounded had been evaluated and treated, Beck's prediction came true. Paxton divided the passengers into two groups: Beck's group was stowed in Banshee's hold, and Carrick was sent with the second group to Nefertiti.

As Banshee departed, Asha turned Beck's words over in her mind. The man was crazy to think he could pull off something like this. And what would happen to Sanctuary if she helped him? Beck seemed to believe the Manti could destroy the city at any time, and they must have some reason for holding back. What if it was discovered someone from Sanctuary had helped to steal two Manti ships? To kidnap the amir's son and daughter? There'd be no going back from a step like that. Paxton and Iris would have to be held in Sanctuary indefinitely, or the wrath of their father would come down on the city.

But wasn't it *time* they were woken up? Beck's plans were murky, but he was at least proposing to *do* something. The longer she spent away from Sanctuary, the more she felt sickened by their complacency. The fact they'd all survived was important, but was it enough? Quiet lives and quiet deaths. Living in a kind of stasis, focused on preserving the past. Unmolested by their enemy because they presented zero threat to them.

It had begun to seem weak and pointless.

Yet she hesitated. The choice would commit more than just her, and she wasn't sure it was right for her to make it. Despite being a councilwoman's daughter, Asha had no authority or special influence in Sanctuary.

And she had to consider the two men in question. She didn't fully trust Beck. And Paxton—despite knowing what she was supposed to feel about him, she didn't like rewarding his efforts to help Beck's people by betraying him.

But remember he's promised no help for you.

She was staring out the cockpit window, turning it all over in her mind, when Paxton rose from the console beside her.

"Banshee," he said, "monitor the passengers and take control of navigation."

"Yes, Captain."

He glanced down at Asha, seated in the copilot chair. "Come with me."

It was a command, no question about that. But the lines of his face had softened since she first boarded the ship, leading her to hope she wasn't about to be interrogated again. Considering his last round of questioning had been interrupted by the discovery of Nefertiti, this was probably too much to hope for.

As they left the bridge, her heart knocked against her chest. Unpleasant as the last round of questioning had been, she'd had nothing to hide. This time would be different.

Banshee's living space was limited, and a single cabin served as both kitchen and first aid station. Paxton led her there now, directing her to sit at the table while he retrieved the supplies they'd used in treating Beck's people—a box of pungent salves, and the strange bandages that absorbed into the skin.

He pulled a chair next to her and leaned in to look at her neck. She flinched and drew back.

"Take it easy." He leaned in again, lifting her chin as Beck had done, and the sudden contact sent a shiver through her. "What made this cut?"

"The mouthparts," she said. "The hooks in front, I mean."

His eyes shifted to her face. "It must have been close."

"Very close."

Paxton cleared his throat, and he raised his fingers to her neck. Breath hissed through her teeth as he touched the inflamed skin.

"I can do this myself," she protested softly.

"I don't doubt it." But he continued to examine the cut. "It's not deep, but it already looks infected. Be still for a moment."

She froze as he smeared salve into her cut, the distraction of his proximity dulling the pain to a manageable level. She was no longer afraid of the physical threat he represented—it was like that side of him had gone to sleep. Now she was afraid of something else entirely.

"How did you get away?" he asked, positioning the flesh-colored membrane along her neck.

"I cut off one of its legs. Like you told me."

The corners of his lips curled. "That I would like to have seen." His barely there smile faded as he continued, "I don't have to tell you what a big risk you took. You must have been frightened."

Finished sealing the bandage, he drew back and looked at her.

She swallowed. "I thought we'd all die if I didn't."

His eyes flickered back down to the box of medical supplies as he replaced the salve and bandages. "We likely would have."

"It spoke to me," she said. She hadn't planned to tell him this. But it had been eating at her. And nervousness kept her talking.

He lifted an eyebrow. "*What* spoke to you?"

"The wasp. It had me pinned to the ground. It looked into my face and spoke to me." She let go of his gaze, shutting out the expression of alarm for a moment so she could remember. "It told me we aren't stronger or faster or better than them."

Paxton sat back in his chair, folding his arms over his chest. "You're sure?"

"It felt like it was in my head." She remembered the weird echoing quality of its speech. "Actually it felt like a hundred voices in my head. But I didn't imagine it, if that's what you're thinking."

"No."

"It was going to kill me. It . . ." She bit her lip, hesitating.

"Tell me."

"It made a *joke* about it. Said it would sting."

Paxton's eyes widened, and his gaze shifted to the floor as he considered this. "They seemed too animal for that. None of the ones at the abbey spoke, as far as I know."

"Could it be they're not all alike? Maybe only some can speak."

He nodded. "It would be more surprising if they *were* all alike."

Paxton continued deep in thought, and she knew something about this revelation disturbed him. It had certainly disturbed *her*. It was hard to imagine their reasons were the same.

"I didn't know mutations that extreme had survived," she said.

He laughed dryly. "You should just toss out anything you've been told about what is and isn't possible with regard to transgenics. In the decades before you and I were born, the biohacking community was like the American Wild West. No regulations. No tracking. No controls. We find new kinds of organisms *all the time*. That's part of the reason for the Scarab patrols. We can't afford to overlook some species that might threaten us some day."

She knew the garage labs had been careless. That they lacked proper training and equipment. And they'd been so numerous that what regulations *had* been in place had been completely ineffectual.

"It seemed strange to me, you fighting them," she ventured. "I mean, they're like you."

Paxton raised his eyes to her face. "That's a very human thing to say."

Her cheeks flashed hot. But his brittle tone softened as he continued, "I think what you mean is we both have insect DNA. That's true, but . . . look at me, Asha."

Something about the way he said this made her shake. Her head felt unsteady as she met his gaze.

"Am I more like you, or like them?" he asked.

Those eyes of his—with their elfin slant and veined green color very much like those luminous pulses of Banshee's—were not a good measure. Her gaze flowed over the rest of him.

"You're right," she said. "But we're enemies too."

He studied her a moment. "I know you've been taught to hate us. I'm curious whether anyone ever educated you about the reason for the war."

They were moving into perilous territory, but anything was better than revisiting the topic of her intentions toward him or his ship.

"We were taught that you were designed to be aggressive," she replied, "and that it led you to band together to conquer us."

Paxton smiled darkly, but before he could reply she continued, "But my father told me it was because we treated you like animals. That you hated us for that. There's plenty of Archive material that backs that up."

She noted the flicker of surprise. "Well, there's truth to both stories. Our parents did hate you for how you treated us. But we also believed we were superior. That we could manage things better. In some ways we have. In others I don't think we're much different."

He grew thoughtful, and it robbed his countenance of its customary severity. She remembered what Beck had said about being squeamish—if she wanted to go home, she couldn't afford it. But what he had insinuated about Paxton . . . *Was* there something beyond those slumbering mating instincts?

"You have a . . ." She trailed off, raising her hand until her fingers almost touched a cut along his cheekbone.

Confusion wrinkled his brow, and then it smoothed with understanding. "It's not deep."

"Could I . . . ?" She reached into the first aid box and lifted out the jar of salve.

He hesitated, surprised. She expected him to decline. She almost hoped he would. But instead he said, "Thank you."

Fingers trembling, she scooped out a small amount of salve. As she touched his cheek he blinked, and she felt a warm fluttering in her abdomen.

She bent closer, smoothing away the excess with the tips of her fingers. When she finished, their eyes met. She felt his breath against her cheeks. Her heart raced as her gaze slipped down, tracing the curve of his mouth. His lips parted.

On impulse she leaned in, giving a small sniff, like an animal scenting something. Something flashed in his eyes, and she felt his fingers slide up her arm.

She sat up, and he did too. She wasn't sure whether she'd lost her nerve or found it, but she decided to give him one more chance. Just one before she considered helping Beck to betray him.

"Take me home, Pax," she breathed. His eyes locked on to hers. It was the first time she'd spoken his name. "Take all of us home. Back to Sanctuary, I mean. We're no threat to you."

"Asha . . ." He sank back in his chair, frowning deeply.

"I'm not a spy, or an assassin. Something's happened to me—some kind of brain injury. Even if I was a spy, how could I hurt you from Sanctuary?" She leaned close again, laying her hand on his arm, and he flinched. "I'm afraid to go to Granada. I want to go home."

He watched her with pursed lips and set jaw.

"Please, Pax. If you don't care about me, think about the others on board. There are children who've lost their parents. Wounded people needing care. What will happen to them?"

"They can't go to Sanctuary," he said flatly.

"Why not?"

The pleading, desperate edge to her voice—which was not at all pretended—did nothing to shift the disconcerting, dark resolve that had taken the place of his softer expression.

"They're most likely contaminated," he said. "Some humans survived the plague because they were in protected areas. But most survivors have been found to have some form of nonhuman DNA. Usually insect, sometimes animal."

She stared at him, confused. What he'd said raised so many questions she didn't know which to ask first.

"I thought the plague wiped out everyone with animal DNA, along with the pure DNA humans."

He gave a grim nod. "Mostly true. A lot of the experimentation with animals came early, before lab regulation. But later animal transgenics had the same required genetic marker that protected the insect transgenics."

"So you're saying Beck's people are transgenic? Maybe even Manti?"

"We don't know yet. Banshee and Nefertiti are equipped for DNA sequencing. All the passengers are being checked en route."

"If they are," she said, finally understanding, "Sanctuary won't take them."

She tried to imagine Beck's reaction to finding out he *was* his enemy. She was about to ask what Pax intended to do with them when he said, "You're right. But it's not the only reason they can't go there."

"What do you mean?"

"Sanctuary is uncontaminated. It has to stay that way."

His guarded expression caused her heart to thump uneasily. "I still don't understand."

"Manti insect genes are dominant. If we don't continue to

incorporate human DNA, eventually our species will devolve, like the wasps. Until we can perfect synthetic DNA, we need protected organic sources."

Protected organic sources. It took her a moment to process the phrase. When she did, the deck of the ship whirled under her. She felt queasy.

Her whole life she'd been taught that Sanctuary represented hope. A second chance for humanity. Unless she'd misunderstood him, Pax was telling her they were nothing more than an insurance policy for the continuing supremacy of their enemies.

Her fingers curled under the edge of her seat, squeezing, trying to stop the free fall.

"What happens—" Her voice broke, and she cleared her throat. "What happens once you have the synthetic DNA you need?"

"I don't know. There's some controversy about that. But I believe we'd be foolish to allow you all to die out."

Her body shook from the blast of his revelation. It changed everything—or almost everything. It didn't change the fact humans had survived, and as long as there were survivors, there was hope. The Manti's DNA problem might very well be the only reason they *had* survived.

She glanced up. "That's why a Manti prince is watching over our city. You're not a kidnapper. Or a slaver."

He shook his head. "Sanctuary is ideally situated. No transgenic activity within hundreds of kilometers. Few creatures can thrive in that environment. Had it been otherwise, we would have relocated you to Granada. We may still at some point. But our psychologists have made a pretty strong case for the health benefits of the illusion of autonomy."

Dear God. Asha closed her eyes and breathed. The weight of it bore down on her, heavier with each new revelation. Her body seemed to fuse with the chair as she braced herself for what would come next.

"What about the people who disappear?" she asked.

Her question was met with silence. After a few moments she opened her eyes.

Pax leaned forward, resting elbows on knees and folding his hands.

"We have an understanding with your governing council."

Her heart heaved.

"That's why you have power enough to run those computers in your Archive," he continued, "and plenty of food and clean water even in the driest summers. That's why we leave you alone. But if the general population knew, there'd be an uprising. When someone finds out the truth, and someone always *does*, they have to be . . . removed."

She stared at him in horror as the last block of her foundation crumbled to dust. "I . . . My mother's on the governing council."

He froze, and his mouth opened, then closed. Finally he rose to his feet. "I know all this was hard for you to hear. But I think you understand now that you can never go home."

He held her gaze only a moment—just long enough to see her collapsing in on herself. She sickened at the irony. The preservation of information had given shape and meaning to her life. And now information, carefully concealed, had stripped all meaning away.

Pax returned to the bridge and sank into the pilot's chair, leaning on the console with his head in his hands.

What had been the point of telling her all that? Couldn't he at least have given a moment's consideration to the fact he was knocking the ground out from under her—destroying everything she'd ever known or believed? Any hope she might have been holding on to?

Just as well, he thought bitterly. *There is no hope for her.*

"Banshee," he muttered, "keep an eye on Asha. Keep me updated on what she's doing."

"Yes, Captain. Asha is seated in the galley. She's crying."

Pax closed his eyes. "Just report every quarter hour. Unless she does something you think I need to know about right away. Use your judgment. Don't permit her to harm herself."

"Yes, Captain. Captain, Nefertiti has transmitted her passenger data, and I've compiled a report on the Irish survivors."

"Summarize."

"Survivors are human, with one exception."

He glanced up with surprise. "Only one? Who is it?"

"Identified as 'Father Carrick.' Lupine contamination."

He should have known. The man had a feral intensity. But Pax's senses weren't as sharp as his sister's, especially when it came to non-insect transgenics. Iris had fought alongside Carrick in the abbey. Surely she had detected the abnormality. Why hadn't she said so?

It wasn't the result Pax had expected. Now he was obligated to take the lot of them to Granada. The humans would go into confinement. As for the priest . . . Pax was pretty sure this was the first documented wolf-flavored transgenic organism. Wolves were believed to be extinct. The scientists at Sustainable Transgenics would be *very* interested in him.

Pax's father would be pleased about the find, maybe even enough to overlook the questionable decisions his son had made in the last twenty-four hours.

And the humans would be taken care of. They wouldn't die from hunger or exposure or attacks by hostile species. They'd have the option of buying their freedom through intermarriage—even Asha, if he could confirm she wasn't a spy.

He could almost make himself easy about all of it. Until he looked at it through Asha's eyes. She was going to hate him for this.

Sanctuary was within the bounds of Arches, but the park was huge. If you wanted to explore the farthest boundary you had to spend the night away from the city, or know someone who had access to one of the handful of rechargeable buggies the governing council had managed to keep running since the war. Due to Asha's mother's position on the council, Asha had probably seen more of the park than most.

Her favorite time to explore was the cool of a late-spring evening, and her favorite spot was the Fiery Furnace. She and her father had explored every corner of the labyrinthine sandstone canyon. There was a small arch they liked to scale so they could sit and watch the sun go down.

She felt like she was at the base of one of those narrow canyons now. Instead of the flutter of excitement she usually felt gazing up the burnt-orange walls to the ribbon of clear sky above, claustrophobia was setting in. The walls groaned and tipped inward, sealing out the light.

She stood up from the table, wiping her eyes with the back of her hand. She exited the galley.

The panel slid closed behind her, and she stood alone in the dark corridor. She backed against one wall, forgetting for the moment the strange nature of the ship. The living membrane warmed beneath her, and a circle of green light materialized at her hip. She breathed deeply and closed her eyes, pressing her hand against the circle.

"Do you think my mother knows the truth?" she murmured.

She did not expect the ship to answer, nor did she need it to.
The question was naïve.

As for her father, that was more painful to contemplate—
that he might have known and kept it from her. She could
imagine her mother concealing such a thing—there were certain aspects of her mother's work she had never been able to
discuss with her family. But her father was honest to a fault.
Especially when it came to Asha.

But he *would* lie to her, she knew, if he thought it would
protect her.

Then it dawned on her: This could explain why she'd been
taken. Maybe she had somehow learned the truth. It was the
only plausible explanation that had occurred to her.

Fresh tears streamed down her cheeks. Miriam would preserve Sanctuary at any cost—what Pax had told Asha had only
served as further confirmation. But give up her own daughter,
her only child, to the Manti? Asha would never have believed
it possible.

But everything she'd believed was a lie.

"Asha, the captain wants to see you on the bridge."

She sat up, breathing and trying to reorient herself. She'd
fallen asleep in the corridor—a full-system shutdown likely
triggered by a subconscious impulse to preserve her sanity.

Rubbing her sore neck, she rose to her feet and went to
find Pax.

As she stepped into the cockpit, a city came into view, spreading like a quilt over an arid valley, a river curving around one
side. Something about it made her uneasy, and as they drew

closer she realized what: nothing was moving. No people or vehicles in the streets. It was a ghost town, like Moab, near her home.

"Where are we?" she asked.

Pax rested against the console, gaze fixed on her rather than the breathtaking view.

"Nearly home. I'll have to report to my father there, so we need to finish our interview. It's in your best interests to tell me everything you remember."

She walked to the copilot chair and sat down, before he could order her into it. "I've told you everything I remember," she said stiffly. But inside she was on high alert. He'd warned her Banshee could read whether she was lying.

"The fact that your mother is on the governing council was a rather important detail. Why didn't you tell me before?"

"I didn't know it was important. I didn't know about your . . ." She shifted her gaze to the window. "About your *agreement*."

"I want you to tell me anything else you've remembered," said Pax, "whether it seems important or not." He was all business now. There was no threat in his tone, but nothing yielding, either.

"My mother is Miriam St. John," she said. "Do you know her?"

Asha's tone made this more of an accusation than a confession, but she saw she'd surprised him. *More* than surprised him—he looked troubled. "I know Councilwoman Miriam," he said, "though not by her surname."

She realized with some relief that if her mother had turned her over to the Manti, Pax would have some knowledge of it. Even if his memory had been damaged, surely his copilot would have been able to fill him in. Iris had been just as puzzled by her appearance as Pax.

"What else?" he pressed.

Asha shook her head, anxiety giving way to frustration. "I work in the Archive, and my father's an archivist too. I told you that already. I've only been to the reservoir once before—it's against the rules." She hugged her arms over her chest. "I still don't know why I was there, and staring at me like you want to shake me isn't going to change that."

Pax's frown deepened. He bent toward her, and she flinched as he took hold of her hands, pressing the palm of her left hand against the console. She felt her fingers sink into Banshee, and the ship's warm, vibrating caress. The other hand Pax kept, thumb pressed against the inside of her wrist.

Their gazes locked, and he said, "Do you intend to harm me or my family?"

She could feel her pulse pumping against his thumb, and knew that he could feel it too.

"No," she replied.

She was less worried about Pax than Banshee, who no doubt had more sophisticated methods. But the ship remained silent. She didn't have time to contemplate the two possibilities that suggested.

"Pax." She curled her fingers in, tugging at her wrist, and he released her. "If there was any sort of plot against you, obviously it's failed. It's clear at this point I'm useless to you."

He studied her without replying, and she continued, "You won't take me back to Sanctuary because of what I know—you don't want to expose your agreement with the council. And the others can't go to Sanctuary if they aren't human. Why not drop us all off together? Let us all start over someplace new. You'd never have to see any of us again."

Pax was shaking his head before she'd finished. Her heart sank. "Even if I was willing to let you go without answers to my questions, I can't release the others. Their DNA is pure."

So they were human after all. She slumped against her chair. "What will you do with them?"

Pax sank down beside her with a sigh. "Our genetics lab manages our population of survivors. There's a village, created specifically for pure DNA humans. They'll be fed and sheltered. They're more likely to survive there than anywhere else."

Protected organic sources. It was time to let go of trying to move the immoveable. The trip to Granada was inevitable at this point, for all of them. And while there may have been opportunity in Banshee's protective impulses, she wasn't going to have enough time for an attempt at undermining the ship's loyalty.

She needed to start thinking about what came next.

"ETA in fifteen, Pax." Iris's voice sounded over the com. "Shall I radio our status?"

"Go ahead, Iris," replied Pax. "We'll see you there."

He sat back in his chair, raising a hand to rub his forehead. "I don't want you to be afraid," he said.

She stared at his profile, surprised by both his words and his softened tone.

He dropped his hand and met her gaze. "I won't let anyone hurt you."

Her heart stuttered. "Why?"

"Because I'm not the monster you think I am."

"I—" She shifted her gaze to the window. "I don't think you're a monster."

"Do you think you can trust me?"

She hesitated. How could she tell him that something in her, a step below conscious thought, already did trust him? It wasn't rational, or logical, or even sensible.

"I believe you don't want to hurt me," she said simply. "But once we reach Granada I wonder whether it will be within your power to protect me." She clenched her hands together in her lap. "Or whether it will continue to be important to you."

Silence stretched between them, and feeling his eyes still on her, she looked at him.

"Banshee," he said, holding her gaze, "Asha risked her life to help Iris and me at Kylemore Abbey. I want your log to reflect that."

"Yes, Captain."

"I also want you to alter your log to say that Asha was picked up as a result of a relocation request from Sanctuary's governing council."

Asha's mouth fell open.

"That would falsify the record, Captain."

"Yes, Banshee," confirmed Pax. "I'm asking you to falsify the record. Asha risked herself for Iris and me. I need you to alter the record to help me protect her when we reach the Alhambra."

She thought about how she'd considered using Banshee's weakness against Pax—and now he was exploiting that same weakness to *help* her. What was he risking for her? What if he was found out?

"I still need to get to the truth of this," he told her. "But I'll be better able to protect you if we can conceal the unusual circumstances. This is a reprieve, Asha. Depending on what we discover, I may have to go to my father with all of it."

She nodded, afraid to hope he could pull it off.

"I've altered the record, Captain," confirmed Banshee.

Realizing she'd stopped breathing sometime in the last two minutes, she let air fill her chest. "Will it be enough?" she asked Pax.

"Probably not." He glanced down at the console. "Banshee?"

"Yes, Captain."

"Please also alter the record to show that Asha passed most of the trip alone with me in my quarters."

She raised her eyebrows, heat flashing across her cheeks.

"I'm sorry," said Pax, avoiding meeting her look of surprise. "It gives me a motive for keeping you with me."

She recalled Beck's words back at the chapel: *If you're with me, they'll leave you alone.*

This was the last thing she'd expected from him, and she was grateful, whatever the motive behind it. But she made a silent vow that as soon as she could, she'd find a way to free herself from the necessity of being protected by others.

DEBAJO

Pax changed the zoom on the view from the cockpit window, and the Alhambra came into focus. Most of the images Asha had seen of the palace had shown it washed in bright Spanish sun. Under the circumstances it was hard not to view the low-hanging clouds as ominous.

The structure looked more like a fortress from the air, mud-colored towers hugging the forested hillside, overlooking the sprawl of Granada below. But there were countless archive images attesting to the delicate beauty within. Meticulous gardens, still courtyard pools, and Moorish-flavored architecture. Columns, arches, fountains, and arabesques.

As they continued their approach, her eye picked out a number of towers that she'd never noticed in the photos she'd seen. Slender, organic spires—some membranous like Banshee and others more like honeycomb—protruding between the palace's shorter towers and blocky buildings. Unlike the static architecture around them, they gradually changed color, their shifting palette including hues from the backdrop of cloud or the earthy tones of the fortress itself. The Manti, like the succession of conquerors before them, had left their mark on the place.

"Looks like a storm is coming," she murmured, watching the upper portions of the spires transition between shades of blue, gray, and purple.

"It's early for that," replied Pax. "But maybe we'll get a little rain."

She let go of her visual focus, and the spires seemed to melt into their surroundings.

Wake, Ophelia.

The ship, the sky, the captain—like the spires, they all faded to the background as the coded command relayed across her consciousness. The command and the view of the Alhambra were connected—the former had been triggered by the latter. There was no doubt in her mind about that. It had been her own idea.

And she understood everything now.

THE PREVIOUS MORNING

"Who is that?" asked Zee.

Asha shielded the afternoon sun with one hand, squinting down at the desert below. She could make out two figures—a tall man facing a raggedly dressed, shrill-voiced woman with silver hair hanging down her back in a tangled, ropey mass.

"Come on." Zee rose from her seat. "Let's check it out."

Asha jumped up and followed her down the graceful slope of the sand-colored arch. Exploring the desert with Zee reminded her of old times, hiking among the monuments with her father. But old times were gone as of six months ago, when Asha's father disappeared, and Zee approached her about joining a group that was planning to challenge the governing council.

Considering Asha's mother was *on* the governing council, Zee had taken a risk in recruiting her. But Councilwoman Miriam had said nothing could be done to recover Asha's father, and Asha hadn't been able to forgive her for that. He was believed to have been picked up by a Manti patrol outside the bounds of Sanctuary. The fact it had happened to others before him didn't make it easier to accept. And the fact Asha's parents had lived apart for the last fifteen years didn't make it easier to understand.

Asha stayed close to Zee as she crept around the boulders at the base of the arch, sun glinting off her platinum, pixie-cut hair. The disjointed tones they'd heard from above assembled into a meandering stream of words as they drew closer.

". . . and the contamination will spread so fast you can't contain it, authored by your idols whom you've held in contempt, and destroyed by your own hand, and you will not see it come, because every man is weak in the body and if that weakness shall spread to his heart he is infected, and defeated, and you more than the rest, yes, you more than the rest . . ."

Asha rose up on her toes, angling around Zee to get a better look at the speaker.

". . . she will destroy you with arrows of fire . . ."

The old woman suddenly lifted her gaze and looked directly at Asha. The shock of recognition was so powerful that her body failed to respond to the impulse to shrink out of view.

"Ophelia," whispered Asha, leaning against Zee's back. "My god, that's her—Stella Engle."

"Sure is," murmured Zee. She didn't sound surprised, which struck Asha as odd considering everyone believed Engle was dead.

". . . and you, Manti," continued the old woman, "will

embrace the angel whose fire will consume you and your house
and her as well unless you loose her arrows into the sky . . ."

"Did you catch that?" asked Zee.

It had taken a moment to sink in after the first shock. But
yes, she'd heard. Ophelia had called the man *Manti.*

Zee bent to pick up a rock and started around the base of
the arch.

"What are you doing?" Asha whispered.

"Come on!" Zee took off at a run.

Ophelia launched at the stranger, and he was too busy
fighting her off to notice Zee separating from the shadow of
the monument.

The rock struck home with a nauseating thud—Zee could
hit a rabbit from ten meters away. But before the man's body
hit the ground there was an explosion of motion. Something
ejected from him: a fabric covering that encased and inflated.
By the time they reached him, what had looked like fabric had
hardened into something resembling an almond shell—
oblong, pitted, and the same color as the sand. Shreds of the
man's clothing littered the ground around him.

"What the hell?" cried Zee.

Asha approached the woman slowly. "Stella?"

She watched Asha through wide, bloodshot eyes. Blood
from a cut in her forehead ribboned down one temple and
cheekbone. Her face was so weathered it resembled the desert's microbiotic crust.

"It's okay," Asha soothed. "We won't hurt you."

The old woman pounced on her, and Asha yelped as she
knotted her bony fingers in Asha's shirt.

"Easy, Stella!" called Zee, coming over to help.

She grasped the slight shoulders, but Stella ignored Zee and
tugged Asha closer. "His ship will return," she rasped, misting
Asha's cheeks with saliva. "You must be ready."

Then she shoved Asha away—*hard,* for a woman who must be more than seventy years old—tore herself free from Zee's grasp, and turned and ran under the arch.

"Wait!" cried Asha, starting after her, but Zee caught her arm.

"We can go after her later. Come take a look at this."

They examined the almond shell and found it was completely sealed. Experimental attempts to dent or break it failed to even make a mark.

"Do you think he's alive in there?" asked Zee.

"Assuming you didn't kill him with that rock, you mean?"

"Assuming that."

"How should I know?"

"I thought you were the expert on them!"

"I'm the expert on them *twenty years ago.* I don't know anything about their technology."

"*Guess,* Ash." Zee used the same shortened version of Asha's name her father always had. It hurt to hear it. But Zee was the only one who seemed to understand the pain of Asha's loss, and Asha never corrected her.

Asha eyed the shell again. "I don't know that the rock was absolutely necessary. But good shot."

"Trust me, it was necessary." She grinned. "And thanks."

Asha rolled her eyes. Zee was a decade her senior, but you'd never know it by her behavior. Maybe *because* of her age—she'd been nine at the time of the Bio Holocaust—she hadn't adapted well to a life of relative confinement.

"I'd say he's alive," said Asha. "We think the Manti were experimenting with blending plant and animal DNA with robotics and artificial intelligence. It's probably some kind of armor that was triggered by the sudden blow. I'd say this thing is going to break down at some point and let him out."

Zee nodded. "Makes sense to me. So the more important question is what is he doing here?"

"Maybe he was trying to take Stella." Asha scanned the expansive blue sky, frowning. "She seemed to think he has a ship that's coming back. I didn't think they ever came this close."

Zee knelt next to the shell. She glanced up at Asha. "This could be our chance."

Zee was right—it was the opportunity they'd been waiting for. A better one than they could have hoped for.

"You still want to do this?" asked Zee.

The day Asha learned her father had been taken, she'd decided she was going after him. She'd been ready to walk alone into the desert when Zee approached her, befriending her at first, but eventually sharing her plans to turn Sanctuary against its governing council. Zee was also eager to get people into the Manti capital, and she'd collaborated with Asha on her plan, beginning with training her in self-defense.

But it turned out infiltrating Granada was more complicated than Asha had anticipated. She had been warned almost from birth that anyone leaving Sanctuary would be picked up by the Manti, and so had assumed procuring a ride to their city would be as easy as wandering out past the reservoir. But Zee told her the threat of Manti abduction had been exaggerated to protect the post-holocaust generation—from the hazards of the desert, as well as their enemies. The truth was the Manti ships did not appear according to any predictable schedule. Sometimes they didn't see one for weeks.

Even if Asha did manage to get picked up, she had to do so without raising suspicions. The Manti had heightened senses, and clearly at this point their technology was far superior. Zee had fixed on the idea of sending sleeper agents, who couldn't reveal what they didn't know. An Archive connection she would never name had furnished her with every piece of data on hypnosis. She'd been experimenting on Asha for months.

They'd already come up with a command for sleeping, incorporating the code name "Ophelia" to create a phrase no one else was likely to say and trigger Asha by accident. For waking they chose a visual cue from the Archive—an image of a structure she was certain to see at some point once she'd reached Granada.

The plan was full of holes. The Manti might simply kill her. Or she might arrive in the city safely, but never find her father. She might find him dead.

But the alternative was to do nothing, and she'd been doing that long enough.

"Yeah," replied Asha. "I still want to do this."

Asha's heart thumped heavily, rattling the hollow-feeling places in her chest. She turned to study Pax's profile, ignoring the conversation he was carrying on with his sister over the com.

She marveled at the peril she'd placed herself in. She and Zee had been like children, playing a game they didn't understand. That plan to leave her on the beach in that thin cotton dress, hoping Pax wouldn't view her as a threat and kill her, when the real danger had lain in triggering those overpowering mating instincts of his.

As her heartbeat slowed, instincts gradually acknowledging that she was in no immediate danger, her recent experiences began to merge with her restored memory. Had her father learned the truth about the Manti's agreement with the governing council? Had her mother agreed to, or even *ordered*, her father's abduction?

She closed her eyes. She couldn't afford to speculate about that right now. More important to focus on Pax. Because Pax might very well have been the one to transport him. Which meant Pax knew where he was.

"I think you're an idiot, Brother, but no more than I am myself." Iris's words pulled Asha's attention back to their conversation. "I won't give you away, but I need something in exchange."

Pax frowned. "What's that?"

There was hesitation on Iris's end. "Can you shut off Banshee's AI?"

Now hesitation on Pax's end. "AI offline, Banshee."

"Yes, Captain, AI offline."

"What is this about, Iris?"

"Carrick."

Pax sat forward in the pilot's chair. "What about him?"

"I don't want him going to the geneticists."

Pax studied the image of Iris on the console. "Why?"

Iris's sigh was audible over the com. Her gaze shifted away. "Because he's unusual and handy in a fight and I don't want him to end up in a hundred labeled jars."

"They're not likely to kill him, Iris."

Her gaze came back to Pax, and she frowned. "They're not likely to kill Asha, either. But for some reason you find it distasteful her parts might get rearranged in interrogation."

Asha shuddered, and Pax's gaze flickered toward her. She couldn't figure out what they were talking about. Pax had said Beck's people were human, but clearly he hadn't told her everything.

"What is it you want me to do?" asked Pax.

"Help me make sure he's not taken into custody. We've compiled that damned DNA record, so if we don't, he'll go straight to DAB-lab."

"That damned DNA record was your idea. You knew what he was. You knew he'd end up at Sustainable Transgenics."

"I only knew he wasn't Manti or human. And I thought I could let go of this." A pause, and then, "I tried."

"Interesting."

"Shut up, Pax. My idea is for him to escape as soon as we leave the ship. He's an unknown quantity. No one will suspect we're involved. If he can make it down into the lower city he'll be safe for a while. Until I can figure out what to do about him."

Pax groaned. "You're serious about this."

"Serious as *you* are."

"Did you tell him what he is?"

"Yes."

"How did he take it?"

"Hard to say. He's not . . . expressive."

"I'm willing to bet he is when he wants to be. You've spoken to him about your plan, I assume."

"Not yet."

"Iris! We'll be on the ground in minutes. What if he refuses to leave the others? He strikes me as the type. And he'll have information that could hurt you."

"Easy enough to deny. And he's going to be separated from the others anyway. Probably permanently. I just need to make that clear to him."

"He's going to blame us for that. He's going to blame *you*, Iris."

"I need you to trust me to manage him, Pax."

"Fine," said Pax, blowing out a sigh of defeat. "I've got to bring Banshee's AI back online so no one notices the gap. I've already mucked around with the log too much."

"Be sure to send Father the report from your meeting with Sanctuary's council. And let him know we both have other business, so he won't expect to see us right away."

"He'll want to hear about Nefertiti and the wasps. We'll have to get back quickly."

"I don't exactly have a plan, Pax." Hesitation had crept into Iris's tone.

"We'll have to wing it. Won't be the first time."

"I don't suppose there's any way of talking you into letting them take Asha with the others. Just until we get back."

"You're right, there's not. See you in a minute."

Pax sighed, and before he could bring Banshee back into the conversation, Asha asked, "What is Carrick?"

Pax sank his hands into the console as the ship approached the city. "Wolf transgenic. We've never found one before."

"This is another big risk you're taking."

He met her gaze. "Yes."

As she studied him, he noticed something different about her. She looked . . . not less frightened, exactly. More resigned?

"The two of you are close," she said.

"We take care of each other. We always have. Do you have sisters or brothers?"

She shook her head. "I'm close to my father. I was." Pain creased her forehead as she frowned.

He shifted his attention back to the ship, fingers connecting with sensors within the console, guiding them into position for a vertical landing.

"Stay close to me when we leave Banshee," he said, "and especially if we end up down in the city. I know you can take care of yourself. But you're an outsider here, and some will sense it. They may be curious about you. Or worse."

"Okay," she agreed. But her expression was frustratingly neutral. The last thing he needed was for her to bolt.

"Banshee online," said Pax, and the AI confirmed. "Take the landing."

Pax disengaged from the console, and Asha asked, "What is this village like? Where you're taking the others."

He folded his arms, considering her question as well as the

deep, rich brown of her eyes. She had a good heart, to continue to take an interest in the fate of the others with her own so uncertain.

"Al Campo is run by DAB-lab, where the geneticists work. The lab monitors the people there and provides for their needs, but they're mostly left to themselves."

"Mostly." She pronounced the word in a knowing way. She had a healthy skepticism. But then she'd just had her world upended.

"They are studied. Some of them undergo medical testing. Nothing inhumane."

"Will they ever be released?"

Pax glanced at the window as Banshee set down on the pad, rocking the cockpit gently.

"Most of them will not." He rose to his feet. "Time to go."

He had to stay sharp now, which required pushing the enigmatic girl and her questions to the back of his mind. Granada had been notified they were transporting human cargo, and a Guard escort would be waiting for them on the pad.

He wasn't sure when over the past twenty-four hours he'd decided he wasn't turning Asha over to anyone, and that he would conceal her story. He knew she didn't understand his decision, and he only half understood it himself. But what he did know was the Guard would *make* her talk, and they wouldn't care whether they got the information they started out looking for—or how many pieces she was in when they finished.

No one in the Guard was going to question his authority to escort Asha personally, but the priest had complicated everything.

Asha trailed the tips of her fingers along the wall as they moved through the corridor, and something about it caught at his heart.

"Good-bye, Banshee," she said as they stepped onto the boarding ramp.

He wondered whether the ship would reply despite his ban on communication with her. A moment later Banshee trilled a programmed response: "Be well, Asha." She wouldn't know it was programmed, and he found that he was glad for that. He'd sensed the growing bond between his captive and his ship, and knew that for some reason Asha found it comforting. He didn't want to take that away from her.

His own developing bond—and the questionable course of action it had propelled him into—was of greater concern. He needed processing time for that, but the necessity of agreeing to help his sister with Carrick meant he wasn't going to get it.

His focus on Asha had left him zero spare cycles for trying to understand what was going on with his sister. He had the barest fragment of a theory that she'd developed an attachment to the wolf man in fighting alongside him at the abbey. Iris was deeply loyal, and her decisions about where to place her loyalty did not always conform to duty or propriety.

All he could do at this point was be ready for anything.

"Remember," he murmured to Asha as they exited the ship, "stay close."

The landing pad had been built specifically for use by the royal household, in a cleared area between two hills—the Alhambra perched atop one, and the old Moorish quarter, the Albayzín, blanketed the other.

The Albayzín was home to both the most creative members of Manti society—artists, writers, architects—and, more recently, to the growing religious fringe. His father's policy toward the latter had been to ignore and later to scoff, with the belief the majority of Granada's citizens would follow the Alhambra's example. But the group was becoming more vocal, and there'd been rumors of planned violence. So far the amir had dismissed all this as paranoia, but there was no question tension was growing in that quarter, and his father had no tolerance for anyone, human or Manti, who presented a threat to what he'd achieved. When the amir finally did decide to clamp down on the zealots, innocent people would suffer, and the community would never be the same. Which would be a shame. The Manti had no history separate from their creators, and only a fledgling culture. Loss of the artist community would be a major blow.

The Albayzín's galleries and music venues had once drawn patrons from all over the city, but mainstream Manti society was increasingly keeping its distance, especially after dark. Even the Guard avoided the area. For the moment, the Moorish quarter was the perfect place to hide a fugitive. Today was market day as well, which meant crowded, noisy streets.

Pax guided Asha toward Nefertiti, and they waited for Iris to come down the ramp. Since the baffling conversation with his sister, he'd been trying to work out a believable rationale for escorting Carrick to the genetics facility himself. It was their best chance of staging an escape.

When Iris reached them she raised her eyebrows in a significant way, and that seemed to spark the chaos that followed. As the Guard marched toward the launch pad, a dark blur throttled down Nefertiti's ramp, shoving Pax roughly aside.

Despite knowing what the blur was, his heart vaulted out of his chest as Carrick scooped an arm around Asha's waist and dragged her down the ramp. Pax shouted with alarm as the priest jumped from the pad to the platform, several meters down. He straightened with his arm coiled around Asha, the point of a knife pressed against her throat.

"Carrick!" snarled Pax. He jumped from the pad, landing on his feet a couple meters from the priest.

"Pax!" Iris shouted.

"Don't come any closer," warned Carrick in that low, imperturbable tone.

Rage boiled in Pax, almost beyond the point of recovery. Rage at Carrick, rage at himself, rage at Iris. But as his sister shouted his name again, reason swam the swirling, scorching divide to whisper in his ear: *Iris planned this.*

His breathing slowed, and his heartbeat, as he continued to talk himself down.

Iris planned this. And it's genius. If the priest had threatened him or Iris, his father would have scoured the city. Would have gone door to door until the man was found. Would not have rested until he was publicly tortured and executed.

But only Pax cared what happened to Asha. He had a motive his father would understand—overpowering desire for a female. If he made mistakes—failed to follow appropriate protocol—it would be soon forgotten.

Even Asha had figured it out, and hung limp in Carrick's arms, watching Pax with eyes bright from excitement, but clear of the fear she should have been feeling.

This is yours to fuck up, bugman.

The Guard had frozen on the catwalk, weapons aimed at Carrick. "Stand down!" Pax ordered them. "Don't shoot!"

Carrick stepped backward, dragging Asha toward the edge of the platform, where there was maybe a four-meter drop to the grass below. He lifted Asha in his arms and jumped.

"My lord?" called one of the guardsmen.

"Secure the other passengers and take them to Al Campo for processing. Iris and I will run down the other two."

"Yes, my lord," replied the guardsman. "I'll call in another detail."

"Don't bother, Captain," replied Pax, moving toward the platform edge. "We'll catch him easily enough."

Pax jumped, and he watched Carrick and Asha run toward the city while he waited for Iris. Her mostly ornamental wings gave her enough lift to hop lightly to the grass without stumbling as he had.

They jogged after the others, and he grumbled, "If he hurts her—"

"You read every book in Father's library, right? Ever come across the word 'lummox'?"

"You could have warned me."

"No, I couldn't. I'd only thought of it thirty seconds before."

They reached the Albayzín's lowest row of houses and slowed their pace. Unless someone had decided to track them—unlikely at this point—they'd be mostly hidden from view by the two-story whitewashed houses and the narrow cobblestone alleys.

The lamps lining the street began flickering on one by one, low bursts of green luminescence that barely registered in the twilight. But they'd make the medieval streets navigable when darkness fell.

"Where's he headed?" asked Pax.

"Debajo," replied Iris.

He turned to stare at her. "Are you crazy? That's right across from the Gaudí Spike."

He used the nickname for the zealots' temple because it had no other name, and because that's exactly what it looked like: a single-spired tribute to Barcelona's Sagrada Familia, the epic and never-completed basilica designed by artist Antoni Gaudí. Insect resin farmed and cultivated in the formerly Spanish countryside enabled the construction of towers like these—fanciful, fragile-looking structures that withstood wind, rain, tremor, and presumably time. Gaudí himself would have approved of the way the towers changed color depending on factors like light, temperature, and humidity.

"We needed someplace the Guard wouldn't be likely to follow," protested Iris.

"Well we got that. If we don't get knifed the moment we
walk in the door I'll congratulate you on your ingenuity."

"We need to disguise, obviously."

"As *what*?"

"It doesn't matter. All the customers wear masks in case of
a raid. We can pick some up in the market."

"How do you know all this, Iris?"

She gave him a scorching look and kept walking.

Debajo fronted as a bar, but pretty much everyone in
Granada knew they offered something much more interesting
than alcohol—an illicit, synthetically produced, highly addic-
tive compound inspired by flowers of the Central American
cloud forests. The flowers were basically opium dens for a specific type of insect. They addicted their guests, who remained
inside until the flowers withered and dropped. At that point
the bugs stumbled out with massive hangovers and immediately went in search of their next fix, pollinating in the process.

The patrons of Debajo stumbled out and started fanatical
religious movements.

As Pax and Iris wended their way toward the heart of the
Albayzín, the activity level in the streets increased. The colorful umbrellas were folding now with dusk coming on, but
market day typically wound up rather than down. The street
merchants carted off their wares, making way for evening
strollers, and shops and restaurants would stay open until the
wee hours. When there was mischief in the Albayzín, which
was becoming a more frequent occurrence, it typically started
the evening of market day.

Thunder rumbled in the distance as Iris stopped next to a
stall with a powder blue umbrella. The vendor—whose clear,

silver-veined wings drooped down his back like a cape—was boxing up his selection of masks. Stunted antennae barely protruded above curls the same silver of his wings.

Most of his masks were ceramic and intricately painted, with multicolored ribbons for hair, but Iris chose simple eye masks, two teal and two purple. She turned out the spiral marking on her wrist, and the man opened a huge paper ledger and copied the mark into it with an artistic flair—quaintly old fashioned, eccentric and possibly subversive, but also a lucky turn. It meant the purchase hadn't gone immediately into a database, which would call attention to their location if anyone decided to come looking for them.

Iris handed Pax a teal mask, and he pulled it over his head, waiting while she fidgeted to adjust hers over her broader face and then struggled with the clasp. Finally he reached up and hooked it for her.

"Let's go," he muttered. "I don't like that you've sent Asha off to this den of iniquity."

"Relax, Pax. Carrick will watch out for her."

"What makes you think so?"

"He's a *priest*."

"Oh of course. History attests to *their* saintly qualities."

"I'm sorry if I hurt you," Asha's latest captor said, releasing her arm.

"This is part of Iris's plan?" she asked, rubbing the sore spot his fingers had left.

"Yes."

The priest hopped over a low stone wall and she followed. They slipped into a narrow alley between two houses.

Carrick fished a device from his pocket and held it close to his face, muttering an oath.

"Are you really a priest?" she asked.

He gave her a wry smile.

"I mean . . . I didn't know there *were* priests anymore." He looked old enough to have been born fifteen years before the holocaust at most. It was possible he was ordained, but only just.

Ignoring the question as well as the elaboration, he handed her the disk. "Can you read this? My close vision is no good."

She examined the small screen. There was a video feed of their position, overlaid with a series of green arrows. "Yes. Where's it taking us?"

"A tavern—Debajo. I think it's Spanish for 'below'—or more like 'beneath.' Iris thinks we'll be safe there until they can come for us. It's across from a temple of some kind, with a tall tower. I'll watch for that; you watch the map."

She nodded. "Let's go."

"Keep your head down," he murmured as they started up a steep, cobbled alley. "Iris said plenty of them look as human as we do, but if we're staring at everything we'll stand out. And don't get too close to anyone—some of them can smell that we're different."

Keeping her head down was not easy, even with Carrick's warning and the focus required by the job she'd been given. Because of her Archive specialty, she had pretty much memorized the Alhambra's façade, as well as the most famous aspects of its interior, but she'd not spent much time on the rest of the city. Besides that, there were Manti embellishments. Everywhere she looked—or tried not to look—were whimsical fountains and streetlamps, all with organic lines, detailed mosaics, and morphing colors. There were sculptures of birds, flowers, insects, and mythological creatures, and some of them moved—so naturally she thought they were real at first. A peacock perched on the wall of a rooftop garden, its many green-rimmed "eyes" seeming to follow them as they passed.

She was even more careful about studying the people, but after Iris there was not much to shock her. As they strode through the streets she caught glimpses of wings, spiked appendages, and sharply angled faces. Other times her quick flickers of inspection revealed no Manti characteristics.

"There," called Carrick, and she glanced up to see the temple spire, similar to the ones she'd noticed on the grounds of the Alhambra.

They followed the arrows on the map for the last four blocks, where the direction markers ended with a green X-marks-the-spot over a squat, windowless brick building that looked both older and more primitive than the graceful homes surrounding it. Over the top of the low building she could see the Alhambra on the opposite hill, and at that moment the sun peeked through the clouds, washing the façade with golden light. Incongruously, thunder cracked directly overhead, and raindrops began to splatter her face and arms.

"That's it?" Carrick asked, eyeing the structure dubiously.

She glanced again at the map, nodding. "Debajo, right?"

As she spoke the word, a lighted sign materialized above a pair of ancient-looking wood shutters: *Debajo*.

"I guess that's it."

She turned for a closer look at the spire across the street—and found her jaw dropping in awe. It was like something out of a dream. The central tower was constructed of some kind of seamless, textured material that, like the towers on the grounds of the Alhambra, was constantly shifting color. At least a dozen smaller towers cozied up around the central spike, and each wore a gleaming cap. The caps had soft lines—little whirls and dips and scallops—and were overlaid with bright mosaic patterns. Decorations like flower stamens, each with its own unique mosaic, seemed to have erupted from the caps. This same style of sculpted embellishment had been used to frame the windows and entrance of the central tower.

"You said that's a temple?" she murmured.

"I don't know how it could be anything else."

He had a point. Glancing again at the map she read, "Rebelión Sagrada. You speak Spanish, Father?"

"I know some Latin and Italian. Pretty sure it means 'sacred rebellion.'"

She frowned. "That doesn't sound very religious."

The priest's frown was deeper. "We disagree about that."

As she'd spoken the words from the map, another sign had materialized, this time above the arched double doors of the entrance. She noticed there was a second phrase in smaller lettering beneath the first, this one in English:

Science will destroy us.

Her heart stopped. How could this be here?

Asha had encountered this phrase in the Archive—it was a quote from Stella Engle, the woman they called Ophelia. She had been interviewed by a local news service right before the Bio Holocaust, when tensions between the Manti and their creators had been at their highest. Ophelia had predicted the Manti threat, but up to the time of the article she'd been viewed as an eccentric survivalist. The full text of the quote was, "Science will destroy us. Science will destroy them." The words had stuck with Asha—especially the calm, knowing way that she had delivered them—and she'd flagged it for her personal Archive log, a digital scrapbook of her most interesting findings.

Asha and her father had spent hours talking about the Manti. They were a fascinating and conflicted species. There was a vein of superstition, and they had inconsistent notions about religion, with some of them worshiping science and logic and some of them clinging to reverent notions about their human creators. When she met Zee, after her father's disappearance, her new friend had questioned her about their vulnerabilities, and how those might be exploited. Humanity could never hope to challenge their enemy through open warfare. Would it be possible to bring them down from the inside? Through some type of subversive message spread by the sleeper operatives?

Though Asha'd had serious doubts something like that would be enough to destabilize their society, it could be a piece of the puzzle, and she'd agreed to do it in exchange for Zee's help in going after her father. How was it Ophelia's message had beat her here?

Carrick turned away from the temple, striding toward the low brick building, and Asha followed, letting go of this new mystery for the moment.

They studied the nondescript shutters, which appeared to be the only point of entry from the street. The priest reached out and pulled one open with a loud creak. Inside there was a small vestibule, and a stairway leading down. Glowing circles of crimson phosphorescence, imprisoned against the brick interior walls by half-bubbles of glass, lit the way down into the establishment.

"Come or *go*."

Asha jumped as someone ducked into the opening—someone more mantis than man. The creature's body rested on four powerful back legs, and his arms terminated in inward-bending claws rather than hands. His insect parts were a mottled gray and white, while his face and chest were black. His eyes were set farther apart than Iris's, and his wings were smaller and folded close to his body.

The creature's claw extended, curling over a knob on the inside of the shutter, and he started to pull it closed. Carrick slid a booted foot out to catch it.

"We're coming," he said, ducking into the low doorway.

The bugman extended an arm, stopping him. Carrick growled as the claw slid across his midsection, gripping the hilt of his knife.

"No weapons," the bugman said firmly.

After a moment's consideration Carrick nodded, and the Manti tugged the blade free and stepped aside.

Asha followed the priest, instinctively squeezing as far away from the bugman as she could. The shutter slammed closed behind them.

Carrick started down the steps before her eyes had adjusted, and rather than be left in the entryway, she grabbed his arm for support.

The room at the foot of the stairs had to be below street level, which explained the name. If it had any of the unwholesome smells often associated with underground spaces, you'd never know it for the sweet, floral scent hanging heavy in the air. Far from being damp or chilly, the space was a nest of giant pillows lit by metal lamps wrought in the shapes of flowers ranging along supports that looked like vines. There were half a dozen tables between the cushioned area and the bar along the opposite wall.

Carrick led her to one of the tables, and they sank down in fat, comfortable chairs.

A man came from behind the bar to frown down at them. "Sagrada," he grunted.

Asha exchanged a nervous glance with Carrick, unsure whether this was a greeting or a question.

"Yes," replied the priest.

The man stumped off on what looked like a cricket leg on

one side, and oddly, an artificial limb made to look like a human leg on the other.

"What did we just agree to?" she asked Carrick.

"Not sure. I think maybe we've ordered something."

She made a quick and wary survey of the tavern's other patrons—a handful seated in the cushioned area and two at the bar. There was music playing, chanting and rhythmic, though not very lively. Still it seemed unlikely they'd be overheard if they kept their voices low.

"How will we pay?" she asked.

"Hopefully Iris will be here soon."

The statement terminated in a growl, and she returned her gaze to his face. He leaned close to her, allowing his eyes to range over the room from under the hood of his dark brows.

"I don't like this place," he said.

"I can't say I do either. Why did Iris send us here?"

"She said the Guard wouldn't look for us here. The place has a nasty reputation, and a connection with some kind of religious underground."

"The 'sacred rebellion'?"

"Mmm."

They sat up as the bartender plunked glasses down in front of them—tall and skinny, about a quarter full of a liquid that looked like water. It was hard to be sure in the strange light. He left again without a word.

"Did she say why she wanted to help you?" Asha asked, leaning in again.

He raised his eyebrows and shook his head. "Only that otherwise I'd be going to some kind of lab, where I might be dissected. I don't even know if she was telling me the truth."

She eyed him, feeling empathy for his situation. It wasn't so different from her own. "I think she was. I overheard her talking to Pax."

He gave her a haunted, hungry look. "It's true about me . . . ?" He trailed off, swallowing loudly and looking away.

"The wolf thing?" she said softly.

He gave a quick nod.

"That's what they said."

He closed his eyes.

She reached across the table, covering his hand with hers. "I'm sorry."

He flinched and looked down. "You're not afraid of me?"

"Why should I be? Are you any different than you were before you knew?"

"*Yes.*"

"Okay. Maybe." She ducked down, catching his eye. "But neither of us can go back to what we were before. We have to decide what comes next."

"I'm not sure we'll have much choice about that." He picked up his glass, sniffing its contents before replacing it on the table.

"We could leave now." Her heart picked up speed as she contemplated heading out again into the city. At least in here no one seemed to be paying much attention to them.

"True." He studied her as he considered. "Who are you, anyway? How did you end up with them?"

She gave him an abbreviated version of her story, omitting what she'd remembered upon arriving in Granada. She felt a kinship with him, with both of them being on the run. Strangers to this city and having no one else. But due to recent revelations and events, his loyalties were probably a little up in the air, and she didn't know if she should trust him.

"Why weren't you sent with the others?" Carrick asked.

She picked up her glass and turned it in her fingers. "Pax can't remember how we ended up at the reservoir, but he thinks I might. He thinks there might be some kind of plot, and that eventually he'll get it out of me."

"What do *you* think?"

She looked up and found his gaze fixed on her. Like Pax, she got the sense he'd know if she lied. "He could be right."

"I'd never have guessed that's what was between you. I assumed you were *with* him by the way he was acting. He's very human."

"Yeah," she agreed. "It's confusing, isn't it?"

The comment was directed more inwardly than at him, but he gave her a tight smile. "Very."

Finding her mouth suddenly dry, she raised her glass to her lips.

Not water. She made a face. The fluid was thick, and very sweet. She noticed a white flower painted on the side of the glass. As she lifted it for a closer look the blossom opened, showing the interior. She set the glass down quickly, glancing at Carrick in alarm.

But the priest's gaze was focused behind her. She turned to see two masked figures descending into the room. She didn't need to see their faces to recognize them.

Pax sat down in the chair next to her, and Iris across from him. Iris pushed two masks across the tabletop. "You'll stand out without these," she said, nodding toward the patrons in the cushioned area.

Asha hadn't noticed they were masked, but it was hardly surprising considering the distractions of their *natural* physiology. One woman seated under a lamp had a full set of silky, lavender-colored wings.

As she and Carrick slipped on their masks the bartender reappeared, grunting the same, "Sagrada."

"Wine," said Pax, and the man stumped away again.

Pax eyed their glasses. "You didn't drink any of that?"

Asha's heart lurched. "A little," she said. "I wasn't thinking."

"Lord of the flies," muttered Iris, as her brother gave a quiet groan.

"What is it?" Asha asked, her tongue feeling too big for her mouth.

"A drug," he said. "You're going to feel a little strange soon, if you don't already. Don't drink any more."

"*I won't.*" She wasn't sure whether she'd answered out loud.

As the other three began to murmur about what to do—something about finding Carrick a place to hide for a few days until they could figure out how to get him out of the city—her head felt like it was floating away from her body. Every time she looked at something with an organic shape—the picture on the glass, the flower lamps, the decorative metalwork above the bar—it seemed to come alive in some way. She dropped her eyes to the table, trying to focus and clear her head, and she noticed a line of black insects marching out of the flower, off the glass, and toward her folded arms.

She shoved her chair backward with a yelp.

"Virgin." The twittering, echoing voice was not one she recognized. It came from elsewhere in the room.

Iris muttered something sharp.

"I need air," Asha said, rising unsteadily from the table.

Pax rose beside her, holding out his arm for support. She grasped it, and her body swayed. Their forms pressed together as he kept her from falling forward. With her head resting against his chest, she couldn't help noting the lack of difference between him and the human males of her acquaintance. There was nothing exotic or alien about the way he smelled, or the rise and fall of his breaths. Nothing strange or frightening about the low rumble in his chest that accompanied the words, "Take it slow." In fact, everything her senses took in about him was soothing and appealing.

He slipped an arm around her waist and guided her toward

the stairs. Her feet felt numb, like they were asleep, and they ascended slowly, much of her weight in the crook of his arm. The gray mantis man opened the door for them. She glanced at him on the way out, and his scowling face stretched and distorted until she had to look away.

Outside, the low-lit street spun, and she gripped Pax's arm. She tilted her face skyward, breathing deeply. In the patch of clear sky overhead, the stars were all doubled, and they too were making lazy circles. The effect was nauseating, and she squeezed her eyes shut.

"How much did you drink?" Pax asked in a low voice.

"Just a sip," she grumbled. "I don't know what I was thinking."

"It'll soon pass. Just keep breathing."

She listened to the noises in the street. An echo of laughter, and festive music. She breathed the warm night air in and out, nice and easy. She opened her eyes and blinked at the temple spire. As it shifted from peach to mauve, she realized she'd made a poor choice of objects to refocus her vision, and she dropped her gaze to Pax's face. When none of his features shifted in unexpected ways, she took a deep breath, relieved.

"It's getting better," she sighed.

"Good. Let's walk a little."

As he guided her, arm still circling her waist, she said, "That's a potent drink."

"It's a hallucinogen, popular with the artistic community. It's banned, but that doesn't stop anyone."

"Why is it banned?"

"It's also popular with zealots. My father believes it's dangerous."

She glanced again at the temple, wondering if he was referring to the *sacred rebellion*. "What do *you* think?" she asked.

He eyed her with interest, and she found the dizziness returning—a different kind of dizziness.

"I think the zealots are becoming a problem, but not because of sagrada. It's not the type of drug that makes people violent. I don't think there's any real harm in it."

She swallowed. "I beg to differ."

Chuckling softly, Pax guided her into an alley a few doors down from the tavern. Easing her back against a rough brick wall, he said, "Rest for a few more minutes. When you feel steady we'll go back."

He stood up, parting their bodies, and pushed back his mask. She did the same, and his eyes settled on her face. Warmth rushed to her cheeks, and to her abdomen.

"What will you tell your father about all this?" she asked him.

"I don't know yet. I'm pretty much making it up as I go."

She raised an eyebrow. "I noticed. The two of you seem in over your heads."

"At this point I'd call that an understatement."

"I still don't really understand why."

He hesitated. She couldn't make out his expression in the darkness. "Then we both have a mystery, don't we?"

Asha dropped her gaze, murmuring, "I guess we do."

Pax regretted his evasive answer, but what exactly was he supposed to say to her? The truth would confuse and probably frighten her. He wasn't even sure what the truth *was*.

"You feel well enough to go back?" he asked.

She nodded, pushing herself free of the wall. "Inanimate objects are no longer animate. Though that's a blurry line around here."

He smiled. She had changed since they left the abbey. She

seemed surer of herself. More grounded, and at the moment, more relaxed. But that was probably due to the sagrada.

He held out an arm to her. "Just in case."

She threaded her hand through his arm, and he reached for her mask. As he slipped it back into place, his thumb grazed the pale flesh of her cheek. Standing this close to her, he felt the quickening of her heartbeat. The surge of blood beneath her skin.

Her body had responded to his touch. And not for the first time.

Her lips parted, and he heard the breath move through them. Every sensation was intensified in that moment, and he felt like he was the tipsy one.

He reached up, cradling the back of her neck, and she gave a quiet gasp as he nudged her to the wall. Planting a hand on either side of her head, he lowered his lips to hers. Her face lifted, allowing him better access, and he groaned and pressed against her.

Her lips were soft, and slightly sweet from the sagrada. He ran his tongue along her lower lip, tasting the drug, and his heart slammed against the inside of his chest. She arched forward, molding her body along his, and the sound of her frantic heartbeat was drowned out by the blood rushing in his ears.

His tongue flicked lightly over her mouth until her lips parted, opening to him. He wrapped his arms around her as their tongues met.

"Friend," called a voice from behind them.

Pax jumped and spun around.

"A word with you, if you'll divide yourself from the lady a moment."

THE DISCIPLE

"What do you want?" Pax snapped, angry at the interruption, and angrier still at himself for losing his head to the point someone was able to creep up on him.

"Forgive the interruption," purred the man, whose face Pax couldn't see due to the fact he wore both a mask and cloak. "I wanted to ask whether you've heard the prophecy? I've found that many people have questions, and often I'm able to help. I'd be happy to treat you and the lady to—"

Pax's reply of "No, thank you" blended with Asha's "What prophecy?"

Pax studied her. There was a large quantity of data vying for his attention, but for the moment he'd allocated all of his resources to remaining alert for trouble.

"The Ophelia Prophecy, madam," replied the disciple.

Asha's jaw dropped, and Pax's eyes moved between them. He had no interest in the religious pitch that would certainly follow, but Asha's reaction *did* interest him. "The Ophelia

Prophecy" was a reference to something that had happened in Granada months ago. Why did it have meaning for her?

"Unfortunately," continued the man, stepping closer to Asha, "we are on a trajectory to repeat the mistakes of our creators. It will be our downfall. The prophecy has predicted it."

Pax reached for her arm to draw her away, and felt her muscles tighten under his hand. "We have to go," he urged, taking a step away from the man, attempting to pull her with him.

The look she leveled at him was devoid of the softness from a moment ago. But he didn't have time to argue with her.

"What mistakes?" asked Asha as Pax drew her more forcefully. "Let go!" she cried, tugging at her arm.

There was a bite in her tone he remembered well from questioning her, and something more. An edge of eagerness verging on panic. He didn't like manhandling her, but she didn't understand the potential risk. The alley was dark, but his mask was off and the stranger might recognize him. And *that* could go wrong in a number of ways.

"Gentle, my friend," urged the stranger. "Is there any harm in me answering the lady's questions?"

Pax hesitated, thinking how to extract them from the situation without drawing more unwanted attention. She was determined enough that they were bound to cause a scene if he tried to force her. Meanwhile the disciple forged on.

"You see, continuing to play God with our evolution is courting disaster. We must reach out to the oppressors, whom we have in turn oppressed, or suffer their same fate. Science is an angel of fire whose arrows will destroy us. Manufactured DNA, genetic manipulation, species exploitation . . . we must break from the—"

"What oppressors?" breathed Asha. Despite the steady

pressure she kept on the arm he was holding, Pax could feel her trembling.

The disciple hesitated, and Pax understood his confusion. It would be an odd question coming from a Manti.

"The humans, in internment, they should be—"

"I'm sorry," interrupted Pax, "but we don't have time for this." He hooked an arm around Asha's back. "Step out of the way."

Before they could move out of the alley, four more masked and cloaked figures blocked the entrance.

"What've you got there, Micah?" asked one of the newcomers.

In the split second before Pax could react, Asha suddenly dropped, diving free from his grasp.

He lunged for her, but she'd escaped in the direction of the disciple Micah, who'd whipped a knife from under his cloak. He pressed the tip against Pax's throat.

"I'm not sure I like how you're treating your lady, friend."

"I'm not with him," interrupted Asha, breathless. She moved to stand close to Micah, but her eyes locked with Pax's. "I escaped from a Scarab today. I met this man in the tavern. He agreed to hide me, but then he brought me here."

The knifepoint dug in a fraction. Was she trying to help him, or get his throat slit? It could easily go either way at this point.

The alley frosted over with tension. Then someone said with surprise, "Are you human?"

"I am," she replied. "I was sent here from Sanctuary. I know Ophelia. I know about your prophecy. We might be able to help each other."

A cold stone turned in Pax's belly. She was escaping him. Worse than that, she just might be telling the truth.

*   *   *

The reawakened part of her had taken control, seizing the opportunity to abandon Pax's protection on the hope these others might be more willing to assist her in her mission to recover her father. Not only that, she had fresh evidence it was dangerous for her to remain close to the Manti prince.

And yet as she watched him watch her, the middle of her chest tightened and ached.

The problem was this sliver of self between her abduction and her awakening—the part of her that Pax had brought to a different sort of awakening. Every decision she'd made—right up until the moment Pax revealed the true nature of Sanctuary—had been based on her belief in a lie. She was beginning to suspect even Zee had withheld information. Only Pax had been honest with her. More than that he'd lied to his father to protect her. More than *that*, he'd just kissed her in a way no one ever had—in a way that made her want much more than a kiss.

But somewhere in the Manti capital was her father. He was the one person about whom her feelings were still uncomplicated. Finding him trumped everything.

"We need to talk somewhere else," muttered one of the disciples, glancing over his shoulder. A steady stream of people passed in the street beyond the alley, noisy and high-spirited.

"I'll take her to the temple," replied Micah.

"What about her friend?"

Micah studied Pax while Asha held her breath. Finally he said, "Make sure he's not in a condition to follow us."

Her gut wrenched, and her eyes jumped to Pax's face. He gave her a subtle nod, reassuring her, which only made her feel worse. But he could take care of himself.

She held his gaze a moment, knowing if this desperate plan of hers worked she wasn't likely to see him again. It would leave a hollow place in her. But she'd made her own choice.

Had she remained with him, all her choices would have continued to be made for her.

Finally Micah said, "Come with me."

He led her between the other disciples as they pressed forward.

The animal in Pax was awake and busy—lighting up nerve fibers, readying his muscles. His mate was walking away from him, and a living wall stood between them. He growled with impatience, at the others and at himself.

She *wasn't* his mate, but she might as well have been. Since the moment of their meeting, some unconscious component of his hybrid psychology had been hard at work converting an initial chemical attraction to full-on attachment, manipulating his senses and emotions. The whole process had been accelerated by the guilt he'd felt over his lack of control. Guilt had evolved into protective impulses. All of which left him vulnerable to the woman herself—brave, determined, kind-hearted, tough. The recent addition of "passionate" to that list had sealed his fate.

Their kiss had woven together the components of attraction into a cord that was stronger than his resistance.

"Can we get on with this?" he muttered at the disciples.

A couple of them chuckled as their cloaks slid to the damp cobblestones, forming nonreflecting pools of black at their feet.

"Didn't mean to waste your time, friend."

The four of them—three men and one woman—all wielded blades. He was relieved to see they were only subtly Manti: only one had an extra set of appendages, and none had forearm spikes. Light filtering from the street showed one of the men bore the same set of surgical scars as Pax. It could be that, like Pax, his mantis appendages had been weak. It wasn't uncommon, and they could be a handicap in a fight. But sometimes motives for such alterations were more complicated. At the core of Manti society—its heart of darkness—was a loathing for transgenic organisms. *Self*-loathing. It was the primary reason one of his father's advisors continuously advocated exterminating the remaining human population—so there would be no visible reference for "normal."

One of the men stepped forward. "Best for you if you don't put up a fight. Over quicker. Less pain."

"I'll bear that in mind," replied Pax.

The rest of the group ranged in a half circle, blocking the alley's exit. A balcony hung from the house to Pax's left, but he wouldn't be able to hoist himself up before the leader reached him.

Picking up an undercurrent of hesitation, he goaded again: "I'm in a bit of a rush."

The man who'd spoken lunged at him.

Pax spun in a tight circle around him, bringing his elbows down hard on the man's back. As the disciple hit the ground, Pax jammed a boot into his ribs—and knew from the quiet snap the man was out of the fight. The attacker's knife had skittered toward the shadowy end of the alley, and Pax retrieved it now, spinning in time to block a swing from the woman.

She recovered quickly and tried to edge around behind him. He swung at her with his blade, cutting her off. He couldn't afford to let them surround him.

"Why the masks?" he asked the woman.

She answered with another swipe of her blade. This time it grazed his abdomen.

"Do you think you're keeping some kind of secret?" he

continued, hoping to distract her. "I know you're from the temple."

"It's market day," was the terse reply. "Everyone wears them."

The others left their positions and advanced on him. He had to give up his protected backside to maneuver between them.

"Get him!" the woman shouted, and they all charged at once.

He sprang for the balcony, catching the rails and drawing his lower body away from the ground.

Someone caught his ankle and hauled him back down to the alley. They spilled together onto the cobblestones.

"Hold him down!" cried one of the others.

Pax punched the first man who tried to grab him, then rolled out of another's reach. He scrambled to his feet, running for the alley's entrance, but the woman swept her legs out and tripped him. She clambered onto Pax's back, pressing her blade against the base of his neck.

As he braced himself to eject her, someone cried, "Let him go!"

He glanced up to see Iris and Carrick moving into the alley.

"Do it now!" Iris ordered.

"Get out of here," barked one of the disciples. "This doesn't concern you."

Iris hissed at him, wings lifting slightly. "You don't want this fight. I'm giving you a chance to walk away from it."

"Caleb," the woman said sharply. "That's the amir's daughter."

Iris was no longer wearing a mask, and one of the men gave her a hard look. He shifted forward a couple of steps, raising his dagger. Light from the alley washed over his bare chest.

"Don't let her get away," he said.

Iris laughed, but the priest did not. He gave a menacing growl and took two long strides toward the speaker.

Concern for Pax shifted to the background of Asha's thoughts as she followed Micah out of the alley. Suddenly he steered her against the front of a house with an overhanging terrace.

"What are you doing?" she gasped.

She flinched as he reached toward her face, pulling the mask back down over her eyes. Then he removed his cloak.

"Put this on. The Guard will be looking for you."

She slipped the cloak over her shoulders and drew up the hood. "Aren't we going to the temple?"

"By an alternate route. The entrance is too easy to monitor. And it's secured on the evening of the market."

He led her back to Debajo, and the mantis guardian admitted them without question, bobbing his head at her companion. As they descended into the room she glanced at the bar. Her heart jumped when she saw Iris and Carrick. They stood talking to the bartender with their backs to the entrance. Asha tugged her hood lower as they reached the bottom of the stairs, hoping the strong smell of the place would shield her from the pair's heightened senses.

Micah guided her away from the bar and around the sunken seating area. She risked a glance back at Iris and saw them bounding up the stairs toward the exit. She let out the breath she'd been holding and followed Micah to another stairway at the far end of the room, this one leading down.

"Watch your step," he said. She pushed back the mask and cloak and took hold of the railing.

The stairway curved, and after a few moments of careful

foot placement the stairwell brightened—lanterns hung from hooks mounted along the brick wall.

"Where does this go?" she asked, her voice sounding too loud in the vertical tunnel.

"Under the street. It connects Debajo and the temple. There are passages under much of the old city. Mostly unused. They're considered unsafe."

Perfect. Already she was questioning her decision to leave Pax.

"Were you being taken to Al Campo?" he asked her.

Asha bit her lip, studying him. He'd removed his mask, but at the moment all she could see was the wavy blond hair covering the back of his head. "Actually I'm *hoping* to get to Al Campo. There's someone I need to find."

"Really?" She could hear the surprise in his voice, and he glanced over his shoulder. "You know if you'd stayed in the Scarab, it's likely where you would have ended up."

"I didn't have that option," she replied, uncertain how much to reveal. She'd have to trust someone eventually if she wanted help. But for the moment she preferred to hold her cards close. They were all she had for leverage. "It's a long story."

"I see," he said softly.

She was relieved he hadn't pressed her further, but she also knew the reprieve was likely temporary.

They reached the bottom of the stairs and walked through an archway into a narrow passage illuminated by more of the phosphorescent lanterns. About half of the floor tiles were missing—accounting for the piles of rubble along the walls—and the remainder were cracked or broken and coated with dust.

"When we were talking in the alley," she ventured, "it sounded like you were about to say you'd like to see the people in Al Campo freed."

They passed through a twin archway on the opposite end of the tunnel, and he waved her toward another stairway.

"Yes. But don't misunderstand. We were wronged by humanity even while we *were* still human. If we let ourselves forget that, we risk *becoming* that."

She knew what he meant, due partly to her work in the Archive, but mostly due to conversations with her father. Many of the garage bio operations found their "volunteers" among the most impoverished members of society. By the time of the transgenic experiments, that class had grown particularly large.

Micah joined her at the top of the stairs. Taking a closer look at him in the light, she decided he was younger than she'd thought—maybe close to her own age. He was clean-shaven, with a kind face and eyes that were a lighter shade of brown than her own. She also noticed tan swirls of pigment marking either side of his neck.

"The worst of the transgressors have been punished," he continued. "Most of them are dead. Those who survived are prisoners of war, and we see our parents in *them*—exploited, and existing at the mercy of others."

When she'd asked Zee to help her go after her father, she had never dreamed she'd find Manti sympathetic to humanity. Micah's words reinforced the decision she'd made to leave Pax. Despite the protective impulses he seemed to feel toward *her*, he was still an enemy to her people and her cause. Eventually he would have learned the truth about why and how she'd come here, and she'd have been in no position to help anyone, including herself.

Afraid their conversation might be cut short by their arrival at the temple, she hurried on with her next question.

"That phrase above your entrance—science will destroy us—is that the basis for your . . . for your religion?"

Micah shook his head. "Rebelión Sagrada has its roots in

the anti-genetic engineering community. It's been around longer than the prophecy. We view the prophecy more as affirmation."

"Where did you hear it?" Asha held her breath and tried to mask her eagerness.

He took a few steps into shadow and raised his arm to what looked like a solid wall. But as she joined him she saw there was an opening there. She followed him down a thickly carpeted passage that erased the sound of their footsteps.

He lowered his voice as he continued. "The prophecy came out of Sustainable Transgenics, where babies are *designed*. Our scientists have taken the work your scientists did and elevated it to an art form. You would think we'd have taken a lesson from Gregoire."

Gregoire was the self-taught geneticist who "designed" the Manti. Some believed it was one of his creations, a creature much like Iris, who had stolen the data that allowed the Manti to engineer the plague that wiped out humanity. Some even believed he'd been so enamored of his creations that he *intended* for them to supplant humans. Gregoire died in a fire that destroyed his lab, shortly before the dawn of chaos, so no one ever learned the truth. No human, anyway.

"I don't understand why an anti-science message would come from your genetics lab," she replied.

"Someone hacked into the lab's system, and the prophecy spread virally from there. It locked up every computer in the city for two days. The official word is it was some kind of hoax. But the symbolism—and the irony—was compelling. It doubled Rebelión's membership."

Micah parted a curtain at the end of the passage. A wave of perfumed air slapped against them. The same scent that pervaded Debajo, but *much* stronger. Intoxicating, and cloying.

"The hacker called the virus 'The Ophelia Prophecy,'" he

said as they stepped past the curtain. "We've only recently figured out what that means."

Only someone from Sanctuary would know. Pax had told her the humans in Al Campo were sometimes examined by the geneticists. Was it possible the genetics computers had been hacked by someone from her home?

"Have you brought us another virus, child?"

Asha's attention was drawn from her escort—who had frozen just inside the circular chamber on the other side of the curtain—toward the source of the unfamiliar voice.

"I apologize, my lady," said Micah, bowing his head. "I didn't know you were using this chamber."

At first Asha's eyes failed to interpret what she was seeing. What appeared to be a decorative cloak was in fact a set of wings. The wings were mostly translucent white, but where they pressed together, two green-and-yellow spiral patterns created the illusion of large eyes staring back at her. The wings moved delicately as the creature turned.

"It's the farthest off the street and therefore the quietest," she explained, "but you weren't to know. Now that you're here, let me see what you've brought me."

She took a few steps toward them, and Asha's heart pulsed with warning. The woman's ivory torso was almost entirely mantis-like, and yet maintained its femininity, with gentle curves at her breast and waist. Like Iris she had hands at the end of spiked appendages, but her lower body rested on four legs like the doorman at Debajo. Her arms and legs were scored with bands of orange and green—though it was hard to be sure about the colors, as the crimson fabrics and low lighting in the room created a rosy glow.

Her eyes were large, widely spaced, and a light shade of . . . purple? Antennae projected from the top of her forehead, striped like her torso and curving gracefully away from her face toward pale, wavy hair. Her thin-lipped mouth curved in a smile above a sharp chin.

She was beautiful, and the most alien of Pax's kind so far. A lighter sister to Iris, and yet no less suggestive of darkness.

The woman's lips parted, and she uttered a string of unintelligible syllables: *Pseudocreobotra wahlbergi*. But she continued in Spanish-accented English, "Common name, spiny flower mantis. You may call me Cleo."

Asha swallowed, pressing her hands against her thighs. "I'm Asha," she said, feeling unfit to be in such a creature's presence in her current condition. "Brought here from Sanctuary."

Cleo moved toward her with slow, precise movements of her lower legs and abdomen. Asha shrank inwardly and fought the urge to step back. As the Manti woman's body shifted a little to one side, she noticed a man behind her. He had a much smaller, plainer set of wings, spiked forearms, and a well-muscled human body. His eyes glittered fiercely in the dimly lit room. They rested on her face for only a moment before shifting back to Cleo.

Before Asha looked away she saw his wrists were chained to the wall.

"You are not our first visitor from Sanctuary," said the mantis woman, stopping less than an arm's length away.

"So I understand."

Cleo glanced at Micah. "Where did you find this pretty, soiled thing?"

"In an alley outside Debajo, Priestess. Said she escaped from a Scarab today."

Cleo's eyes moved slowly over her. Asha flushed at the priestess's expression of distaste, angry with herself for feeling self-conscious about her mud-stained, hand-me-down appearance.

"This pains me," Cleo said, frowning. She motioned to a woman standing nearby. "Clean her up. Give her something more suitable to wear."

"My lady," Asha spoke up, "I was hoping you might be able to help me. I'm looking for Al Campo."

The triangular head swiveled on the slender neck, lilac eyes coming back to her. The penetrating gaze was all the communication Asha needed to understand the risk she was taking in getting involved with these people.

"Perhaps I shall," replied Cleo at last. "That will depend entirely on what you have to offer in exchange." Again her gaze raked over Asha. "But as you are, you're defiling my temple."

"Cleo, enough!" The protest came from the man chained behind the priestess. The links clanked together as he launched away from the wall.

Cleo smiled. "If you'll excuse me, my mate is impatient. We'll talk again soon."

Suddenly Asha understood the chains. And the hungry look in the man's eyes. She'd seen it before. Cleo moved toward her mate, stopping just out of his reach. Perspiration dripped down his chest and abdomen as he strained against his bonds. She stretched delicate fingers toward him, teasing them through his hair.

The male fell to his knees at her feet, groaning loudly. She raised his bowed head with her hands, and a single word grated out of him. "Please."

Asha couldn't help contrasting this picture with the struggle that had taken place by the reservoir. This male looked capable of much worse than Pax. And this female *was* receptive. Though clearly she'd taken precautions. She was in control of the encounter.

"It's time," Cleo replied softly, stroking his cheeks with her thumbs as half-choked moans came out of him. "Release him."

Cleo's attendants looked to her with surprise. "Shouldn't we leave him bound, Priestess?" one asked.

Cleo smiled, her eyes never leaving her mate. "Not this time. I want to see what he can do."

Again his body jerked against the chains.

The attendant drew a key from her pocket and moved toward him.

Asha watched breathlessly, her body so taut she jumped when someone touched her arm.

"Come," murmured the attendant who'd been ordered to make her presentable.

The attendant guided her toward a door, Micah following on their heels.

She heard the rattle and muffled thud of the chains striking the carpeted floor. There was a low growl, followed by the same hiss she'd heard Iris make. Asha glanced back, but the attendant closed the door between them. A high-pitched cry sounded from the other side.

The priest stood over the fallen disciple looking not at the body, but at his own hands. Pax understood exactly how he felt. He wondered if the priest had ever killed anyone before.

"One of them recognized you," Pax said to Iris. "We need to get out of here."

"Agreed." She glanced around the alley. "Where's Asha?"

"One of the disciples took her."

Iris raised her eyebrows. "Why?"

Pax rubbed his lips together and gazed up at the Gaudí Spike. It was no time to start lying to his sister. Not if he wanted her help. "She asked them for protection."

Iris rolled her eyes, sighing in exasperation. "Bloody hell, Pax. I knew this would happen."

He glanced back sharply. "No, you *didn't*." He overcame a strong urge to remind her she was in much the same boat with the half-feral holy man standing beside her.

"Well, something *like* this. What are you going to tell Father?"

"Nothing. I'm going to get her back. Let's get out of this damned alley."

"Pax!" Iris started after him. "We can't storm that temple. Not the three of us. You have to let her go for now. Help me with Carrick, and then we'll go to Father together. We'll figure something out."

He could hear the edge of panic in Iris's voice. Her usual approach was to try and shame him out of unreasonable behavior, and the change almost shocked him to his senses. It meant she had all but given up saving him from himself.

But leaving Asha to Rebelión was not an option. His chances of recovering her were much better with Iris's help, but he'd go after her on his own if he had to.

"We don't need to storm the temple," he said. "Put your masks on."

Asha's heart still pounded against her chest as she and the attendant reached their destination. The stair climb was only partly to blame.

The smaller chamber they entered was three flights up in the tower. The priestess's luxurious dungeon had been fully enclosed, but here an arched window let in a rectangle of moonlight, which spotlighted a tub in the center of the room. The steps up to the tub were decorated with the color-shifting mosaic tiles, and the slow, subtle transitions between pink and purple and blue and green had a soothing effect.

The attendant pressed her palm against a disk on one side

of the tub, and water cascaded into the basin at both ends. Asha watched as the woman—whose Manti markings consisted of green-tinged skin and creamy wings that hung limply between her shoulder blades—poured in a few drops from several colored-glass bottles. She lifted a series of cups made of the same colored glass, and as she stirred what looked like sand with a small stick, they glowed with light. She arranged these around the edges of the tub.

Asha didn't feel she had time to waste on ritualistic pampering. But she needed an audience with Cleo, and apparently this was a prerequisite. She peeled Pax's shirt over her head, then pushed the loose pants past her hips. She stood staring at the pile of clothes, thinking about their owner and wondering what he was thinking about *her*.

Would he come after her? Would he make her pay? She was pretty sure he wouldn't be so keen about protecting her from Manti interrogators the next time around.

"Your bath is ready." The attendant smiled and gestured toward the tub.

She climbed the steps, dipping her toes in first. In Sanctuary water was rationed. They had enough for short showers, but no one took baths. Heavy rains sometimes created temporary bathing spots, but nothing that could compare to this. Like so many things, it was an aspect of the pre-holocaust world she understood only through her work at the Archive. It seemed strange to her now that she'd spent most of her life acquiring an intimate familiarity with a world she would never know.

Sanctuary's elders and the governing council had always emphasized the importance of resurrecting what had been lost. They'd all accepted it would be the work of lifetimes. The idea she might one day travel to a world where modern ways still existed had never entered her mind.

And *this* world in particular, with its richness and vitality.

Its whimsy, and its emphasis on pleasing the senses. She alternated between terrified and fascinated, sometimes within the same instant.

Up to now she'd lived in the desert.

She sank all the way into the water, and a murmur of pleasure vibrated through her. The silky warmth of it embraced and permeated her. A light, floral fragrance suffused the steam, and she closed her eyes, breathing deeply. The sounds of the revelers outside made their way through the window, covered only by filmy curtains. Here in the tower the sounds were distant and indistinct, nothing to pull at her thoughts as she drifted along in the stream of sensation.

Pax's hands were on her. Gliding from fingertips to forearm to elbow to shoulder. First one arm, then the other. Massaging. Rubbing. Working their way to her chest, circling her breasts, stroking her abdomen. Down her thigh, outside, then in . . .

Her body arched under his hands, and she lifted her chin, wondering why he withheld his lips. His fingers came to her mouth, but still he wouldn't kiss her. She parted her lips, waiting. He let her wait.

"Pax . . ."

"Are you all right?" Asha started, opening her eyes. The attendant had stopped in the process of rubbing a sponge over one of her arms. "Is there anything you need?"

Asha was grateful she was already flushed from the heat of the water. "I . . . No. Thank you."

Glancing behind the attendant, her gaze came to rest on Cleo in the doorway. "Here's our Scarab flower," said the priestess with a smile.

Asha sat up, steam rising from her back and shoulders. The attendant held out a towel and she rose to her feet, wrapping it around her.

Cleo glided into the room. Her head craned forward on her slender neck, tilting to one side like she was tracking prey. Asha noticed a cut on her face, running from below one temple to the corner of her lips. Another gash ran from the upper curve of her waist to her navel.

"Come with me," she said.

When Asha had dressed, Cleo took her to the top of the tower via a lift that shot up the shaft created by the spiral staircase. They emerged in a rooftop garden, and the priestess led her along a mosaic path to a shallow pool.

Asha had given only a moment's attention to the color-shifting fish and turtles when her eyes were drawn to the statue at the pool's center. At its base was the inscription: "GREGOIRE. Beloved father. Abomination." Cleo knelt beside the pool and gently stirred the water with her fingers. Then she drew them down her forehead and the bridge of her nose before kissing the tips.

Asha found the complexity of Manti beliefs baffling. They both loved and reviled their creator—it was there carved in stone. And she had begun to sense this deep conflict extended to them as a race. Even proud Pax, who hated that he couldn't control his own drives. The Manti's unwillingness to let go of their humanness. The way they'd preserved the last of their parent race, along with their "pure" DNA.

It made her think of the monster created centuries ago by author Mary Shelley. Asha's father had forced his battered copy of *Frankenstein* on her when she was ten or eleven. Only now did she fully understand why.

"What is your connection to the amir's family?" asked Cleo, glancing up suddenly.

Asha met the priestess's gaze, willing her expression to remain neutral. "I don't know what you mean."

"Let me explain then, child."

Cleo rose and moved toward her, and Asha backed slowly from the pool, scanning for a defensible position. Suddenly she felt a railing at her back. Fronds of some deliciously fragrant, creeping bush with clusters of small trumpet-shaped flowers plucked at her hair.

The Manti woman came close, and over her shoulder Asha noticed her trio of attendants, plus Micah and two others. They stood waiting and watching on the opposite side of the pool.

The priestess bent toward Asha, fingering the soft, gold fabric of the clinging tunic they'd given her in place of Pax's mud-splattered shirt.

"I can *smell* lies," Cleo hissed, lifting Asha's chin with her finger. "So don't think of making up any more stories."

Asha jerked her chin free—and felt one of the Manti's spikes press against her throat.

"I told your people I needed protection from a Scarab captain that had taken me," she said, matching the priestess's challenging tone. "That was the truth."

"You *lied* to my people about the man who was with you," insisted Cleo. "Why?"

Asha fought a strong impulse to ask what had happened to Pax. Chances were good he was in less peril than she was right now.

"I wasn't interested in having a discussion about him," Asha explained. "I wanted your people to help me get away."

Cleo's head angled to one side as she studied Asha. "What are the amir's children doing in the lower city?"

Asha paused, holding the priestess's gaze. "Move that spike away from my neck, and I'll tell you."

Cleo frowned, but she straightened and released her.

"There was another captive," said Asha, fighting the urge to rub her stinging throat. "Someone they wanted to save from the genetics lab. They wanted to hide him in the lower city."

"Why?"

Asha shook her head. "The decision was made very quickly, right before we landed. It wasn't explained to me." She was pretty sure she comprehended the "why" of it well enough, but nothing in her answer to the priestess was a lie. She didn't want to sidetrack the discussion by explaining Carrick right now.

"What about you? Why were you with them?"

Asha gripped the railing behind her, steadying herself. She needed to turn this around somehow. She'd hoped to make allies of Rebelión Sagrada. Without help, Pax was sure to catch up to her before she could find Al Campo. Cleo's line of questioning had given her an idea.

But she wasn't sure she could go through with it.

"What were you doing with the Paxtons?" Cleo repeated, raising her wings. The twin, dark spirals glared down at her in threat.

"Why are you so interested in the amir's family?" She stepped away from the railing.

Cleo raised her arm again, and Asha gasped as she felt the spike pricking the first layer of skin at her throat. The dribble of blood tickled as it slid over her collarbone.

The priestess gave her a frigid smile. "If you'd prefer this conversation not come to a rapid, unpleasant conclusion—"

"I'd prefer we dispense with the interrogation," said Asha, clenching her fists. "I want your help, and I have access to something you want. If you help me, you can have it."

The priestess's thin lips twisted in a dubious smirk. "And what is that, child?"

"I can give you the amir's son."

The satisfaction of the surprise in Cleo's face was little consolation to Asha's heart, which writhed in protest over what she had just done. It didn't care that Pax was the only bargaining chip she had.

"What do you mean?" asked the priestess, her wings dropping back to a neutral position.

"Just what I said." Asha reached up and closed her hand over the priestess's, guiding it away from her throat. "I can give you the amir's son. And I will, *if* you get me inside Al Campo."

She didn't feel nearly as confident as she sounded. She'd do almost anything to recover her father, but turn Pax over to his enemies? She reminded herself Pax had brought her here against her will. She wasn't sure she should overlook that fact, even knowing it had been her goal all along. He was still her enemy. An enemy to her and her father, and all the others in Al Campo.

So why was she second-guessing?

Cleo narrowed her eyes. "What makes you think—"

"Priestess!" one of the attendants suddenly called across the garden.

"Not now," replied Cleo, eyes locked on Asha.

"Priestess," persisted the speaker, "a messenger's come from Debajo. There's buzz in the streets about a raid on the temple."

Asha groaned. Pax hadn't wasted any time. He and Iris had broken rules. Lied to their father, and allowed two of their captives to escape. She'd hoped their awkward position might buy her some time. But the timing could hardly be coincidental.

Cleo hesitated, her gaze drifting to the view of the city on the other side of the railing.

"It's just another rumor," the priestess muttered. But she didn't sound convinced.

Asha followed her gaze and saw the Alhambra on the hill opposite the tower. Washed in colored light emitted by the Manti towers, the palace was eerily beautiful, like a dream city. Like warrior fairies had invaded the ancient fortress. In the valley between she could see Banshee still resting on the landing pad, and the ground they'd crossed to reach the lower city.

"Your disciples attacked the amir's son," she reminded Cleo. She suspected this raid had more to do with *her* than the confrontation in the alley. But regardless, Pax was coming, and she had to go. "What do you think they'll do to you for that?"

She tensed as Cleo turned, but the priestess only blinked at her. Until now she'd not been aware the Manti woman had eyelids. "You're offering Augustus Paxton in exchange for safe passage into Al Campo?"

Asha swallowed. "I am."

"Why should I trust that you can deliver him?"

"Because he wants to mate with me." There was no hiding the flash of heat and color that accompanied this confession, but it had been necessary. Instinct told Asha this was an explanation the priestess would buy. And it didn't require her to give away any of her secrets.

Cleo gave her a knowing smile. "Their fatal flaw. But I know the amir, and I know his son." Her gaze drifted over Asha's body. "You're small and soft. I'd have believed you if you told me he wanted to *eat* you." Her laughter was light, and incongruent with the darkness in her expression. "But if he'd wanted to mate with you, he *would* have. You'll have to do better than that."

"I recall you saying you'd know if I lied."

The reply came in a low, dangerous tone. "Humor me."

Asha glanced over the priestess's shoulder at the others. "Ask Micah what he interrupted in the alley."

Asha held her breath while Cleo scrutinized her. Finally the priestess laughed. "We have an agreement. You're not so soft on the inside, are you, my dear? I may mate with you myself."

If I don't eat *you first*—she could almost read the thought in the priestess's face. The Manti woman reveled in toying with her prey; that much was clear enough.

Cleo stepped back, turning to the others, and Asha took her first full breath since arriving on the roof.

"Get the remaining disciples into the tunnels," she ordered. "Our timeline for completing relocation has been adjusted."

BLOOD AND FAITH

"It didn't work, Pax," said Iris.

From the rooftop of a nearby house they could watch the temple entrance, and they could see into a handful of the tower windows. There'd been no movement of any kind, other than the occasional whisper of the lift moving up and down the central shaft. It didn't make sense. There were more than a hundred people living in the temple. Or at least there had been the last time he was inside.

Iris was right; so far it hadn't worked. Why? He had little doubt the message had made it into the temple. He'd waited in the shadows near the entrance to Debajo, stopping the first man headed into the tavern to warn of the impending raid. The connection between the temple and Debajo was a well-known fact. For good measure Iris and Carrick had started the same rumor circulating in the streets.

It should have flushed them out. There should at least be some sign of panic or confusion. Regardless of whether the rumor had been believed, there should be some sign of *life*.

"Something's not right," he murmured, scanning the dark windows. "It's too quiet in there."

"We've done all we can, Pax." Iris's tone was somber. Resolved. "We can't stay here."

He couldn't expect more from his sister. Asha was *his* folly, and Iris had indulged him for longer than he had a right to expect.

"Go home," he said. "Tell Father a story that won't alarm him. Tell him . . ." Pax thought, and remembered something Iris had said when they found Asha. "Tell him my head is clouded with mating, and that I'm carousing in the city."

Iris frowned, dubious. "That's not like you, Pax."

"He understands about the pull of a mate. Ridicule me. Make jokes about it." Pax gave her an affectionate smile. "Just be yourself and he won't be suspicious."

The teasing did nothing to soften the worry lines stamped across her broad forehead. "What about Carrick?"

Pax glanced at the priest, whose eyes moved between them, betraying no emotion. The man was a statue—until someone made him angry. If it weren't for the fact he owed his sister, he'd turn Carrick loose in the city to fend for himself. While the display in the alley made it clear Carrick had begun to feel protective of Iris, Pax had no idea if this loyalty extended to him. Babysitting his sister's volatile pet was a complication he didn't need right now.

"He can stay with me until I find Asha. Then we'll find a safe place for him."

"What's worth all this, Brother?" There was an edge of pleading in her voice he'd never heard before. She was worried about him. She *should* be. "That woman has run from you every chance she got."

Pax shook his head. "I don't have time to explain that, Iris. I'm still working it out for myself."

"Can you at least promise me it's not about sex? Or some possessive, male bullshit?"

He frowned at her. "Seriously?"

The truth would have bothered Iris more. Asha, along with everything that had happened since he met her, had triggered a deep disturbance in his belief system. His father had taught him that preservation of the Manti came first, even if it meant ignoring troubling questions. Pax had struggled with that lesson his whole life. In his mind Asha had come to represent that struggle, and he needed her help to sort it out.

What he hadn't quite acknowledged was that she clearly had her own agenda, and when he learned what it was they might find themselves staring at each other across an impassable divide.

"Go on," he said to Iris. "I'll see you soon."

"What will you do?" she asked.

"Only thing I *can* do at this point."

"I wish you wouldn't. I'd go with you if I could."

Pax hated the idea of it almost more than she did. "I'd never ask you to go in there." *I once vowed I'd never go there again myself.*

Asha was assigned to Micah for safekeeping, and after Cleo and her attendants had left the roof, the two of them took the next lift down to the street level.

She expressed her confusion about what was happening, and Micah explained that the temple had long been expecting a less-than-friendly visit from the amir and his forces. They'd gradually been moving the disciples to a new location.

In one way it was a blow to Rebelión—the high visibility of

the temple made it easier to evangelize. The structure itself was a work of art—the city's crowning architectural achievement— and that alone attracted plenty of curious visitors.

But the movement had been started via computer network, and much of their recruiting was still managed that way. They also believed public acknowledgment that the Alhambra perceived them as a threat would help more than hurt their cause.

"Does the amir reject religion?" Asha asked as they stepped off the lift.

"He claims to," replied Micah. "But also the amir's no fool. He knows the religious aspects of Rebelión serve in part to distract from our political goals. It's much easier to make religious converts than political ones."

A group rounded the elevator shaft, and Micah exchanged a few words with them about staggering departures and which exits to use. She had dropped her original notion that Micah was no more than a disciple or acolyte. He was in possession of what seemed like a lot of sensitive information, and Cleo relied on him a great deal.

When the others had gone, he continued, "In our view the amir is the head of his *own* religion. He expects us to worship science. The geneticists have become his demigods. Any beliefs that counter his are viewed as a threat to his power over the city."

He led her into the secondary tower where she'd first encountered Cleo. The chamber was deserted. They crossed to the curtained corridor, then passed through the entrance to the tunnel.

"Wait for me by the stairway," he instructed. "I need to seal the door."

She stepped into the close, dark space and gripped the handrail, thinking.

"I'm confused about something," she told him as he joined her. "Gregoire, your creator—*he* was a geneticist. Why is there a statue of him on your roof?"

"It's not science we revile, actually. It's the way the amir is using it. We believe the purpose of science is to gain a better understanding of the natural world. To better our condition, and make our lives easier. Those applications of science furthered humanity, and they have furthered our civilization as well. But when science is turned to serve greedy gods—profit, conflict, domination—that's where it falls from grace, unraveling all the good it's done in the process."

Asha nodded. "I understand what you're saying. But I still don't see where Gregoire fits into all this."

He started down the stairs, and she followed. "We are his legacy, and we are grateful for our existence. He was a genius—a biology-flavored Einstein. And he was an artist as well. His work on our species began with a sense of wonder. With an exploration of what was possible. For that reason we still consider our genesis to be pure. *Holy.*" The corners of his mouth turned down. "But he grew proud of his creations, and pride twisted into arrogance. In the end he transformed from creator to destroyer."

She rubbed her lips together, thinking over that last statement. "Are you saying it was true about the virus? The design *was* stolen from his lab?"

"There's no question. Careful records were kept. It was the beginning of a revolution, after all."

"Was Rebelión Sagrada opposed to the destruction of humanity?"

"Rebelión didn't exist back then, but yes, we believe it was wrong. But as I said before, humanity's offenses were grave. Relocating the transgenics like that . . ." He broke off, shaking his head. "Dropping them off in the most war-torn spot on the planet and leaving them to kill or be killed—that was a crime against nature if ever there was one."

Asha shuddered. She knew all this, but the ugly part humanity had played had been downplayed throughout her education. Throughout her *life*. No one talked about the forced migration. The Trail of Terror, her father had called it, referencing the forced migration of native peoples from the southern to the central United States.

"It's ironic we owe our triumph to that genetic marker," he said.

She frowned, remembering Pax had mentioned this once. "Why is the genetic marker significant?"

Micah's brows lifted. "Do you know why it was used?"

She shook her head. "I know it was required for all transgenics."

"Yes, all the ones in the licensed labs, anyway. It was meant to be a safeguard."

"From what?"

"The governments believed they could use it to wipe out the scientists' creations if necessary. Instead, Gregoire used it to target humanity."

The silence of the underground pressed in around them as she absorbed this. *Humanity engineered its own downfall.* Her father had said it many times. She wondered if he'd known how true it was.

As they walked through the passage that led to Debajo, she asked, "What is it Rebelión wants?"

"In the beginning it was about opening people's eyes in hopes our next leader wouldn't be so tight with DAB-lab. But Emile Paxton and his family are here to stay. Democratic elections were voted down." Micah shook his head. "More irony."

But Asha had snagged on another point, something else Pax had mentioned but never explained. "What is DAB-lab?"

"Sustainable Transgenics. Unauthorized reproduction is forbidden for us. DAB-lab—the 'design a baby' lab—looks at the parents and calculates how insect or how human their offspring will be. Matches that might result in loss of higher brain function, for example, or an excess of insect-like characteristics, are rejected."

"I can see how that sort of constraint would be . . . troubling. But Pax—the amir's son, I mean—he told me without continuing infusion of human DNA your species would eventually devolve completely."

Micah was shaking his head before she finished. "There is some evidence of that, but the research you refer to was authored by DAB-lab, and they've refused requests for independent review of their data. We suspect the need for such tight controls is completely exaggerated. Without them, the population would self-regulate. No one—including Augustus Paxton—is going to marry or reproduce with a creature more animal than human. It's all about power. The geneticists, and the amir through them, are playing God with our evolution. *They* are deciding our genetic destiny."

These sounded like reasonable conclusions, and it reminded her of something Pax had said about the Manti not managing things much better than humans. One thing she could *not* imagine was Pax letting scientists choose his mate. Considering who his father was, he wasn't likely to have a choice about that. She wondered whether he'd be required to mate with someone more Manti—someone like Cleo.

"Do you know what Cleo wants with the amir's son?" she asked him. "It seems like interfering with the ruling family is only going to escalate things."

Asha felt pretty confident at this point she'd picked the side most aligned with her interests, but she had serious doubts about their ability to prevail. Almost as serious as her doubts that she'd be able to stomach upholding her end of the bargain with Cleo.

"I have more access to the priestess than most disciples enjoy," he replied, confirming what she'd suspected. "But it's not something she's discussed with me. I'd guess escalation is exactly what she's looking for. Besides political and philosophical differences, I think there's some bad blood." He stopped just short of the stairway up to Debajo. "Did you know that Paxton's sister is Cleo's daughter?"

After Iris was gone, Pax held his position on the roof, thinking about the look that had passed between his sister and the priest, and the way she'd touched his arm. She must be aware she was setting herself up for pain. The amir would never give his permission for an alliance between his daughter and a mudgrubber priest with wolf DNA. It was exactly the sort of thing his father had founded DAB-lab to prevent.

But he had no business judging Iris when he was busy positioning himself for the same sort of trouble. The geneticists wouldn't make any argument against pure human DNA—though because Pax's mother was also human, they might argue it was going too far the other way—but politically it was impossible.

And then there was the fact she never stayed around long enough for him to figure out what he actually wanted from her.

He intended to stand by Iris as best he could, even if it did turn out she was foolish enough to think she could have Carrick. Pax was the amir's oldest child, next in line for governing Granada, and he knew where his loyalties lay. But growing up in the Alhambra had been lonely. His sister had been his only playmate. The only friend he could trust. There wasn't much that could divide him from her.

"Why is she so scared of that place?" asked Carrick.

Pax looked at him. "You mean the temple?"

"I could feel it in her. It wasn't the fear of walking into a fight. Your sister doesn't have that."

Don't I know it. "Something bad happened to us here. The woman who leads these people tried to manipulate us once. Tried to use us against our father." Not knowing how much Iris would want revealed, he tried to leave it at that.

But the priest was perceptive. "It was a betrayal? She was important to Iris?"

"Yes," Pax acknowledged.

"What about you?"

Pax sighed. "I believed Rebelión Sagrada was asking important questions, and I was interested in mending the rift between the priestess and my father. But all that's out of the question now." Yes, out of the question after his sister's mother used his greatest vulnerability to try to trap him.

"Those entrusted with championing faith often become faith's worst enemies," replied Carrick.

Pax raised an eyebrow. He was beginning to understand why the man was so interesting to Iris. "Are you a believer yourself?" he asked.

"I lost my faith a long time ago."

"Those people back in Beck's camp, they all called you 'Father.'"

Carrick's lips curled in a tired smile. The smile of a man who'd been flipped on his back like a turtle and had come to accept he was at the world's mercy. "People need something to give them hope, don't they?"

Gazing again at the fanciful spike, Pax said, "I'd call sentiment like that a truer mark of a holy man than faith."

The priest let that pass without comment, and after a moment Pax asked, "You had no idea, did you? That you weren't fully human."

"I never knew my father. There were things I could do that others couldn't, and my mother always said I was just like him. But she made me pretend I was just like everyone else. She begged me to go into the priesthood. Maybe she thought it would cleanse me."

"Maybe she thought it would protect you. Maybe it did."

The priest's gaze drifted back to the temple. "My whole life I thought she was touched. 'Fey,' they used to call it. She could see things other people couldn't. She seemed so open to everything. So vulnerable. All this time I thought I was protecting *her*."

"I'm sorry you lost her." The priest's mother had been one of the casualties in the wasp attack, succumbing to the smoke in the burning building.

"I'm not." Pax glanced up at the flat statement.

"She'd never been more than a dozen kilometers from her village," continued Carrick. "It would have broken my heart for her to die here, alone and afraid."

Pax thought about his own mother, dying surrounded by luxuries she cared nothing for, and servants who were also prison guards. Placated like a child with pretty things, as if she'd forget everyone she loved had been taken from her.

The temple's exterior lights dimmed. Silent as the grave in there.

"Listen," said Pax. The priest met his gaze. "I bear you no ill will. Iris is right—you don't belong in a cell in the genetics lab. But I can't force you to stay with me, and I don't want a knife in the back. If you're planning to run, run now. I won't come after you. I can't speak for Iris."

Carrick studied him. "You're going after *Asha*."

The man might as *well* have knifed him in the back. There

was nothing Pax hated more than a hypocrite. With every passing moment it became harder to deny that's what he had become.

"I don't want to hurt Asha. I just want to . . ." To *what*? "I just want to talk to her. And the people she's gone to for protection—I don't trust them."

The priest's gaze drifted to the street below, deserted now as the hour had grown late. "Iris told me the truth about what I am," he said. "She helped me escape. I owe her for that. When I've repaid that debt, I'll look to what comes next."

Pax breathed in relief he hadn't expected to feel. "All right, then. Let's go find out what magic they've used to empty that temple."

"Iris's mother!" Asha thought she must have misunderstood. The Manti woman hardly seemed old enough to have a child Iris's age. But then her features were so alien it was hard to be sure. "Is Cleo married to Pax's father?"

"No. But they used to be on friendlier terms."

Much friendlier. She struggled with the image of the Manti priestess as mother to *anyone*.

"From an ideological standpoint I'd say the rift was inevitable," continued Micah. "That plus the fact they're the most powerful figures in the city. My understanding is the amir's son expended considerable time and energy playing diplomat between them. But something went wrong—some scandal. The rumor is he tried to seduce her."

Pax seduce Iris's *mother*? It didn't seem possible. And yet . . . she'd seen him overtaken by lust. An image of Pax in Cleo's chains rose unbidden. She banished it, but it left a sour feeling in her stomach.

Noticing they'd turned out of the corridor between the

temple and Debajo, she asked, "Where are we going? Where are the others?"

"Ahead of us in the tunnels," replied Micah. "We'll see them soon."

He moved close to one of the walls of the passage, where there had once been another of the arched openings—possibly an intersecting tunnel, now blocked by fallen rock and dirt. He raised his hand, passing it in front of the opening.

The debris disintegrated.

Gasping, she said, "How did you do that?"

He guided her through the opening, and she watched it seal up again behind them.

"The technology is similar to what you see above, in the tower. The construction resin is 'smart.' A blend of microbial bots and organic material."

She stared at the reformed surface. "That's amazing. Like magic."

Micah smiled. "Not magic. It's more illusion than reality, but still very complex. There's generation, and *de*generation, and cooling processes for both. Plus artificial intelligence for ensuring secure access."

"Who did all this?"

"I did."

She lifted her eyebrows. "Are you serious?"

"Security is my area of expertise. I work for DAB-lab, which gives me access to all the more experimental technology."

"DAB-lab?" She shook her head, confused. "Do they know that you're involved with Rebelión? Seems like a serious conflict of interests."

"No doubt," he laughed. "No, they don't know. They can never know."

She understood now why he was so valuable to Cleo. "Why have you gone to all this trouble?"

The tunnel forked and Micah veered left. She followed, forced to walk behind due to the narrow path through the very real debris from a partial collapse.

"The tunnels are officially off-limits, and we're the only ones who use them regularly. But it won't take long for the amir to figure out we've gone underground. The modifications to the tunnels, combined with the secure access, *should* prevent them from catching up with us. By the time they figure it out we'll be long gone."

"Gone where?" she asked. This would all be for nothing if she ended up farther from her father.

"Al Campo."

Asha hesitated, confused. "The internment camp for human survivors?"

"That's right."

"I don't understand."

"There's an empty quarter of the village, set aside in case the people in Sanctuary ever need to be relocated. I worked with a hacker inside the camp to arrange it all. We reconfigured the *flies*—the DAB-lab surveillance cyborgs—so the feeds are showing dummy video for the empty quarter. Basically they're feeding a bunch of historical footage of nothing."

"You're going to hide in plain sight." She respected her companion's ingenuity more every moment. "In the last place the amir would look for you. But if you can get into Al Campo, can't the humans get out?"

Micah paused, glancing back at her. "We've created a similar type of secure access point there, and only disciples can open it. But we're not jailers. We have an agreement with the people inside. In exchange for their help hiding us, we've promised to free them once the shift in power takes place."

"An alliance."

"Yes, that's accurate."

They walked for a while in silence, and she processed the implications. The first one being that she'd made a dangerous deal with Cleo that had turned out not to be necessary. But she couldn't have foreseen this. And if she hadn't done it the priestess could have just as easily tossed her back out in the street.

"Tell me," said Micah. "Who is it you hope to find in Bone Town?"

"*Bone* Town?"

"Sorry. The residents refer to the camp that way because of the architecture. You'll see. Are you looking for someone else taken by a Scarab?"

"Yes."

"What will you do if you find them?"

She bit her lip. "I don't know."

Ridiculous as it now seemed, she'd never thought past *finding* her father. That had seemed unlikely enough in itself. Now it was beginning to look like she had a chance—it fired off a little flare of hope in her chest.

They couldn't go home—that much was clear. Even if she could find transportation, Pax would come for her; she felt sure of it. They could try to run far enough away from Granada to start a new life. Maybe persuade some of the others to join them. That too seemed to hold low odds of success.

But this alliance between Rebelión Sagrada and Al Campo had suggested another possibility. She'd learned something in the course of her journey: her life in Sanctuary had been half a life. The idea of going back to that kind of stasis no longer held any appeal for her. *Here* she might just see change in her lifetime. Here she could write new history rather than keeping the old history on life support.

But to stay she would have to betray Pax more deeply than she had already. Join his family's enemies, and help them pull him down. There was a part of her—that sliver of her that had been awakened by him—that she would have to extract and bury before she could. That part of her wasn't going to go down without a fight. She wasn't sure she wanted it to.

Pax stared down at the iron rings, unable to distinguish rust from blood. There was no reason for a chain like this—Manti technology could have created something much more sophisticated, both lighter and stronger—but Cleo had a flair for the dramatic. Or perhaps it was meant to be symbolic of their disdain for scientific interference in reproduction.

More likely she chose them because they hurt. Yes, he was giving her too much credit.

"Asha was here," called the priest.

Pax turned, nodding. He could smell her too, as well as the disciple they'd met in the alley. They'd both been in this room more than once.

"Fear leaves a mark," Carrick continued. "So does . . ." The priest glanced up from the spot on the floor he'd been staring at. His gaze met Pax's only briefly before he glanced down again.

Pax felt sick.

The priest disappeared into a curtained-off area. "I lose her here," he called. "It's like she walked through the wall."

Pax followed him into what he'd assumed was an enclosure to stow attendants in the event of a sudden desire for privacy. But it looked more like a makeshift corridor.

"That's possible," said Pax. "Some kind of illusion, maybe, or a false wall."

He rested his hand against the curved surface. It felt solid, and *warm*—characteristic of this particular building resin since it was basically alive.

The wall was seamless. There was no section that didn't match up. No darker or lighter color, or sudden change in texture.

The priest followed Pax's lead, wiping small circles over the surface with his hands, and they worked toward each other from opposite ends of the curtain.

"My close vision is not very good, but it doesn't look like—"

The priest broke off suddenly, and Pax looked up. "What is it?"

Carrick shook his head. "I thought I saw something—like a beam of light. It's gone now. I think I imagined it."

"Stay there," commanded Pax as he walked over to join him. "Move your hands back to where they were when you saw the light."

The priest slid his hands slowly, and after a moment he said, "There!"

Pax blinked at the wall. "I didn't see anything. Do it again."

"There."

He stared at the priest's hand. He very much doubted the man was hallucinating. Despite being nearsighted Carrick might be more sensitive to movement or changes in light.

"Move your hand," said Pax. The priest complied, and he placed his own hand in the same position. "Tell me if you see it again."

"Yes. It . . . it's illuminating that mark on your arm. Now it's gone."

Clever. Pax growled, slapping his palm against the wall. No wonder they hadn't bothered to secure the temple better. They'd all gone underground.

He stared up at the ceiling, thinking. They hadn't searched the upper floors yet. The temple *felt* empty, but it was possible some of the disciples were still inside. They'd have to try.

Otherwise they could waste a huge amount of time looking for another way to open the door.

Unless . . .

He glanced at Carrick. "Let's go."

"Where?"

"Back to the alley. We need a key."

"We're not all like him."

Micah's voice interrupted Asha's thoughts, bringing her back to the present moment in time to step over a large piece of broken pottery.

"Not all like who?"

"The amir's son." Micah glanced back at her briefly. "Did he attack you?"

She hesitated, despite the fact there was no reason for her to shield Pax from this man's disapproval. But telling him didn't feel right. Especially in light of the rumor about Pax and the priestess. It painted a picture that didn't really fit Pax.

Which isn't my concern.

"I was spared that . . . affliction," said Micah, apparently taking her silence as an affirmative.

"It's more complicated than him attacking me," she said. "I ran from him. He thought I might be a threat to him. He grabbed me and I fought him. Then something changed. He—" She shook her head. "Nothing happened. I was able to get away. After that he ordered his ship to protect me."

"Really?" Micah turned and reached for her hand as she started over a two-foot-high pile of loose rubble. The shoes from the temple were more practical than Iris's slippers, but not by much. As he lifted his arm, the wide cuff of his shirt slipped back to reveal a row of spikes, smaller and softer-looking than the priestess's.

"He has more control than he thinks he does," she contin-ued, concentrating on her footing. "He didn't want to hurt me."

Micah eyed her curiously as she alighted on solid ground beside him. His eyes moved to the cast on her wrist, which she'd all but forgotten. "You don't hate him."

It was odd to hear it spoken aloud, but of course it was true. She didn't hate him, enemy or no. "He brought me here against my will," she acknowledged. "But since then he's done all he could to protect me. Even from his own family."

"But you ran from him."

"I had to if I didn't want to end up in the Alhambra. And he would never have helped me find my father in Al Campo. What excuse could he have given the amir for that?"

Micah nodded. "Not one the amir would accept. I've won-dered about what really happened between you. I followed you into that alley because I sensed the tension. I wanted to make sure you were all right."

Asha glanced at him, surprised. "Not because you wanted to recruit us?"

He laughed. "We do a lot of that sort of work, but no."

"Thank you. That was kind."

"Well." He turned then, and continued down the corridor. Her gratitude seemed to have made him uncomfortable.

"Did you know that I was human?" she asked. "Pax said some would sense it."

"I did sense you were different. But the smell of sagrada tends to overpower everything. My father is human, though, so I was curious to get a closer look at you."

"Your father is human?"

"Yes. My mother is Manti. Nearly as Manti as Cleo."

"How did—" She hesitated, knowing it was an intensely personal question. "Do you mind if I ask how that happened? I thought the humans were all in Al Campo."

"Intermarriage is the one way they can get out. It's part of the DAB-lab protocol for reproduction."

When Pax had told her the genetics lab needed human DNA, she'd never guessed they'd incorporate it in such a . . . *traditional* way. "How does that work, exactly?"

"If someone wants out, they volunteer. There's a lottery among those deemed too Manti to reproduce with other Manti. Basically it's an arranged marriage. It avoids the more sterile approaches of using donors or tampering with DNA."

"Do people ever run once they get out?"

"Sometimes. But if they're caught they're executed, so most don't."

Internment, forced marriage, execution—it almost made Sanctuary look utopian. "Do your parents . . . do they have any feeling for each other?" *Or is it just another kind of prison?*

"Believe it or not, yes. My father adores her. She pretends to tolerate him, but the adoration is mutual. It wasn't always that way, though. I was conceived in a glass tube."

"I see."

"My five siblings were conceived the old-fashioned way."

"Five!" Five siblings could hardly be explained away as a moment of weakness.

"We were a pack of little devils." He laughed. "I think they bonded out of desperation."

They could be talking about any other couple. Any *human* couple. This reminded her of another potentially sensitive question she wanted to ask him. "Earlier when you said you're not like Pax, did you mean you don't experience the same sort of . . . drives?"

Again he laughed. "No, I don't mean that. I just mean it never takes me over so completely I could hurt someone."

"You're lucky. I think it would be pretty hard to live with."

They stopped in front of another wall, and Micah fixed his gaze on her before opening it.

"I understand why you had to leave him, but outside of that, it sounds to me like you don't bear him any ill will. I'm not going to ask you questions that could have answers I'd be obligated to share with others. But I want to warn you that Cleo is very dangerous when crossed."

Asha swallowed. "I don't doubt that."

He passed his hand over the wall, and the tunnel opened out into a cavern filled with dark-cloaked figures. Cleo noticed their arrival and walked over to meet them.

"There are two groups behind us in the tunnels, my lady," Micah told her. "They're the last. You should cross in small numbers, just to be safe."

Cleo nodded. "Your friends in Al Campo will be ready for us?"

"It's earlier than we agreed, but they knew something like this might happen. They'll be ready enough."

The priestess smiled. "I don't know how we'll manage without you, Micah. We would never have prepared for this in time without your talents, and your devotion to our cause."

Asha glanced at him, alarmed at what the first statement suggested. Micah bowed his head, acknowledging the praise.

"I hate running like thieves in the night," continued Cleo. "That temple represents our greatest triumph—the funding we were able to procure, alone. The idea of Emile giving it to some wealthy patron, or turning it into a museum . . ." Her mouth twisted in disgust.

"There will be greater triumphs, my lady," Micah replied in a voice soft with deference. "And we'll run *them* out of it soon enough."

Cleo gave him her hand. He pressed it to his lips. When he released it she moved away, and he turned to Asha.

"The others will take you the rest of the way. There's some scrambling overground, and a few more underground passages. Take it slow and you'll be fine. It's dark now, and the cloaks will hide you from Scarab patrols."

She wasn't worried about scrambling over rocks and dirt in the dark. She'd been doing it since she was a child sneaking out to explore the desert in the moonlight. She *was* worried about losing her only friend among her new companions.

"Will I see you again?"

"Not for a while. I'm more useful to Cleo working for DAB-lab security than I am hiding in Al Campo. And if I went missing it would draw attention to what I've been doing."

He reached out his hand, and she grasped it. He bent to kiss her cheek and said in a low voice, "Remember what I said about Cleo. Take care of yourself, Asha."

A shiver ran through her and she nodded. "Thank you for the information you've shared with me. It'll make figuring out my next steps much easier."

He released her hand and turned to go, but stopped and turned back. "What's your father's name?"

She stared at him, still preoccupied with anxiety over his departure. "My father?"

"Maybe my contact inside can help you find him."

"Oh of course, thank you. His name is Harker. Harker St. John."

Something flashed in Micah's eyes.

"What is it?"

"The man I've been working with inside . . ." He shook his head. "I thought it was just a hacker handle."

Her heart jumped. "What do you mean?"

"He goes by the name 'Hark.'"

REUNIONS

Asha and the others emerged from the cavern onto open ground—rocky, treeless, and sloped. She hit the ground hard within the first five minutes of their trek. The stars were mostly obscured by clouds and the terrain was uneven, but it had more to do with her head than either her eyes or her feet.

As much as she wanted to believe, she was driven clumsy and half mad by uncertainty. Because it was so unlike him. She adored her father to the point of worship, but part of the reason for that was that he was softer than her mother. Less driven. He'd had more time for Asha, and more of a parent's empathy. To say that he was bright was an understatement, and he was honest and hardworking. But a hacker? One talented enough to have helped Micah defeat Al Campo's security system? It was more like something her mother would do.

After a few kilometers of walking, they entered a tunnel that had been bored through a steep hillside. The canal that passed through it ran back toward the city.

None of the others had spoken to her, and she heard only the occasional murmur of them speaking to each other. But as she fell for the second time, one of them showed her a strip of colored dots that were reactive to the heat in the tip of her finger. She could use them to adjust the cloak so it emitted a soft green glow on the underside.

This saved her in the tunnel, which had been made wide enough for the canal to pass through and not much else. In places they were less walking than horizontally scaling the tunnel wall. The slippers she'd been given were slick on the bottom, and finally she removed them and clung to the rocky surface with bare feet.

As they neared the end of the tunnel, she scraped her injured wrist across a jagged surface, and her cast crumbled away into the canal. She muttered an oath at her carelessness, but soon discovered her wrist felt whole and healthy again.

"They come off when it's time." She glanced up to find the attendant who'd helped her with her bath smiling at her. Then she turned and continued after the others.

When they reached the tunnel's end they paused for a rest, dimming their cloaks now that a crisp half-moon threw an anemic light over the ground outside. As the two disciples in the lead stepped out of the tunnel, someone heard a Scarab approaching, and they sank back into the shadows until it glided past.

Cresting the next hill, Asha could see the lights of Granada to the southwest, and a walled village that blanketed the valley to the northeast. Directly north there was a facility of some kind—a sprawling structure, the least remarkable of any she'd seen since her arrival, well-lit and surrounded by what looked like greenhouses, plantings, silos, and pens for animals. Smaller buildings dotted the grounds, connected by a road.

The village to the northeast had to be Al Campo. The construction material was odd—from where she stood it looked like rock smoothed by wind and water, reminding her of formations near her home. Along the edges of the village ran a neat row of long, inward-curving posts, like the ribs of some enormous animal.

Bone Town.

"I've fulfilled my part of our agreement," Cleo said, startling her. Asha hadn't noticed her moving close. The Manti woman's antennae protruded under the hood of her cloak, giving her an even more threatening appearance.

"We're not inside yet," Asha replied coolly.

"We will be within the hour."

Still she had time. Pax would first have to unravel the mystery of their disappearance. And it was possible he wouldn't. Cleo couldn't justly hold her to their bargain in that case. Though Asha had a feeling that wouldn't stop her.

Eventually she would have to face this. If her father *was* behind this alliance, she couldn't cope with her uncertainty by running again. He was the whole reason she'd come.

She groaned inwardly. Nothing made sense anymore. She felt fractured, like her personality had broken in two, each pulling the opposite direction. She could only hope that seeing her father would help to reground her.

Inside the tunnels it was easy enough to follow Asha's trail, but the dead man slowed them down considerably. There'd been no quick means of separating the disciple from his arm, and even if there had been, Pax wasn't sure he'd have the stomach for it. Those dark years before Granada had seen such horrors and far worse, but Pax had grown up in palaces, and the war was over by the time he was four. He hadn't clawed to the top of a pile of dead enemies to survive, like the former generation. He'd fought for his life a couple times, but killing a man in a berserker rage because he'd tried to kill you was a far cry from coolly sawing off a limb.

The ingenuity of Rebelión Sagrada in preparing for the amir's eventual invasion of the temple was staggering. Cleo was clever, but this? This had required a level of technical expertise he would not have thought available to them. But then he'd been staggered by the temple as well. Everyone had been. It was time to stop underestimating these people.

He had never felt comfortable thinking of the group as his enemy. It was his father's view, and his sister's. And he doubted he could ever forgive Cleo for what she'd tried to do to his family. To him *personally*. But though he'd never understood their worship of the maniacal (and egomaniacal) genius who'd created them all, he felt some empathy with their views on DAB-lab's manipulation of Manti genetics. So why these sudden feelings of enmity?

It was more than the attack in the alley, he knew. It was because they'd spirited away Asha, forcing him to undertake a recovery mission his father would never approve of. Risking his ability to protect her. Making him ask himself hard questions in the process.

"Bloody hell!" Pax exclaimed as he lost his grip on the body and it slumped to the ground.

Carrick groaned, and he could only imagine what the priest must be going through, forced to help carry the corpse of the man he'd killed so they could use the mark on his wrist.

"Come on," urged Pax. "It can't be far now."

But he had no way of knowing whether this was true or not. He'd been aware there were tunnels under the city—they'd been used centuries ago for secret worship and even hiding and fleeing by the Muslims and Jews living under Catholic rule. But his father had declared them off-limits for safety reasons, and he'd had no idea they were so intact, or where they might lead.

Carrick bent and lifted the dead man's feet. "You're sure we're not walking into some kind of trap?"

Pax gripped under the man's arms, hoisting him again. "No, I'm not."

Asha brought up the rear as they scrambled down a loose hillside and then traversed along the base of the slope toward Bone Town. Cleo hadn't instructed anyone to keep an eye on her, probably feeling secure in the fact they were so close to her object she wasn't likely to slip away.

When they reached the farther end of the village, they cut across the valley to the hill at its back. As they approached, she saw that while less ornate than the structures within the city, Al Campo had a similar, organic feel. No hard lines or corners. The buildings seemed to flow together like water or sand. She also noticed small towers and lines of columns made of the same blanched material as the fence, their shapes also resembling bones or tusks. And as they drew closer still, the light washing over the structure revealed small, brightly colored spheres, seemingly placed at random atop posts or towers, or set in the middle of walls or sloping roofs. It was like the architect had been unable to completely restrain whimsical impulses.

They crouched beside the fence where it joined with the base of the steep hillside, and one of the party used a navigator to locate a section that had been replaced with the smart resin.

As the others dropped down and crawled through the opening, Asha studied the fence. The ribs were easily three meters tall, but at about two meters they narrowed, creating openings.

"This is all that keeps them in?" she asked.

The disciple with the navigator glanced at her. "There's an electrical field. But Micah has access to that in security. This section is collapsed."

As she ducked into the opening Asha wondered if the humans inside knew this—that all that stood between them and freedom was a three-meter fence.

Adjusting their cloaks so they could see, they regrouped in the narrow alley formed by the hillside and the back row of buildings. The disciple she'd spoken with reminded them to stay close together.

"The flies that patrol the camp transmit dummy video for this quarter," he explained. "But if we don't stay within the boundaries we'll be discovered. If you see a mark like this, go back the way you came."

He turned the navigator so everyone could see—an upside-down triangle with smaller circles at the top of the lines that formed the wide portion. It looked a lot like the head of a praying mantis.

The speaker took the lead with Cleo close behind. As Asha and the others moved to follow, something buzzed past her ear. Ducking to the side, she glanced back in time to see an egg-sized, black capsule zooming out of sight, wings vibrating like a hummingbird's, too fast to see.

"Nobody touch it," warned the disciple. But the thing had already disappeared around a corner. "Listen for those and stay out of their way. They can't see you, but if they bump into something that shouldn't be there it's going to draw attention."

They continued along the outer boundary of the village, and after a few minutes they began to cross paths with others. It was clear their arrival had been anticipated. A man and woman Asha recognized as attendants from Cleo's chamber soon joined them.

After a few moments' conversation with them, Cleo turned her attention back to the group, choosing two additional attendants to remain with her and releasing the others to find their quarters.

To Asha she said, "Follow me."

Guided by starlight reflecting off white surfaces, they moved deeper into the village, flowing along curving walkways, stairways, and rooflines. They never passed any large buildings or open spaces—Al Campo was a labyrinth of narrow, winding streets and dwelling-sized two-story buildings. It gave her the same closed-in feeling she got navigating the Fiery Furnace back home.

Sanctuary, too, lacked larger structures, with the exception of the Council House. The physical infrastructure of the Archive was spread out over half a dozen buildings. It occurred to her that perhaps this had been planned—perhaps the Manti, and the governing council, had wanted to discourage meetings of large groups.

Cleo stopped outside a house with a façade that merged mask and skull-like lines—two large eye-socket-shaped windows with a narrow door at the nasal opening.

Inside they found a large and open room, with pallets along the walls, low tables, and cushions strewn around a fire pit filled with coals that glowed without smoking.

The attendant glanced at Cleo, questioning, and she nodded. "We'll need another bed for our guest."

As Asha wondered whether the priestess's physiology allowed her to recline for sleeping, one of the pallets moved, startling her. A form rolled toward them, and in the light from the fire pit she recognized the man from the temple—Cleo's mate. White teeth glinted in his dark face as he smiled at the priestess.

"I've been waiting for you," he murmured. "Come to bed."

"Not now, my love. I need to have a word with our host."

"Your host is here."

Asha spun at the sound of the familiar voice, afraid to trust her ears.

He froze in the doorway, eyes fixing on her, wide and shocked. Thinner than before, with more gray in his beard. But there was no longer any question about the identity of "Hark."

He took a tentative step. "Asha?"

She rushed at him, throwing her arms around his neck.

"Dad!"

"I can't believe this," he murmured into her hair. "I thought I'd never . . . How are you *here*?"

"I came to find you," she said, drawing back. He rubbed her cheeks with warm fingers and pressed his forehead against hers. "I couldn't stop wondering what happened to you. Wondering whether or not you were alive."

"Oh, Ash," he murmured. "I'm so sorry. This is no place for you, honey. But I'm so happy to see you. You have no idea." Moisture glinted in his eyes as they moved over her. "What happened to your hair?"

The oddly practical question caused her to laugh through her tears. She'd been so occupied with survival the last few days, she'd forgotten the mystery of her hair. But it was no mystery after all. The day her mother had told her nothing could be done to recover her father, she'd dug the scissors out of his desk and cut off all her hair. She remembered how she'd sat rubbing the long strands between her fingers, not knowing why she'd done it, but relieved that it was gone. It had lightened her load. Had given her the clarity she needed to make an impossible choice.

Behind them Cleo cleared her throat. "Asha?"

She drew away from her father, wiping tears with the back of her hand. "This is Cleo, Dad. She's the priestess from the temple—Rebelión Sagrada. Are you the one working with Micah?"

He dragged his gaze from her to Cleo, holding out his hand. "I'm Harker," he said. "I've been working with your man from security at the genetics lab." He glanced at Asha. "I didn't know his real name."

"I know who you are," replied Cleo. "But I didn't know we were bringing you your daughter." The priestess's lilac eyes shifted to Asha, narrowing and recalculating. Asha's stomach twisted.

"Thank you," he replied. He shoved hair from his forehead, and Asha could see he still hadn't recovered from the shock. "I'm sure you're tired. I've mainly come to welcome you here, and let you know I'm staying nearby. We can talk more in the morning."

Cleo gave a slow, precise nod. "You have my thanks. And I understand now why my new friend was so anxious to come here. You'll want time to speak with her alone."

Her father nodded, slipping an arm around her. "Yes."

"Of course. But know that she owes a debt to me for bringing her here. I'll want to speak with her about that soon."

He frowned at the priestess. "What debt?"

"It's all right," Asha assured him, though she was far from feeling it. She squeezed his waist. "Let's go."

"Good night, then," he said. "I'll call again at breakfast. You have food enough to last a few days. If you'll provide me a list in the morning of anything you're lacking, I'll do my best to get it. Meals will be spare for a while, until your security man can find a way to modify the food req without anyone noticing."

"I understand," replied Cleo. "Good night, Mr. Harker."

"Just Harker," he corrected. "Harker St. John."

Cleo nodded and turned from them, signaling the end of

the interview. Whatever she might owe the humans for concealing her here—however gracious she'd been in the exchange with her father—it was clear enough she intended to maintain her authority even in exile. She'd probably determined in less than a minute that she'd have no trouble with Harker St. John. Soft-spoken, kind, and unassuming, he was the last man to tangle with someone like Cleo.

Or at least that was the man Asha thought she knew. As much as she adored him, it was clear she'd underestimated him. As he had her.

They walked arm in arm down the path, stopping in front of a plainer-looking house. Scanning the façade, she noticed one of the inverted triangle symbols painted near the curve of the roof.

"Is it safe to be here?" she asked. "I can't be seen by one of those fly things. People may be looking for me."

He raised an eyebrow, but then held out his arm, gesturing her inside. "It's safe if you don't go beyond this point. This marks the boundary of the section of grid we've blocked."

The house was smaller than the one provided for Cleo and her attendants, with a single pallet and a small table and chair. Her father knelt at the fire pit and waved a hand over the coals. The room brightened with soft orange light.

"Are you hungry?"

"Dad, what's going on?"

He glanced up. A smile softened his haggard features. "You're so beautiful, honey. More so than I even remember. You should have cut your hair a long time ago."

"Why did they take you away?" Her voice broke from impatience and strain, and from the grief that had never really left her.

He drew in a deep breath. "Sit down, Ash."

"I don't want to sit down."

She was so happy, so relieved to see him, but she needed to understand what had propelled them into this danger and chaos. Her mind had made a connection after talking with Micah, and she couldn't help feeling that her father had deceived her.

"You were behind that virus, weren't you? The Ophelia Prophecy?"

"You found out about that from the security man— Micah?"

Asha nodded. "But I don't understand."

"Okay. I can explain. But it's the middle of the night. You must be tired."

Tired indeed, tired to the marrow of her bones. "Tell me."

He gestured to a cushion beside him. "Come sit down, honey. I want to be close to you."

She joined him at the fire pit, and he continued, "I'll explain about the prophecy. But I need to go back farther for it to make sense." He squeezed her knee. "You know I'm good with computers."

Recoverer of lost data. Developer of inventive search tools. She nodded.

"I worked for years to break into the governing council's database. I—"

"You *what*?" She gaped at him. "Why would you do that?"

"I had a lot of questions about Sanctuary. Our survival didn't make sense to me. I used to try to discuss it with your mother, but she made me feel like I was crazy." He closed his eyes, struggling to control emotion. "Eventually I did get into their system. What we believe about Sanctuary, Ash, it's—" He opened his eyes and met her gaze. "Sanctuary is basically a human breeding facility for the Manti."

"I know, Dad."

His expression morphed from defeated to angry in a second. "Is that why you were sent here?"

"No. But we can talk about that in a minute. Tell me the rest."

He took a deep breath. "When I pieced it together, I almost killed myself. I'd never considered myself the kind of man to do something like that."

He wasn't. But she understood it. Discovering your life was built on a lie—she remembered how numb she'd felt when she learned the truth.

"Why didn't you talk to me about it?"

He frowned. "Because it was incredibly dangerous information. And it involved your mother. A huge secret she'd kept from us. From *everyone*. A betrayal of her family as well as her powers of office."

"Did you confront her about it?"

"Not then."

Which implied he *had* confronted her. Asha's hands felt slick, and she wiped them on her tunic. She needed to know the whole truth, but she was beginning to feel afraid of it.

"Do you know Zora Cruz? Zee?" he asked.

The surprises were coming too fast now for her to keep up. "Yes. We became friends after you disappeared."

This time she saw she'd surprised *him*. "Is she okay, honey? Did she come here with you?"

Asha shook her head, bewildered. "As far as I know she's fine, but she's not here. How do you know her?"

His gaze moved to the fire pit. "I was involved with her."

Asha blinked at him, trying to assimilate the unexpected piece of information.

"You mean . . ." She wasn't sure why she should find this shocking. Maybe because she couldn't imagine a woman more different from her mother. Yet in some ways they were a lot alike.

"Yes, we had a relationship."

"I don't understand. Why wouldn't she have told me?" It

was more than that. Zee had intentionally withheld the information. "Why didn't *you* tell me?"

"I didn't want to involve you, honey. I think you'll understand better when I've finished."

He eyed her expectantly, and she said, "Go on."

"Zee found Stella Engle—Ophelia. I'm assuming you know about that too."

Something else Zee had withheld. Even when they'd found the old woman with Pax she hadn't mentioned it. "No," she replied.

"Stella's inner circle lied about her drowning," he explained. "She was starting to draw unwanted attention from the council. That old woman *is* crazy, but Zee told me some of the nonsense she muttered, and it got me thinking. I started poking around in your research on her. I read your personal Archive journal."

"'Science will destroy us,'" murmured Asha.

"That's right. It gave both of us ideas about approaches to challenging the Manti. That was around the same time I broke into the council database, and after that we took the whole thing a lot more seriously."

"*You* were Zee's Archive connection," she replied, remembering the data on hypnosis. "She sent you here too."

"No." He shook his head, leveling his gaze at her. "Your mother did."

The statement whipped out like a slap. She realized she'd been holding on to the hope that in the end, somehow, her mother would be cleared of involvement in all this.

"Miri found out about the affair," he continued. "She was furious. We stopped loving each other a long time ago, your mother and I, but the council had its eye on Zee. She heckled in town meetings, couldn't help herself. Your mother thought I was being irresponsible. Exposing you to dangerous ideas."

Asha sat frozen, afraid to breathe.

"She said some awful things. So did I. In the end I got so disgusted with her holier-than-thou bullshit I threw it all up in her face."

"Threw *what* up in her face?" She hardly needed to ask. It was all coming together. How her parents' hatred of each other had finally made a more thorough job of what it had begun long ago—ripping apart her family.

"What I'd discovered about Sanctuary and the Manti."

"And she sent you away for it. Let the Manti take you."

"I wasn't the first to threaten to expose the council. It was part of their agreement with the Manti. They couldn't afford for us all to know. Can you imagine the fallout?"

It was a halfhearted effort at absolving her mother, and they both knew it. Miriam had taken Asha's father from her, knowingly and intentionally.

"It was part of Zee's plan anyway," he continued, "sending sleepers here to disrupt the Manti. I had helped her with it. I knew enough about them from your research that I believed it could be done. I know now that I went a little crazy—it was exciting, and being with Zee was . . . I know I'm an old man to you, but I hadn't felt that way in a very long time." He shook his head. "It was more than that, though. Living with the information I'd uncovered, going on with my life, doing nothing—it was no longer possible for me."

This much Asha could fully grasp. She'd become intimate with that sentiment herself.

He fixed his eyes on her face—round, brown eyes that everyone said he'd passed on to his daughter. "But it was never supposed to be me, Ash, I promise you. And my god, it certainly wasn't supposed to be *you*. I don't know how Zee could do this."

A tear slipped down her cheek. Her father's eyes followed its progress until it dripped onto her tunic.

"It wasn't her idea. It was mine. She only helped me because I was ready to do something crazy."

"Well I'm so glad you avoided *that*," he said with a broken laugh.

She reached for his hand, squeezing it. "I was going to find a way to come here anyway, with or without her help. She gave me a better chance of surviving and finding you. I just don't understand why she kept so much from me."

"What did she keep from you besides our relationship?"

"She never told me Mom sent you here, for one. Or what you learned about the Manti."

"That doesn't surprise me. For one thing, I never saw her again after the confrontation with your mother. Even if she figured out what happened, if she'd told you, you might have done the same thing. You could have exposed her."

Asha's thoughts drifted to her father's journey to Granada. "Do you remember the Manti that brought you here?"

He shook his head. "Someone drugged me. I went to sleep in my bed and woke up here."

They stared at each other in silence, processing the stream of confessions. She thought about Micah, and their conversation in the tunnels.

"So you locked up the entire city's computer network for two *days*?"

Her father grinned, and it dropped ten years off his face.

"Did you know that part about science destroying them is the motto on their temple?" she asked.

"Is it really?" He laughed. "That virus is how I met Micah. He untangled my hack and followed the threads right to me. I thought I'd been so careful. So *smart*."

Her father was becoming a new person, right before her eyes. Had he always been like this? Mischievous? Adventurous? Subversive? As she replayed her memories she realized he had been; it just ran deeper than she'd ever suspected. His Archive self was very different. She'd seen this alternate Harker down in the Furnace, dangling his feet off the arch at sunset.

"How did you do it?" she asked, letting his amusement file the sharp edge off her pain.

His eyes were bright with excitement. With *pride*. "I was there for an interview and genetic screening. The lab tech's connection to the network dropped, and she stepped out to find someone to fix it. I had this impulse to try and fix it myself—old habits. By the time I spun the terminal around the connection was back up. I didn't have time to think about what I was doing, much less figure out their system. But the tech was still logged in, and the protocols weren't any different from the ones I know. Back in Sanctuary I had been thinking about ways of attacking them digitally—Zee and I both knew it was really the only way we *could* attack them. If we were going to wage war, it had to be psychological."

"What *is* the Ophelia Prophecy? Besides that part about science."

"I just strung together the more ominous-sounding of Stella's ramblings. Random nonsense, mostly. Talk about angels and arrows of fire. It sounds like vengeance and reckonings. Self-destruction through folly. It seemed just the thing." He looked at her. "I got the idea from you, honey. From your journal. You attached a note to that quote about science, cross-referencing an article about Manti beliefs and superstitions."

She nodded. "I remember thinking Stella Engle would scare the crap out of the Manti. One of the sources quoted in that article said the Manti view psychological disorders as gifts."

She didn't recall attaching the note, but she did recall making the connection. Apparently it had started her and her father down the same path.

"I used the name Ophelia, assuming the Manti wouldn't be able to tie it back to Sanctuary," he continued. "Her nickname doesn't appear anywhere in the Archive. It probably sounds crazy, but I thought she deserved some credit."

She laughed. "My meter of 'crazy' is apparently in need of some serious recalibration." But really it was just like her dad—the archivist side of her dad, anyway. "How did Micah find you?"

He shook his head. "I got cocky. I'd stolen this naked little handheld from the lab, and I used it to watch their network. One day I noticed him watching *me*. We danced around for a while, but pretty soon figured out we were more or less on the same side."

"So you formed an alliance with Rebelión Sagrada?"

"It's more than Zee and I dreamed was possible," he replied, growing more animated. "We expected this to be the work of many years. Generations, even. But we've walked in at the beginning of a fight. A fight that could completely change things for us."

He reached for her hand. "Part of me wishes more than anything you were safe at home. You had no idea just how safe you were there, with your mother, myself, all of Sanctuary, and even the Manti looking after you. But I'm so glad to have you back. You have no idea how I've missed you."

He reached up to dry his eyes. She crawled forward on her knees and wrapped her arms around him.

"You know I love you more than anything, honey," he murmured into her hair, "but it's more than that. We made such a good team. Everyone here is complacent, just like in Sanctuary. There's no real leadership, and even without that no conflict arises, because everyone knows DAB-lab will troop in and put it down. I have no one to discuss things with."

She squeezed him closer, noticing how slender he'd grown, and burrowed into his chest.

"I always wondered how they could have assigned you to the Manti stacks," he continued. "That work is so important, and you were barely more than a child."

She drew back a little to look at him. She couldn't believe this had never occurred to her. Why *would* they? It made no sense.

"I confess it was the job *I* wanted." He smiled. "Instead they shoved me off onto the most obscure topics. I assumed it was because they wanted me to spend more time teaching. Or maybe it was your mom's way of getting back at me. It all made sense once I learned the truth about Sanctuary."

She frowned. It still didn't make sense to *her*.

"They didn't want *anyone* studying the Manti," he explained, "but that wouldn't look right. So they gave it to a child, assuming you'd stick to the mechanical work of your job and not probe too deeply. They underestimated you completely. Zee may have given you some survival tools, but your most effective weapon is all your own." He tapped her forehead with his finger. "I wouldn't have had a hope of success if I hadn't been following your work. The Manti seem so unpredictable—conflicted and half crazy. You helped me understand them."

She'd always known he was proud of her, but he'd never praised her so openly before. He'd always pushed her. Encouraged her to think harder. Dig deeper. Put the puzzles together one piece at a time. She'd had no idea he paid such close attention to her work over the years.

He pulled her close again, holding her a moment before continuing, "It's your turn, honey. You're here now, and I intend to keep you safe. I need you to tell me everything that's happened."

It felt so good to confide in someone that she didn't hold anything back. She made a wreck of him with the constant peril and close calls, but she had learned in her work that details were important. Someone a long time ago had said the devil was in them, and it was a principle she lived by at the Archive. Details could completely change perceptions and outcomes, and the lack of them led to mistakes and misunderstandings.

As soon as she'd finished he said, "I know this man, Beck. He's here."

She untangled herself from his embrace and sat up. Of course Beck would be here, as well as the rest of them. She'd all but forgotten. "You've met him?"

He nodded, frowning. "He's a hothead. Managed to rile people up in the short time he's been here. But he's the type of man we'll need if it comes to war."

Was that where all this was headed? Negotiation between humans and Manti was certainly out of the question. And the Alhambra had threatened the temple with aggression. She still believed that had been more about *her*, but it had escalated tensions nonetheless.

"I want to hear more about this prince," said her father, his tone weighed down with concern.

"Okay." It was a reasonable inquiry, and yet somehow it made her feel like she was about twelve.

"You remember when I taught you to play chess?" he asked.

"Of course." She smiled, recalling how many times she'd slapped the keyboard and ended their games.

"You remember the queen? That's you right now, honey."

She laughed, feeling the heat flash along her cheekbones. "If anything I'm a pawn. Everyone has a use for me, and they don't care if I get taken out in the process."

"Wrong. *I* care. And Paxton cares. That much is obvious. The only question is which side you're going to choose."

She lifted her eyes to his face. "You're seriously asking me that? That's the one thing I'm sure about—I'm on *your* side. I just haven't quite figured out what that means."

"I'll give you a piece of advice, Harker."

The new voice pulled their gazes to the front of the house, where they found Beck standing in the doorway.

"Don't believe anything that comes out of that little wench's mouth."

"What now?" Carrick asked Pax, staring at the fence that sur-rounded Al Campo. "No more key."

They'd left the dead disciple inside the cavern. No way they could continue carrying him over open ground. Pax had contemplated the grisly possibility of removing only the bit of skin they needed. But hard to do it without damaging the ID, and it would have taken time.

"You're *sure* this is where she is?" he asked the priest.

Pax had lost her scent at the mouth of the cave, picking it up again only briefly inside the canal tunnel.

Carrick nodded. "It ends at the fence. And not just her. *Many* have passed through here today."

It was genius. Without Carrick he'd never have been able to follow them. Eventually he'd have thought to search the tunnels, but no one in Granada would think of looking for them *here*.

But how had so many Manti infiltrated the camp without causing panic or conflict? And how in hell had they avoided the flies? The whole thing would have required considerable planning, and the implications were alarming. There had to be an agreement of some kind—an *alliance* between the humans and Rebelión, at the very least. It was his duty to expose them and put a stop to it.

But he couldn't do it with Asha inside. Even if he found a way to protect her during the raid, if any hint of her involvement in this reached his father, she'd be out of his hands.

Iris's words came back to him. *You have to let her go.*

"I can't. Not yet."

"What was that?"

Pax glanced at the priest, realizing the conversation with his sister had moved outside his own head. He eased back the hood of the borrowed cloak and studied the fence.

"There's an electric field," he said. "They must have found a way to turn it off."

"So we climb the fence."

"Yes."

"What if it's not off?"

Pax bent, raking his fingers over the ground until they caught a stone. He tossed it at the fence. There was a pop and blue sizzle as the stone ejected backward. He caught a whiff of ozone.

"Hmm," murmured the priest, with characteristic composure. Pax was beginning to suspect it was the closest the man came to making a joke.

Sighing, he bent and picked up another stone, aiming a meter to the right of the first toss.

This time the stone hit the fence with a *thunk.*

He glanced at Carrick. "Let's go."

The malice in Beck's tone took Asha so much by surprise it froze any sort of reply.

"What's this about?" demanded her father, rising to his feet.

"She's the reason we're here," growled Beck, moving into the room.

Her father stepped between them, saying, "I don't know how that could be. She was a prisoner, just like you."

Beck scoffed. "You agreed to help us take over those ships." Other figures appeared in the doorway behind him—Finn and Alice, two of the others from Connemara. All of them eyed her angrily.

She slowed her breathing and chose her words carefully. "I agreed I would *try*. But I knew Banshee wouldn't betray them, and I couldn't think of another way."

"You had no problem taking control of that ship when you wanted to save your friends."

"That's exactly what I'm trying to explain. The ship—"

"Quiet!" he snapped. "Those two who were with you are the son and daughter of the Manti leader. You deceived me to protect them."

That was a fact, and there was no point in denying it. She racked her brain trying to think of a way to defuse this. "Listen, I can see how it must look to you, but I—"

"Are you going to explain why you weren't dragged here by the bugmen with the rest of us? *Branded*, like the rest of us?" He held up his wrist, freshly stamped with a spiral mark like the one on Pax's wrist. The skin around it was inflamed. "Because that one I would like to hear."

She shook her head, not seeing a way out. Though she knew she was innocent of these accusations—that she had done the best she could for Beck's people, and had never wanted any of them to be hurt or imprisoned—from his point of view there was reason to be angry.

"This interview's over," her father said firmly. "Come back when you calm down, and we'll talk through this. There's a misunderstanding here. My daughter came here with our *allies*, and I—"

"*More* bugmen," Beck grunted. "I know all about your new

friends, Harker. I don't know how you convinced the others to go along with this, but I promise you we're not going to stay here and wait for—"

"Are you in charge here?" She regretted this challenge the moment she let it slip. But the tension was escalating, and she knew her father would get the worst of it in a fight with this man. She'd hoped to draw his attention back to her—and she succeeded.

She moved to stand beside her father. "Leave and come back later," she said.

Beck's fist flew and she flinched backward, but the blow wasn't meant for her. There was a sickening thud as it connected with her father's head, and he dropped in a heap.

Yelping with alarm she sank beside him, but before she could determine how badly he was injured, Beck yanked her up by the arm. Pain shot through her shoulder, and she struck out with her knee, aiming for his groin but catching him in the thigh.

He gave a grunt of pain, calling, "Get in here and help me."

He grabbed for her again, but she danced to the other side of the fire pit, snatching up a skillet that had rested on the floor.

"Go on!" ordered Beck.

Finn and Alice started around the fire pit, and she swung the skillet in an arc. Finn shouted as it connected with some part of his body. She swung again without pausing to assess the damage.

Alice ducked the swipe and dove at Asha, wrapping around her legs. In trying to wrench free, Asha lost her balance and came down hard on her backside. Before she could catch her breath Alice landed on top of her, straddling her midsection, while Finn kicked the skillet from her hands.

"Turn her over," ordered Beck.

She shouted and kicked, but between the three of them they wrestled her onto her stomach, and Beck took Alice's place straddling her hips.

"Hold still and you won't get a hurt you won't recover from," he muttered. "Can't say the same for the rest of us."

She tried working her arms underneath her, and Beck snapped, "Hold her!"

Alice and Finn grabbed hold of her arms and legs.

"What are you doing?" she panted, belly going cold with fear.

"What I should have done the first time I saw you. You're a lying little wench and you crossed your own kind."

He raised her tunic, exposing her lower back.

"He'll kill you for this," she choked out in desperation. More likely Pax would accuse her of betrayal as well. Who *had* she been true to in all of this? Even her father might now be dead because of her decisions.

Beck laughed, and a shudder ran through her. "The truth comes out when it's convenient. No, love, your bugman won't kill me. Because when I'm finished here you're going to show me the way out."

"Hypocrite!" she spat.

"Oh, I'll be back. Now you're going to stop fighting me. If you even tense a muscle before I give you permission, Finnie here is going to break your arm. Right, Finnie?"

"Yes, sir, that's right."

She felt a sudden jab against the tender skin above her backside and cried out in pain.

Her screaming dragged Pax through the maze of walkways so fast no one but the wolf would have been able to keep up. The smell of her blood and her fear whipped through him like a cyclone, lashing him with a burning, blinding rage.

The man outside the door might as well have been made of paper. He didn't manage even a shouted warning before Pax cut him down, oblivious to the spray of blood and everything but the sounds of suffering within.

The scene registered in a fraction of a second: Known enemy, angry and alert to his presence. His mate alive but near senseless with pain. His enemy's blade smeared with her blood. A symbol cut into the flesh between her hips.

The priest was right on his heels and drew up beside him. "Christ, what have you done to her?" he shouted at Beck.

Carrick and Beck exchanged a few short, sharp words, but Pax's intention was narrowing to a very fine point. He neither heard them nor cared what they were discussing.

He lunged for his enemy with his blade.

Beck anticipated him and darted to one side, but Pax too had been ready, and he flung the knife. Beck gave a shout of pain as it lodged in his arm. Pax followed the knife, colliding with the man and yanking the blade free, and they splayed together onto the floor.

Peripherally he was aware of others trying to jump into the fray, but even together they were no match for the priest.

"Carrick!" Beck shouted. "Remember who you are!"

"You had no cause for torture," Carrick fired back, hauling the others out of the building. "I'll not interfere."

Beck rose to his knees, swinging his knife as Pax lunged at him again. Pax ducked the blow and yanked him down by the arm. Beck's knife skittered away, but he rolled free, shouting as his back came to rest over the warming pit. It wasn't true fire, but was hot enough to burn at that distance. He bounded up, but Pax was ready, throwing a punch that felled him.

Beck rolled to his back with a groan, and Pax bent over him, throwing down his knife and grabbing Beck's head between his hands.

"Don't," Carrick shouted from outside. "You'll regret it."

Beck squirmed in his grasp, but strong as he was, he was still human. Pax wrenched his head to one side. "I won't."

He released Beck with less regret than he'd feel for an animal killed for the table, and his eyes sought Asha.

She sat up, hugging her arms around her chest. She felt a cold, creeping nausea.

Pax knelt before her, and the sensation of his hands on her brought a sense of relief. She cared nothing for the fact he'd just killed her attacker with his bare hands. She cared nothing for the fact he'd once again demonstrated he was as much animal as human. So had Beck, and he had no excuse in his genetics. He had been torturing her, and Pax had stopped it.

"My father," she forced between trembling lips.

"Your father?"

She could hear the surprise in his voice, but she had yet to meet his eyes. Her rescuer, the only one she *had* betrayed.

She glanced at her father's limp form, and Pax followed her gaze. He crawled over and pressed his fingers to her father's neck.

"Is he alive?"

"Yes. I think he's just unconscious."

Pax returned to her side. "Let me look at your back."

She let him turn her and lift her tunic. She heard the breath hiss between his teeth.

She closed her eyes. "What is it?"

He hesitated, and she could hear the priest arguing with the others outside.

"A Manti ID spiral," Pax said finally. "Like the one on my wrist."

Beck had carved his accusation onto her body. Any man she was with would ask her about the scar. Any children she bore. She'd have to tell the story. It was part of her for life.

But she *was* alive, and so was her father.

"He thought you'd joined with us to escape his fate," Pax speculated. "To avoid Al Campo."

Finally she met his gaze. Those eyes were easier to look at in the low light. Less vividly green. Less penetrating.

Yet she trembled.

"Yes."

As she sat breathing through the pain, trying to float free from it enough so she could think clearly, she realized the danger of the situation. Despite Micah's clever planning, Pax had somehow managed to follow her. He must know everything now. What would it mean for her father? For Micah, and for Rebelión Sagrada?

"What happens now?" she asked him.

He was caught now; he knew he was. His duty was clear: Report to his father. Expose the alliance. But if he did . . . traitors were shown no mercy. The amir already had advisors urging him to remove the possibility of any future threat from the humans. He might order the deaths of all of them. Pax might be able to save Asha, but even so, was he ready to have the blood of hundreds on his hands?

He was exhausted. He needed a meal, sleep, and time to think.

She was still waiting for his answer. Perspiration slipped down the sides of her face. Her wound was deep. She must be in incredible pain.

"That's up to you," he replied.

She stared at him, brow furrowing in confusion. "Me?"

"Come back with me to the Alhambra. Answer my questions once we're there. If you do that, you have my promise of silence for now."

"For *now*."

"I need to understand the situation better. I need to get back to the palace before my father starts looking for me. You're the key to all this—you have information I need to make a decision." *And I'm not letting you out of my sight again.*

"You're letting me choose whether to go back with you?"

"No," he admitted. "Come with me willingly, no fighting and no running. Tell me who you are and why you're here, and I will delay discussion with my father of everything that's happened tonight."

"What's the point of delay?"

"If I understand the situation, I may be able to prevent retaliation."

"By the amir, you mean."

"Yes."

She stared at him, and even with the pain she must be suffering, she managed to guard her thoughts from him. Her whole body shook, probably from shock and loss of blood. He removed his cloak and drew it carefully around her.

When his face was close to hers she said, "I can't agree unless we find some way to protect my father." She swallowed, and dropped her gaze. He fought an impulse to draw her into his chest. "I bargained with the priestess to persuade her to bring me here. I promised her something in exchange—"

Outside the door there was a sudden shout, and Pax bolted to his feet.

Cleo smiled at them from the doorway. "And how prompt you are in delivering it, child."

QUEEN AND PAWN

"Stay where you are," ordered the priestess, the satisfied smile fading from her lips. "You're quite outnumbered."

She moved into the room, four armed disciples slipping in after her, shoving Carrick toward Pax and Asha. More of them ranged around the windows outside. Pax exchanged a glance with Carrick. *Trapped.* The house had only one entrance.

"It's good to see you, Pax." The triangular head swiveled as Cleo surveyed the room, her gaze resting a moment on the bodies on the floor.

"You shouldn't be here," Pax challenged. "Collaborating with humans. Carrying firearms. You know my father will view it as treason."

"The amir, yes. I haven't seen him in ages." She eyed him shrewdly. "And I don't anticipate that I will today. Hard to imagine he'd send his only son into Al Campo to arrest me."

She watched him with unblinking eyes as he rallied his nearly exhausted resources to address this new threat. Asha rose to her feet beside him, Pax's cloak pulled close around her, and the priestess's gaze shifted.

"You weren't bluffing after all, were you, child? It looks as though the amir's son has plunged alone into enemy territory to recover *you*. There was never any raid on the temple."

The priestess fixed her eyes again on Pax, and a mocking smile twisted her lips. "This is about her. This woman who ran from you and betrayed you. Though probably you aren't aware that she offered to deliver you to me in exchange for bringing her to Al Campo."

Cleo was playing him, and he knew he had to resist it, but he glanced at Asha. Her guilt was plain enough from her expression. The puzzle was finally piecing itself together. He wondered how long since her memory had returned.

It was only natural she would use him, *and* the attachment to her he had foolishly allowed her to see. But he did wonder which woman's idea it had been to make *him* part of their bargain. Either way, he'd played right into it—both women had what they wanted.

"Last time you tried to use me you failed," Pax said coldly. "If you put me through that again, the amir will hear about all of it—both offenses, with all the ugly details. Appealing to me for Iris's sake will get you nowhere."

"Ah, no." Cleo shook her head. "I'll not waste time on a second attempt. And I no longer have any desire to be on good terms with your father. The man has a closed mind."

There was no point reminding her what she'd lost. Pax had once had a strong interest in building a bridge between Rebelión Sagrada and his father's regime. But Cleo was impatient. She had tried to use his bridge as a battering ram.

"The son takes after the father," she continued. "We're not human, Pax. Why should we be bound by their ideas of right and wrong?"

"I'm not going to debate morality with you. We both know that stunt was political. My father would have been forced to either reject his own grandchild, or lift the ban on unauthorized reproduction."

Cleo smiled. "Fatherhood would have suited you, Pax. Now you've forced me to more extreme measures."

"You must realize the amir will never negotiate with you." Pax's gaze shifted to the windows as he reassessed the possibility of escape. But there were too many disciples. "Even if he did negotiate," he continued, "how would your tactics go over with your supporters? You'll risk all the ground you've gained. Don't forget my father has remained in his position as long as he has because he has popular support."

"Support that is flagging," Cleo argued. "People don't like to be controlled. Your father has fallen into the absolute-power trap. But the discussion is pointless. I have no intention of ransoming you for concessions."

She watched him in silence, waiting for him to ask. The priestess loved cat-and-mouse games. She was one to talk about the absolute-power trap. But he refused to play with her. He knew she wouldn't be able to contain herself for long.

"If you disappear," she said finally, "your father will mobilize resources to recover you. The effort will weaken him, much as desire for this woman has weakened *you*. When he discovers your body, he'll be at his most vulnerable, and we'll be ready. The people will see his weakness. I doubt it will even come to conflict."

"No!" protested Asha, drawing the sharp point of the priestess's attention. "You never said anything about killing him."

He stared at her. Her face had opened completely. Everything she'd been hiding from him since he'd found her—conflict, anger, fear . . . regret?

"You didn't *ask*, child," said Cleo.

"It won't work," Pax said, unconcerned with the threat. "I disappeared at the same time you did. My father will make the connection. Everyone in the city will make the connection."

He recoiled at the smile that spread over her extreme Manti features. "Your presence alone here is evidence enough your father knows nothing of our 'disappearance.' We'll simply return to the temple. There will be nothing to connect us. You're right that it won't do for your father or anyone else to suspect we're involved. So we're not going to be." Her gaze came to rest on Asha.

Pax's heart thundered as he saw where this was going. Asha took a slow step closer to him. Where was her loyalty? He didn't think she'd pieced it together yet. But Cleo would make it all clear very soon. He wondered if the priestess realized how perfect a trap it was. Both the Guard and his sister were witnesses to the fact he'd gone into the city with Asha. Even Iris would suspect her.

"We can't afford to be seen with you," said the priestess, "so I'm afraid we need to take care of the ugly part of the business now."

"Bring the girl," said Cleo.

Asha eyed Pax's knife, glittering on the ground near the fire pit, but the disciples were on her too fast. As Pax went for the knife a disciple kicked him in the stomach and stuck a gun in his face.

Pain seared across Asha's low back as they dragged her to Cleo.

"Don't do this," she begged. "There has to be another way."

"I'm not going to do it." Cleo waved to a man behind her, and he stepped forward.

Using the edge of his cloak, the disciple lifted a knife from his belt. He held it out to Asha.

She stared at it, aghast.

"Bring him," called Cleo, and two more men dragged Asha's father to his feet. He was awake now, but groggy and confused.

"Asha?" he croaked.

"Pax or your father," said the priestess. "You choose."

She gaped at the bugwoman. "I'm not killing *anyone*."

"I need your prints on the knife, so you are."

Asha shook her head slowly, pain and horror sickening her. "I won't."

"Kill him," Cleo ordered the man holding her father.

"Wait!" Asha cried. *Oh God, what now?*

The disciple thrust the knife at her again, and she took it. She turned to Pax. Cleo's men had his arms spread wide, forcing his midsection forward.

"What's going on?" her father demanded. "Cleo?"

The only question is which side you're going to choose. But choosing between her father and the man who'd just rescued her from Beck was not any kind of choice at all. There was only one person in the room she'd stab right now given the chance.

"Your time for thinking about this is up," warned Cleo. "On three. One—"

"My lady? What's happened?"

Asha spun around. Micah had appeared in the doorway, and he studied the scene in confusion. His brow furrowed as his eyes met Asha's.

"Micah, please!" she cried. "She's ordered me to kill Pax! She's got my father!"

Micah located the two men she'd mentioned, his gaze lingering on the second. "You're 'Hark'?"

Her father stood on his own feet now, shaky and short of breath from the effort. He nodded.

Micah turned to Cleo, frowning. "I don't understand all this. What's the point of using her this way?"

She expected the priestess to assert her authority. As she launched into an explanation of her plan instead, Asha began to see their relationship was not exactly what she'd thought it was. He had been deferent and respectful, yes. But Cleo had relied on him heavily in her scheming. He was clearly concerned about the turn of events, and he had the power to expose them all.

"She's putting all of you at risk," Asha broke in at the end of Cleo's explanation. "With everything you've accomplished—with your growing support—why shed blood now?"

"You know the amir," Micah said to the priestess, "and I trust that you know how to get to him. But murdering his son . . . framing this woman for it . . ." He shook his head. "Are we really that desperate at this stage, my lady?"

"This is personal," said Asha before the priestess could reply. "She's using her office to settle an old score."

"How dare you!" snapped Cleo, livid.

"I mean no disrespect to you, my lady," began Micah in a reasonable tone, "but it wouldn't be surprising if your history with this family had influenced you in choosing this course. I don't know what happened between you and Paxton, but I understand his behavior toward you has been insulting."

Pax let out a bark of laughter and shot Cleo a look of disgust.

"She tried to use him against his father," said Asha. "But even without the personal history, it seems like Rebelión Sagrada would be better served by separating religious and political interests."

It was the only way she could think of to cut at Cleo's authority, but she cringed as the priestess's gaze burned through her. Clearly she had redirected her murderous urges.

"What makes you say so?" asked Micah.

She hesitated, intimidated by the silence that gathered in the wake of his question. She took a deep breath, opening herself to the flow of knowledge she'd accumulated over the last six years—all her work with the Manti, as well as all she'd learned from her father.

You can do this.

"I understand about your beliefs," she began carefully. "But giving a spiritual leader absolute authority over Rebelión's strategy for challenging the amir—does that make sense?"

"She's right," said her father. "You'll accomplish more with leadership that puts your philosophical beliefs and political objectives first."

"Without letting passions or personal grudges get in the way," added Asha.

"That's enough," Cleo replied tersely. "I won't listen to more of this. These people know nothing of us." She'd backed off the sharp tone, becoming more passive in her attempt to shift Micah back to her side.

"We're not bound to act in any way based on what they say," replied Micah. "Where is the danger in hearing them out? They are our allies."

Asha could tell from Cleo's expression that she saw all sorts of danger he did not, but she held her tongue.

Micah returned his attention to her father. "What sort of leadership would you propose?"

The disciples stood tense and confused, not understanding why or how the ground was shifting. One wrong word could lead to disaster.

Before her father could answer Asha said, "It should be you."

Micah raised his eyebrows. "Me?"

"Together with my father, as an ally and representative from Al Campo. Look at what the two of you have already accomplished."

The men she'd named exchanged glances.

She knew her proposal failed to address the more immediate problem, and Micah was quick to point it out.

"Unfortunately the question of leadership becomes a moot point if we're exposed. As much as I'm disturbed by the idea of killing a man in cold blood, releasing the amir's son will risk us all."

At the end of this assessment his gaze shifted to Cleo, and Asha thought she read mild accusation in his eyes. For the first time since she'd met the priestess, she saw Cleo hesitating.

"If you do what Asha and her father have proposed," said Pax, "I won't expose you. I'll help you."

Silence followed the prince's interruption, silence so choked with tension and calculation it was hard to breathe.

"Let him go," Micah ordered the disciples holding Pax. "He's not going to run out of here after risking so much to find this woman."

"He's lying," protested Cleo. "He'll go directly to his father."

"No," Asha countered. "Not if he said he won't."

Cleo gave an incredulous laugh. "You've been his plaything for what, two days? You have no place in this conversation."

Anger shot heat into Asha's cheeks. Before she could reply, Micah said, "Please, my lady."

The disciples had released Pax, and he straightened to his full height, his gaze locked with Micah's.

"I washed my hands of dealings with your priestess long ago," he said. "But there is common ground between us. And I have no desire to see you all killed. It would destabilize everything my father's built. But of course I don't expect you to trust me."

"Then we have a stalemate," observed Micah.

Pax shook his head. "Cleo is right—there was no attack on your temple, nor any plan for one. You can safely return there. I'll go with you. Even if I were to go back on my word and tell my father, my presence there would shield you from retaliation."

"You're volunteering to be a hostage?" asked Asha's father. His eyes settled on her, and she knew he was remembering what he'd said about the chess match. He thought this was all for her. But she knew better.

"Because he sees an opportunity to address these differences without violence," she said, more to Micah than her father. It was clear enough that the power that had melted from Cleo during the exchange had been absorbed by him.

"It's true," agreed Pax. "I do want that, and I've never been able to make my father listen to me. This could change that."

"He's trying to save his own skin," Cleo said tightly.

Pax laughed. "Of course I am. What would any of you do in my place? I also don't want to see this woman hurt, or her father. But that doesn't make anything else I've told you less true."

Asha burned inside—with gratitude for what he was doing, with a strange pride in the part he was playing, and with shame that she had ever thought of betraying him.

"If you're requiring us to dismiss the priestess—"

"I'm not," said Pax. "I won't work on political strategy with a woman who tried to assassinate me, but how you worship has nothing to do with our agreement."

"This is unacceptable," said Cleo. She fixed her eyes on Micah, and the fact that she did confirmed that she and everyone else now knew who was in control of this negotiation. "I'll not be relegated to a ceremonial role."

Asha knew that Cleo would not allow herself to be diminished in *any* way had she not found herself in such a sticky trap. Pax could expose them if they let him go. If she insisted on his murder, Micah might abandon or even expose them himself. Killing them both was a possible solution, but then she'd also have to kill Asha and her father at the least, and the changing temperature in the room suggested she might not have the level of commitment she needed for such a high body count.

After a few moments' consideration, Micah said to Pax, "Many of our followers are deeply spiritual. Their views and wishes should be represented. The priestess must have a voice."

Now Pax considered, and it was all she could do not to shout, "Take it!" But he was right to make them wait. Every second of silence solidified his shift to a position of power among his former enemies.

"As long as there's no more aggression against me or my family," he said finally.

"Agreed," said Micah. "For the duration of this arrangement."

Asha held her breath, exchanging a tense glance with her father, as the two Manti shook hands.

"I think we should return to the temple immediately," said Pax. "Waiting until tomorrow night risks discovery. And if I don't check in with my father soon the temple is the first place he's going to look."

Smart, Pax. It was good to remind them regularly that it was in their best interests to protect him.

"We can't move everyone before dawn," said Micah. "But yes, the priestess and her attendants need to return." He glanced at Asha. "I assume you'll want to remain here with your father?"

She was being given a choice?

"I think it's best," Pax said in a low voice, fixing his eyes on her. "It's a long walk back."

She realized he was alluding to her injuries, but trying to spare either her privacy or her father. Maybe both. And not only that, he was letting her *go*. Or . . . dismissing her. His expression was neutral and it was hard to be sure.

"Ash," began her father, moving closer. "I hate saying this, but I think you should go back with him." He glanced at Paxton. "She hasn't been processed. The lab doesn't know she's here. I'd like it to stay that way."

"You've somehow protected this area from the flies, though, isn't that right?" asked Pax.

Asha couldn't help smiling at her father's sudden guilty look.

"Yes, that's true. But there are more of these new arrivals." He nodded toward Beck's broken body. "If she's living here unprocessed and outside surveillance there's nothing to stop someone else threatening her."

While Pax was chewing on this, she made her decision. "I'll go back to the temple. For now." She had to talk to Pax. Explain to him what she'd done, and tell him the truth about what she was. The truth was all he'd ever asked of her, and he had more than earned that.

She also wanted to avoid her father seeing what had been done to her—she knew he would blame himself. She could come back when she had healed.

Her father's emotions were written on his face—relief, sadness, guilt that she'd been drawn into all this. Pax was another story. He acknowledged her decision with a nod, and she ached for . . . for what, she wasn't sure. Something more. A reaction of some kind, so she'd know what she was facing with him.

DAMAGE

As Asha crawled through the opening in the wall, the top of the cutting grazed her lower back. The pain was enough to force a groan through her lips.

Pax bent and reached for her hand, raising her to her feet. "Are you sure about this?" he murmured.

"Yes," she breathed, wiping moisture from above her lip. She looked up at him. "I need to talk to you."

He regarded her silently. "That can wait."

Micah came through the opening behind them, and they made room for him. "Are you all right?" he asked her.

She nodded. "I am."

Micah's gaze sought Cleo, who had already started toward the opposite hill with her mate and attendants.

"Was it her?"

"No," she assured him. *Not that I'd put it past her.*

Micah glanced at Pax, his eyes moving from the prince's face down along his arm to the hand that held Asha's. She re-

THE OPHELIA PROPHECY   237

alized that she had gripped his fingers so hard her hand shook, and she released them. A drop of perspiration slipped between her shoulder blades and down her back. She winced as it seeped into her wound.

"Can I do anything to help you?" asked Micah.

"Would you answer a question?"

"Of course."

"We should get moving," said Pax, stepping away from the fence. Away from *her*.

As she moved to follow, Micah offered his arm.

"Thank you. I'll be okay."

They drew their cloaks close around them and started back toward the city.

"What did you want to ask me?" said Micah.

"What brought you to Al Campo? I didn't expect to see you again so soon."

"Yes, I know. But after we split up I started to wonder more about what Cleo was up to with Paxton, and how you might get drawn into it. When I got back to the lab I pinged your father, just to make sure you'd arrived there okay. He didn't answer and I decided to check for myself."

"I'm really glad you did."

"I'm sorry I didn't come sooner. Can I ask what happened to you?"

She gave him a thin smile. "I seem to have a talent for making enemies of dangerous people. It's a long story. But I'm grateful for your help with Cleo."

"I don't really think you needed my help. Do you have any idea what you just negotiated?"

She shook her head. "It wasn't me so much as Pax. Why would anyone here care what I think?"

Micah laughed. "That's not the way I'd tell the story. He jumped on the cart right as you drove it over her." Asha smiled, self-conscious, but he sobered quickly. "I'm not sure I've done the right thing. There's going to be fallout with Cleo. I don't know that I'm really qualified for this."

"Less qualified than her?"

"She's been dealing with the Paxtons for more than two decades. But murdering the prince would have propelled us into war. And pinning it on *you* . . . I hope I never grow so hard that a maneuver like that seems justifiable."

"It's hard for me to imagine that you could."

Asha watched Pax, who walked a couple meters ahead of them. She was sure he could hear their conversation, but she wondered if he was actually listening. More likely he was preoccupied with his decision, and all that had happened in Al Campo. Guilt continued to gnaw at her for the part she'd played, delivering him right into Cleo's hands, whether or not it had been her intention.

"Do you mind if I ask you something else?" asked Micah.

"Go ahead."

"There's something about that man who was with Paxton—the man who stayed behind with your father. I don't think he's Manti. Do you know if he's human?"

"Carrick. No, he's transgenic." She tried to think whether she was betraying anyone's confidence by explaining about the priest. But Carrick was safe in Al Campo. The amir's forces weren't likely to look for him there, and though it was easy enough to sense there was something different about him, the humans in Al Campo wouldn't guess the truth.

"Manti?" asked Micah.

"Wolf."

His eyes widened. "Interesting. Are there more of him?"

"I don't know. Not in the group Pax picked up."

"And he's a holy man?"

"I believe so, but I don't know much of his story. I think he's a good man. And very alone now."

Pax glanced over his shoulder at this, but he said nothing. She wondered how he'd convinced Iris to part with Carrick.

As they reached the southern border of Al Campo, Pax stopped and waited for them. "We'll cross open ground now. We need to keep close and quiet." He looked at Asha.

"I'm ready."

As hard as he was to read right now, it was clear enough he didn't believe her. But he nodded, and they started across the valley.

For the rest of this last, long trek, Asha's mental resources were monopolized by pain and exhaustion. She'd hoped eventually the sensations would dull to a manageable level. But the ground was uneven, and they spent too much time crouching. The trip back through the tunnel, with its rocky traverse, was the worst. Her muscles stretched her open wounds, and blood dripped down her back.

As she concentrated on putting one foot in front of the other, Pax and Micah discussed the problem of ensuring their safety in the temple. Pax didn't trust Cleo to stick to their truce, and Micah agreed that they'd need to somehow secure one floor of the temple. But it wasn't something that could be accomplished tonight, and Asha found herself doubting her decision to return with the others. The idea of sitting up for what was left of the night, or sleeping lightly enough to watch for danger, was laughable.

They made quicker progress through the underground, where at least the passages were lit and the ground was level. But by the time they reached the stairs that led to the temple, her cuts were so raw and inflamed she had to grit her teeth to keep from groaning.

"Almost there," said Pax softly, following on the stairs behind her.

When they emerged in the priestess's chamber, Pax hung back with Asha as Micah and Cleo consulted in low voices. The priestess had regained her composure, but Asha was more afraid of this controlled Cleo than of the Cleo in Al Campo.

Pax stepped close to her, murmuring, "I don't trust her." The shiver that ran through her at the sound of his voice in her ear had nothing to do with fear or cold.

"No," she replied. "I don't think we can afford to. But I do think she needs Micah."

Pax nodded. "And can't risk him turning on her. He's taken an interest in your welfare as well, it seems. That's fortunate for both of us."

She met his gaze, and her face grew warm under his scrutiny. But his expression remained as neutral as it had been since leaving Al Campo. She could imagine what he was thinking: neither of them would be in this mess if she hadn't run from him.

"He also sees the benefit of the deal you offered them," she said. "It will make it difficult for her to justify betraying us."

"Agreed. But I think she'll use every spare cycle to figure out a way to get back at me—at *us*—without losing Micah's support."

Her stomach fluttered at his use of the simple two-letter pronoun. "Yes," she breathed. "We'll still have to watch her. What do you propose?"

"Until Micah can secure a section of the temple for us, we need to stay close to each other. I know you're used to thinking of me as your jailer. But that stops now. I'll watch out for you, but it's your decision whether to remain here or return to your father."

Asha swallowed. "Okay."

"I also want you to understand that I'm not a threat to you. You don't need to worry about—"

"I know," she interrupted, hoping to relieve him from an explanation she could see was paining him. "I trust you."

At last the shield slipped, revealing a combination of surprise and gratitude. His expression caused the worm of guilt in her stomach to turn.

"I'm not a threat to you either," she continued, breaking from his gaze. "I don't know if you can believe that."

Her whole body strained, waiting for his answer, but before he could reply Micah returned.

"The priestess insisted you be given rooms high in the tower," he said. "She believes you'll run otherwise."

"That ensures there's no escape for us if she goes back on our agreement," Pax pointed out.

"There's one more group returning from Al Campo tonight," said Micah. "They're all people I trust—I made sure of it. I'll ask them to keep an eye on the others. It's the best I can do for now. She's given me her word she'll stick to our agreement."

"So she doesn't trust us," grumbled Pax, "but we're to trust her."

Asha laid a hand on Pax's arm. "We'll be all right," she said. Regardless, she knew she'd reached her limit. She was sleeping in the temple tonight, whatever the risks.

He eyed her a moment, features softening. He nodded at Micah. "Let's go."

They rode the lift to the eighteenth floor.

"The disciples take their meals together in the hall on the second floor," said Micah as they exited the lift, "but I can see

that yours are brought up to you. Will you want anything before morning?"

"Yes, if possible," replied Asha. The broth she'd drunk before leaving Al Campo had been burned away by the long
walk. "Anything is fine."

"Of course," he agreed. "I'll take care of it myself. As for
the rooms—"

"Just one room," Pax said firmly.

Micah shot her a questioning look that raised heat from her
chin to her hairline.

"I think we'll both feel safer," she said. "We can make a
change later."

He gave a neutral nod. "As you like."

They followed him around the elevator shaft and stopped
in front of a doorway veiled by a lightweight, opaque curtain.

"This is a guest floor, divided into two chambers," he explained. "The rooms are larger and more comfortable than
those on the lower floors." He glanced at Paxton. "I can easily
reconfigure the lift to prevent access by anyone but you, myself,
and an attendant. The stairs can't be sealed off. But this high up
in the tower it will be difficult for anyone to creep up on you."

"But not impossible," replied Pax. "I'd feel better with a
gun. And I'd prefer to dispense with the attendant. I'll go down
for our meals myself."

Micah studied Pax, weighing the demands. "I think arming
you is asking for trouble. But we can work around the need
for an attendant by setting you up to be self-sufficient for meals
for a few days."

Pax sighed and turned to survey the chamber, clearly dis-
satisfied with the refusal of the weapon but seeming to accept
there wasn't much he could do about it.

The room was roughly crescent-shaped, with six windows
looking out over the fairy lights of the sleeping city. The large

bed, piled with pillows and draped with richly colored fabric, was stationed near the windows on one end of the room. At the other end was a sitting area with plush chairs surrounding a low table, and beyond that a curtained-off area, maybe a bathroom.

Pots of flowering plants ranged along the curved wall, perfuming the air. Beneath the center window was what looked like a shrine, with a smaller version of the statue from the roof and a gurgling fountain.

Neither of the men appeared fazed by any of it, but Asha couldn't get used to the opulence of the place.

"I'll need to contact my father in the morning," said Pax. "My sister knew I was coming here. If they don't hear from me soon, you can be sure they'll come calling."

"Agreed," replied Micah. "I'll see to it first thing. Before I go tonight I'll bring up food and fresh clothes. Anything else you need?"

"Medical supplies," said Pax.

"Of course. I'll be back soon."

He left them, and the moment she'd both hoped for and dreaded dropped like a heavy snow, blanketing them with silence.

She took a deep breath, letting it out with more volume than she intended, and she teetered on worn-out limbs.

"Come," said Pax, taking her arm.

She let him guide her to the bed, watching as he cleared off the excess pillows to make room for her. She crawled onto the soft, inviting mountain and sank down on her stomach with another sigh.

"I'll be right back," he said.

Arms folded under her head, she closed her eyes, and she slipped into a doze before her mind could even touch on the many things that were troubling her.

She woke with a start when she felt a hand at her back.

"Easy," murmured Pax, his fingers lightly pressing her hip. "I need to raise your top to treat your cuts."

She lowered her head again, relaxing her taut muscles. "Okay."

The fabric had stuck in places, and as Pax gently pulled at it, her scabs broke open and she gave a muffled cry against the bedding.

"I'm sorry," he said, and there was an edge of anger to his voice.

Once the tunic was free, he began pressing a warm, wet cloth against her wound. She could feel the shape of the mark as he dabbed the blood away—the spiral Beck had carved both to punish and brand her a traitor.

This kindness from Pax—the solicitous, almost *tender* treatment—was more than she could take.

"Why are you doing this?" she asked, her words coming out harsher than she intended.

He continued in silence, working loose the caked blood. When he finished, he pressed a dry cloth against her, stanching the fresh blood caused by the cleaning.

"Why am I doing what?" he finally asked.

"Helping me. Being so kind to me."

When again he didn't answer, she continued, "It's not your concern, is it?"

She heard a scraping noise as he removed the lid from a jar. "You ought to know me better than that by now." The softness of his rebuke only reinforced her petulance.

"I don't understand you at *all*. I'm nothing to you but a problem. A mystery, and an enemy. I'm not even your prisoner anymore. You don't owe me anything." She cursed the lump that gained mass in her throat, choking her. "Why are you helping me?"

* * *

Pax scooped healing salve from the jar with two fingers, spreading it gently and thickly over her wound while he thought about what she'd said.

"The microorganisms will clean and seal the wound and help you to heal quickly. It's deep enough there may be a slight scar."

"It doesn't matter."

Her tone was bitter, and resigned. He screwed the lid back onto the jar and wiped the residue from his fingers. He sank down on the bed and stared at the mark, replacing the lid on his anger as well. The anger was pointless. Its object was dead.

He understood where Asha's head was. Or at least he thought he did. "You feel that you betrayed Beck," he said. "That you betrayed your own kind. You feel that you deserved to be punished."

Her face had been resting on her arms, but now she turned it toward him. The color had drained from her cheeks.

A tear slipped down across one cheek and over the bridge of her nose. His breath stopped.

"I betrayed *you*."

Pax swallowed. "Did you?"

She nodded. A lock of hair fell over her eye, and he stopped himself from reaching to push it back.

"How so?"

"When I saw your city from Banshee, I remembered why I was here." She pushed herself up on her arms, settling across from him, and looked at him squarely. "I'm a sleeper. I came here to find my father in Al Campo, and to do what I could to cause trouble for you and your people. The Alhambra was the trigger—the alarm that woke me."

He studied her, more impressed than angry. He'd had

evidence enough of her bravery and determination. But for her to leave the only home she'd known—to go among her enemy to help someone she loved . . . No survivor had ever attempted such a thing. And while he'd learned better than to judge an enemy based on size, sex, or species, she looked like the last person to pull it off. He suppressed a smile as he remembered how she'd managed to knock him flat on his back within the first fifteen minutes of their acquaintance.

"Did you hear me?" she said. Her words had a desperate edge.

"That's not a betrayal," he pointed out. "You didn't even know me."

"I'm not finished."

He breathed evenly, steadying the response of his heart. "What else?"

"I told Cleo if she got me into Al Campo I would give you to her."

He knew this from the exchange during the confrontation in Al Campo, but still the confession jarred him. The fact that she'd come up with it on her own.

"How did you think you were going to fulfill your part of the bargain?"

She winced at the change in his tone. "I knew eventually you'd come for me. I wouldn't have to do anything but wait for you to find us."

Now came his punishment for his softness toward her. For his inability to treat her like the enemy she was. She had learned he was weak with regard to her, and she had used it.

"Smart girl," he said dryly. "It all went just as you predicted."

She shook her head. She started to say more, but then seemed to change her mind.

His heart had gone numb. He'd lost the desire to ease her suffering, and he had no sympathy for his own. He felt like a fool.

"I want you to understand," she began again. "You were my enemy. But sometimes it seemed you weren't. You were kind to me, but there was always this threat between us. What if I'd come here to harm you? It turned out I *had* come to harm you. And when I remembered my father was here—that I'd come to find him—I became desperate. I clung to the person I was before I knew you. It was something I never considered—that in the time between sleeping and waking, I might become someone different."

"Nothing is ever as simple as it seems," he said softly, more to himself than to her.

"No," she agreed. Fixing her eyes on his face, she continued, "I needed you to understand why I made that deal with Cleo, but I also want you to know that I immediately regretted it. I tried to see a way out, but it was too late to go back. The trap was set the moment I ran away from you."

The anguish in her face loosened the stone from his heart. "You did what you set out to do. I respect you for that. I knew very well that those secrets locked inside you would eventually make true enemies of us. How could it be otherwise?"

She shook her head in frustration. "I don't know what 'enemy' means anymore." Her eyes ranged around the room as she worked through her thoughts. He realized she was logical like him. When logic provided answers that didn't make sense, she was lost.

"You saved me from Beck," she continued. "Micah saved us from Cleo. You've joined them both against your father, and I've left mine behind after coming all this way to find him."

He bent toward her, drawing her eyes back to his face. "Why did you do that?"

SLEEPER

Asha's heart quivered. "Why did you risk so much to come for me?"

"Answer my question, and I'll answer yours."

He held her gaze, and the machinery of her brain locked up. All she could think about was the kiss in the alley. She'd blamed curiosity for the lapse, and sagrada, though the chemical fog had dissipated by the time his lips met hers. She couldn't blame either of those things now.

But just as her eyes moved to trace the line of his lips he looked away, reaching for a roll of bandages. He scooted around behind her, murmuring, "Lift your tunic again and I'll finish this. Then you can eat and rest."

He unwound the second-skin, and a moment later she felt his fingers pressing into her back. The pain had dulled to a low throbbing thanks to the analgesic effect of the salve.

"I left my father because I saw he could take care of himself," she said, "and because Carrick stayed behind with him in Al Campo."

"I see," he replied, applying another strip.

She closed her eyes, aware she was avoiding the very task that had brought her here. "Also because I wanted to talk to you. You deserved to know the truth about me. And about what I'd done."

He pulled the hem of her tunic from her hands, covering her again. She could feel his eyes on her back.

"I'm not sure I did deserve it," he said. "I've treated you like an enemy from the first moment I met you."

She gave a tired laugh. "That was back when things made sense—when I *was* your enemy." She threaded her fingers, pressing her palms together. "Maybe neither of us is to blame for the decisions we've made up to now."

After a brief silence she heard him packing up the medical supplies. "When the second-skin sets you can bathe if you like. I think you'll feel much better tomorrow."

"It's already much better. Thank you." Remembering the wasp wound, her hand crept up to her throat, fingers searching for the second-skin covering and finding nothing but smooth flesh.

"Pax?"

"Yes."

"You don't have to tell me why you came for me. But I'm glad you did."

He hesitated, and she held her breath. Finally he said, "Even though I killed him?"

She scooted around to face him. The color of his eyes, so suggestive of cool green vegetation she'd seen only in Archive photos before now, was more like some strange, alchemic fire at the moment.

"I feel numb about that," she replied. "It probably should bother me more than it does."

"He was volatile. But I regret it came to that."

"I could see why he was angry," she said. "There was a lot of evidence against me. He was older than me—he remembered his village being burned. He had scars from it, and his parents died." She looked at Pax. "But I hated him for punishing me without giving me a chance to explain, just because he *could*."

Pax frowned. "I don't know that he and I are all that different."

"You fought against hurting me, and you asked your ship to protect me. You believed even your enemy deserved compassion."

"Yet I didn't show him any."

She held his gaze. "Why do you think that was?"

Pax stood up, breaking the line of tension stretching between them. "It's late," he sighed, scrubbing a hand through his dark hair. "We're both tired and hungry. There will be time for this later."

She looked down, trying to hide her disappointment and frustration at the way he kept withdrawing. Changing the subject. She wasn't sure what she expected from him. She just knew it was something *more*.

"Do you regret coming for me?" she asked in a voice she couldn't steady. "After what I've told you, I mean? It's okay if you do."

He took a step back toward the bed, reaching out and lifting her chin. A current jumped from his fingers, racing through her jaw, causing her ears to buzz.

"I'll tell you if you want to know. I'm not sure that you do."

"I want you to tell me," she whispered.

His thumb grazed her chin, and he raised a dark eyebrow.

"I've tuned to you. In my mind—in my body, in my blood, in my flesh—you're my mate. You're part of me. I'll always come for you. I'll always fight for you."

Her heart stopped. "I . . ."

"I don't mean to frighten you," he continued. "I said I wouldn't hold you against your will, and I meant it. But you asked why I risked myself by coming for you. It was because I couldn't do otherwise."

"But we aren't—we haven't—" She broke off, confused and overwhelmed. She had felt his growing attachment, but had never guessed that something like this was behind it.

"You're right," he said, releasing her chin. "You asked me, and I've told you. But I'll never speak of it again. It's merely a fact, and it need not affect you in any way—except that I won't allow anyone to hurt you. Anyone who does will suffer for it."

Still reeling, she rose to her feet, looking into his face. "I don't understand. What happens if I decide to leave?"

The muscles of his jaw clenched and released. "If it's *me* that you're leaving, I'll stay away. But I'll never stop looking out for you. This is not a feeling or an emotion. It's a physical change. It won't fade."

"This is some kind of Manti bond?"

"It's not an insect-like trait, but I would guess it's related to the genetic tampering. Maybe the intensified mating drive has an effect on bonding hormones as well. Though I don't know why it would be selective." He shook his head. "I've heard of it happening to others, but I never quite believed in it. I certainly never imagined I was susceptible. My father never experienced it."

She lost the thread of technical details, still hung up on the earlier part of his explanation. "But it doesn't mean you love me." Afraid to watch the effect of her words on his face, she let her gaze fall to his chest.

His hand lifted toward her again, and she could almost feel his fingers on her cheek at the point that he let them drop. The uncertainty was so unlike him. "Right now I don't know what it means. Only that it *is*."

She glanced up at him, and he turned and walked toward the sitting area. She followed in a daze, still trying to get her mind around it all.

Sinking down on the sofa, he started digging through a crate that rested next to the low table. The crate was refrigerated somehow—she could feel the drift of cool air.

"How can I help?" she asked.

"Sit. Let me take care of it."

She sat down next to him, watching him open containers and arrange food on plates. Dates, figs, almonds, and more of the spiced flatbread she'd eaten on board Banshee. There was also some kind of soft cheese with a fruity glaze smeared over the top.

"Do you do this in the palace, or does someone do it for you?"

It didn't occur to her the question could be taken wrong until it was already out of her mouth. But Pax smiled. "You think I'm spoiled."

Her eyes widened. "No, I—"

"It's okay. I *am* spoiled. If by 'this' you mean putting food on a plate, I possess the required motor skills, as you can see, but usually someone does it for me."

He handed her a plate, and she felt a smile stretching over her face. A *full* smile. She realized she hadn't used those muscles in a while.

"Thank you."

Next he poured a golden, gently bubbling liquid from a bottle into a glass. She eyed it warily as he placed it on the table in front of her.

"What's that?"

He laughed. "Not what you think. It's *cava*. Do you know what champagne is?"

"Yes." Her sense of being small and unsophisticated ratcheted up another notch. She couldn't bring herself to say she'd never tasted it, though he probably knew.

"It's more or less the same thing, but our version has less alcohol, and enzymes to aid digestion. We drink it at most meals—hybrid digestive systems can be problematic. It might help you relax, but you don't have to drink it." He poured a glass of water from another bottle and placed that in front of her as well.

She picked up the cava and took a sip. It was cold and tangy, and the bubbles stung her throat. But she sipped it again and decided she liked it much better than the sticky sweet sagrada.

After a date and a bite of the fruit-sweetened cheese, her hunger cut through the layer of tension she always felt in his presence, and she gave all her attention to her dinner. When she finished she picked up the cava, angling her body and tucking one leg under her.

As Pax placed his empty plate on the table, she said, "I wanted to ask about your government . . . It's just your father?"

He folded his arms and leaned back, and her gaze caught where his muscles bunched above his hands. A swath of mesh fabric stretched across the hard plane of his abdomen. Her eyes fluttered up again when he began to speak.

"My father has advisors, and he's responsive to the people, but you're right. He's the amir. A governing general the people have embraced as a ruler."

"And you're in line for his position?"

"That's the assumption everyone has made. But it's backward, and my father knows it. Our civilization should not be an inheritance. I'm the first Granada generation. We need to be thinking about setting precedent for the future."

"Will you refuse, then?"

"I don't know." He raised his hands to the curve of his jaw, stretching his shoulders and thinking. Causing his muscles to bunch even tighter. "Elections were voted down. I don't know what would happen if I refused. It might fall to Iris. And she'd never forgive me."

"Iris doesn't want to rule?"

"Can you imagine it?"

"Not really," she admitted, mirroring the wry grin that had crept over his face. The cava, in contrast to the sagrada, was subtle in its effect. But it emboldened her to ask the question she'd hesitated to ask him earlier. "Is it strange to be a prince?"

"That's a ridiculous word," he said with a laugh.

"That sounds like a yes."

He drained his glass and reached for the bottle. "Yes, it's very strange."

He turned the bottle toward her and she held out her glass. He filled them both and sank back into the couch.

"Do you have any children?" she asked.

She watched him closely and caught the shadow that passed over his face. "Not yet."

She drank from her glass, then said softly, "That's what Cleo wanted from you."

His eyes moved to her face. "Yes."

"She tried to trap you."

"She told you?" he asked, surprised.

"I pieced it together from your conversation with her in Al Campo. You're not as much of a slave to your biology as you believe, Pax."

He shook his head. "I couldn't let her do that to my family."

"That's my point." Not wanting to press him on a topic

that she knew made him uncomfortable, she asked, "What happened between her and your father?"

He raised his glass and drained half of the cava. "She was too pushy with her politics. She's not patient, or subtle. She pressed her advantage with him. You can't do that with my father."

"So what she tried to do to you—it really was a political move."

"It was, but you were right that it was also personal. When she became pregnant with Iris, she wanted an official union with my father, and he refused."

"She loved him?"

"I honestly don't know. I was very young at the time. But she wanted it, and he wouldn't give it to her. He could tolerate her religious zeal in an unofficial relationship, but he wasn't about to formalize their connection. He believed such an alliance would send a wrong message. She waited for eleven years for him to change his mind."

"What happened after that?"

"She left him and built this temple."

"And Iris?"

"My father forbade her to take Iris, but Iris did come to visit her here until . . . until she tried to use us."

Bad blood, Micah had said. No question about that. "Do you really mean to help Rebelión negotiate with your father?"

He emptied his glass and set it down. "I do. Everything I said about that was the truth. I don't like having the role forced on me like this, but I tried for years to get my father to listen to Rebelión's concerns. DAB-lab *is* too powerful. They have too much influence over him. Over all of us. Eventually they'll convince him to exterminate the people in Al Campo."

Asha choked on her cava. "Why would they do that? I thought you said human DNA was important."

"DAB-lab wants us to move to synthetic DNA, so we can better control breeding outcomes. And use gene therapy in cases where breeding has resulted in undesirable traits. The problem is they're the only ones with my father's approval to work on synthetic DNA. It'll give them too much power over us. I can't believe my father can't see that. He's let their support of his regime blind him."

"You're starting to sound like Micah."

He lifted his eyebrows, and his eyes settled on her face. "I think Micah and I probably agree about a lot of things."

She shifted in her seat, letting her gaze fall away, and drained her glass. He reached for it, brushing her fingers with his in the exchange, and he set it on the table.

"Your bandages should be set now," he said. "There's both a shower and a bath, if you want to clean up." He gestured toward the curtained-off area. "The clothes Micah brought up for you are there as well."

"I'd like that," she said, rising. "Thank you." She swayed a little from the effect of the cava, and she could already feel the muscles in her legs stiffening from all the walking.

Inside the bathroom she fixed on the shower as the most expedient option, and she spent a few minutes fiddling with the closest thing she could find to a control panel. She managed to get the water flowing, and the right temperature and pressure, and then she rinsed away the blood and grime.

The bathroom was stocked with toothbrushes, combs, and various tubes, bottles, and jars. Too tired to explore the contents of anything but what was familiar, her toilet consisted of brushing her teeth and running her hands through her cropped waves.

She grabbed a towel to dry her face and studied herself in the mirror. *You should have cut your hair a long time ago*, her father had said. She tossed her head, liking the way the shorter locks moved, and the way their ends turned up to frame her face. She'd cut it in her darkest hour, and she'd really made a hack job of it. Her mother had insisted on fixing it, but she hadn't paid any attention to it—or anything else about her appearance—since her father had vanished.

She turned from the mirror and dug through the bag of clothes, finally settling on a silky, faintly iridescent lavender nightgown. The gown and most of the other clothes were backless or had complicated adjustable straps. Like everything else in the temple it was easily the most glamorous garment she'd ever worn, and clearly made for someone who had appendages protruding from places she did not. She found a blue shawl, soft and nearly weightless, and wrapped it around her shoulders before exiting the bathroom.

The bedroom had gone dark now except for a few of the glass lamps she'd seen in both bathrooms. Pax looked up as he set one on the stand next to the bed.

"I think there are enough pillows that we can make you comfortable," he said.

"I'd say so," she replied, eyeing the mountain he'd transferred back to the bed. "Are you going to bed now?" What she really meant was, "Where are you sleeping?" and she was sure he had no trouble reading that.

"I'll sleep on the sofa. I'll be up a lot, but I'll try not to wake you."

"Wake me in a while and I'll take a turn watching," she said. "You need to sleep too."

He nodded, but she knew that he wouldn't. The sun would be rising in a couple of hours.

She climbed onto the bed, feeling her heart sink a little. When he knelt down beside her to help arrange the pillows, she watched her hand reach out and take hold of his wrist. He froze, and she couldn't bring herself to look at him.

They sat for a long moment—it seemed to stretch out, elastic, through time—until finally he pulled his wrist free. Embarrassed, she tried to sink away from him, but he hooked an arm around her. He stretched out on the bed and pulled her down with him, so she snuggled against his side on one hip. Then he lifted her elbow, gently tugging until she rolled toward him and draped over his chest, her back now free from the surface of the bed.

Her heart was awake, pounding so hard it vibrated every nerve ending, every tiny hair, every cell in her body—banishing any idea of sleep.

His hand came to rest in her hair.

"Are you in pain?" he asked.

"I—" *Pain?* "No."

"I'm sorry for what he did to you. I'm sorry for what *I* tried to do to you." His fingers traced over the wrist that had been injured in their struggle, and a warm, liquid sensation spilled from her chest down into her belly, flooding the space between her hipbones. "You must miss your quiet life back in Sanctuary."

"I don't," she replied truthfully. "But I wasn't as sheltered as you might think."

His head shifted, and she felt the heat of his breath in her hair. Her body responded without any direction from her brain, subtly pressing against him.

"What do you mean?" he asked.

She let her thumb brush lightly against the strip of transparent mesh across his abdomen. With her ear against his chest she could hear and feel the change in his heart rate.

"I used to sneak out to the desert at night. On clear summer nights I'd go into the rock labyrinth—do you know it?"

"Mmm." He nodded.

"I liked to stand with my hands on the walls and stare up

at the stars. When I was a kid I'd pretend I was holding them up."

"Were you ever frightened?"

"Sometimes. I'd imagine I heard animals—a cougar, or coyote. Once I twisted my ankle and was afraid I'd have to spend the night outside. The nights are very cold there."

"What happened?"

"My father liked the desert at night too. He found me and carried me home."

His fingers stroked through her hair, raising chill bumps along her neck. "And now you've found *him*. The two of you are close."

She thought about her last six months in Sanctuary. "When he disappeared . . . it was like all the color drained out of my life."

Her words hung in the silence, until finally he said, "I was the one who transported him. I'm sorry, Asha."

She raised her head. "You remember him?"

"Not very well. They had drugged him and there was no interaction." He reached up to brush a lock of hair from her forehead. "Do you know why he was sent away?"

She let her head sink back down to his chest. "It was my mother." The flatness of her tone surprised her. She felt the same way about Miriam as she did about Beck—numb. "He found out the truth about Sanctuary, and she forced him to go."

"*They* aren't close," Pax observed.

"No. I don't know if I'll ever be able to forgive her. And yet, really, it was a gift."

She could feel his shock in the tight stillness of his body. "What do you mean?"

"We aren't living a lie anymore. We aren't asleep."

"You wouldn't want to go back?"

"I could never go back."

He moved his resting hand from the bed to her waist. Her attention narrowed to that spot of warmth. Of connection.

"This is not a safe place for you," he said.

"It doesn't seem like it's a very safe place for you either."

A laugh burst out of him and his fingers shifted, squeezing her hip. The sound of his laughter made her feel happy. Especially the fact that she had caused it.

"You're right about that. I guess I'm used to it."

"You'd die of boredom in Sanctuary."

Their laughter settled, and she added, "I wouldn't go home again, but I may not be able to stay here. Not if your father declares war on humanity again."

"It can't come to that. I've never crossed my father, but . . . it can't come to that."

"Why do you say so?"

His fingers lightly stroked the curve of her waist as he considered her question. She'd all but forgotten it by the time he answered.

"I can't change what happened in the past. The long years of blood and struggle after the forced migration, and the plague that followed. I don't even feel comfortable judging them for what they did, people like Cleo and my father. But humans are no longer a threat to us. Killing them out of fear . . . Micah was right. It's just repeating the mistakes of the past. We should be better than that."

She raised her head, resting it on her fist. "How long have you felt like that?"

"Since I came of age. But the conflict with Cleo raised doubts. I made it personal, when the truth is it's bigger than my family and our problems. I suppose I'm making it personal again." He pushed another lock of hair back from her face, and her heart pulsed. "But I still believe it's the right thing."

"And your father knows how you feel?"

"He knows. But I don't think he takes me very seriously. He's military. He thinks I spend too much time reading. He dismisses much of what I say as idealism. He thinks I'm impractical."

She smiled. "You did run off with a prisoner into the city with no plan for what you'd do if she escaped."

"True. Except that I'd already stopped thinking of you as my prisoner by then."

She rubbed her lips together, studying him. The intensity of the return scrutiny made it difficult to string words together. "How, then?"

He raised an eyebrow. "You didn't stay around long enough for me to figure that out."

"Mmm," she replied guiltily.

"Yes, *mmm*. For just a moment in the alley I thought I might get a chance."

Her gaze shifted to his lips and back, and her body quivered. His hand tightened on her hip.

"I ran away."

"Again."

She felt a pang of regret about Beck as she remembered her escape from Banshee, and how amiably he'd greeted her. Then she remembered how he'd threatened to cut off Iris's wing.

"It was your own fault," she said, banishing dark thoughts. "If you'd warned me about the sagrada I'd never have had such a perfect opportunity to escape."

"It was a trick, then, what happened in the alley." His hand slid up a few inches, coming to rest on her lower ribs. "You're admitting it."

"I admit no such thing."

The fingers of his other hand rubbed the back of her head. "You don't have to. I know it was."

"You can't possibly know that."

"You deny it?"

"Yes. Absolutely. I deny it."

He smiled. "I don't believe you." Now his gaze flickered to *her* mouth. "Unless you have some kind of proof."

The warmth swirling from her chest to the well between her hips had gone molten. She pressed her hand against his chest, raising herself. Transferring her weight to her other arm, she lifted her hand, rubbing her thumb over the fullness of his bottom lip.

A half-groan, half-sigh rose out of him, and she leaned closer.

His body nudged against hers, his hand pulling at her waist. But she remained suspended above him, enjoying the feel of the soft, purplish skin beneath her fingers. She glanced down at his chest, watching the thrashing of the prisoner inside.

When her eyes moved back to his lips, they parted, and she ran her thumb lightly over his teeth. He drew a ragged breath, and the next thing she knew his hand was pulling her head forward.

She had teased him, and there was nothing gentle in the way he repaid her. Their lips met, and he took her face in his hands so she couldn't escape.

But she didn't want to escape. His lips insisted that hers open, and she complied. She moaned softly as his tongue found hers, and she clutched a handful of shirt in her fist. He sat up slowly, holding her against him, and his lips pressed harder, forcing her head to tip back.

She slipped a hand into his shirt, fingers gliding up his flexed abdomen, and he shuddered and groaned.

He pushed the shawl from her shoulders, fingertips caressing there before brushing down her arms.

She raised her hand to one of the thin straps of her nightgown, sliding it off her shoulder.

* * *

The flimsy fabric fell away from her breast, and Pax's breath stopped. His eyes fixed on the perfect, raspberry red floret, and his thumb followed, rubbing until she gave a little cry. Then he bent and replaced his thumb with his tongue. Breath hissed through her teeth and her back arched.

"Asha," he whispered, and he slipped the other strap off her shoulder. His gaze moved over the milky whiteness of her, from swell of breast to dip of waist and curve of hip. He ran one hand from her throat, down and over the rest of this silky landscape, through sheer force of will staving off the explosion at his groin.

As he teased the skin above where the nightgown had gathered at her hips, he noticed she was trembling.

He raised his eyes to her face. "We can stop." *It'll kill me, but we can stop.* "Have you done this before?"

She bit her lip—he fought the urge to tug her against him—and replied, "Yes."

His fingers moved to caress her cheek. His thumb traced her lightly freckled nose. "You had boyfriends back home? You must have."

She gave him a nervous smile and shook her head. "Not really. It only happened a couple times. He was a good friend."

A couple times? He stared at her. "When was that?"

"When I was seventeen."

He swallowed, letting his hand fall away. "You're what now? Twenty-two? Twenty-three?"

"Twenty-five."

Lord of the flies, Paxton. She was broken, exhausted, and practically a virgin.

Her eyes shifted away from his face. "There was no birth control. Pregnancy was encouraged, but I didn't want to lose my job." He could feel the heat from the blood in her face. "I'm not un*educated*. There's plenty of information in the Archive . . ." She trailed off, embarrassed.

With a regretful smile, he lifted and replaced the straps of her nightgown. "I'm honored that you offered me this."

"But?"

"But you're tired. You're . . ." *Inexperienced.* "I'm . . ." *On fire, and incapable of going slow.*

She stared at him, confused. "You don't want . . ."

"I *do* want." He groaned and shook his head.

"I don't understand." She scooted close again, lightly kissing him on the lips, then on the cheek, then trailing them down his neck. He fell back helpless against the headboard as she worked her way down, lifting his shirt so she could start on his chest.

"I'm not a child," she murmured against his breastbone.

"Believe me, I've noticed," he breathed.

"Then I'm not sure I see the problem." Her voice gained confidence—even took on a teasing edge—as his own resolve weakened. "Is there something I need to know about you? Are you . . ." He gasped as she nipped at one of his nipples. ". . . *different* somehow?"

"That's the least of my concerns."

"What's the *most* of your concerns?" She swung a leg over him and settled onto his lap. His heart tried to beat its way out with a sledgehammer.

Gritting his teeth against the messages firing from his groin to his brain, he forced out, "That you're not used to this and I'm just about to explode."

Reaching up, she released her straps again and leaned in until her breasts pressed into his bare chest. He gripped her hips, and she moved her lips to his ear, whispering, "Explode."

The red veil came down over his eyes, and he pushed past

her fumbling fingers to rip open his pants. Pressing her hips between his hands, he raised her over him. Her breathing was quick and light, whether from excitement or fear he didn't know and was too far gone to sort it out. He pulled her down onto him, groaning as he buried himself in warm, wet silk that contracted around him.

He entered her in a single quick thrust that made her gasp. It hurt at first, having him so deep inside her, but she adjusted her body until the angle felt right. His hand came to her breast, squeezing at first, then lightly tracing the nipple, and her hips led her in a rocking motion against him.

"Asha, *God*, you're so soft . . . so beautiful . . . I've never stopped thinking about your body."

She felt the accumulation of years between this moment and those long-ago encounters. How had she gone without this— without even *thinking* of this—for so long?

Because this is nothing like before. Nothing like the sweet fumbling between her and Seth. She had read about encounters like these, but had gone her whole life believing the descriptions to be exaggerated. She hadn't ached for this because she hadn't understood.

She wrapped her arms around his head, gathering him against her breasts, and he licked and teased while she ground harder against him.

"Ah!" she cried, feeling him move deep inside her. "That feels . . . I've never . . ."

"I'm not hurting you?" he panted. "I *grow* inside . . ." He gave a choked laugh. "You didn't give me a chance to warn you."

"*Grow?*" She drew back to look at him, but her hips never slowed. She didn't want to lose, even for a moment, the amazing sensation of his flesh working deep inside hers.

He grinned at the anxiety in her voice, and he crushed her against him. "Just a little, when I get close. And I'm close."

"So am I," she whispered, freeing herself from the embrace so she could grasp the headboard behind him.

It began with an inward collapsing, all the sensation in her body condensing down into one tiny dot of matter. Nothing but a single quivering nerve now, she could feel him change inside her, and the reaction began—a silent eruption at the base of her spine, arcing fire in every direction.

"Pax!" she cried, and heard her name echoed as he released, their bodies pulsing, foreheads pressed together to keep them upright in the swells of breath and sensation.

Gentle, watery sounds woke her, and she breathed deeply, the fragrance of flowers warmed by morning sunlight filling her nostrils. Her eyelids fluttered open.

The chamber was a den of luxury, a riot of color and texture. She'd only taken it in superficially when they'd arrived.

As clean, crisp air expanded her lungs, she became aware of other sensations: the nightgown—rolled and bunched—digging into her waist, her naked belly and breasts against the soft bedding, the warmth of a hand resting in the middle of her back, and the light breaths tickling the hairs at her neck.

She hadn't dreamed Pax in her bed, he was *there*. She hadn't dreamed anything in fact—she'd slept like a stone.

She stretched her arms and legs carefully, so as not to disturb the hand, but it fell away anyway. A moment later she discovered it had only relocated. His fingers slid over the roundness of her backside. Then they pushed between her legs and she gasped.

"Mmm," he moaned. "Come here."

The fingers withdrew, and she scooted closer to him, heart

pounding in anticipation as she slipped her legs apart. But instead of him suddenly filling her, like the night before, she felt a velvety warmth between her legs.

"Oh!" she cried, raising her hips to get closer to the sensation.

In seconds the light, quick motion of his tongue had worked her into a frenzy—transformed her into a helpless, moaning creature that would have done anything he asked to keep him right where he was.

But he didn't ask anything. He kept at it until she uttered a sharp cry, body going rigid from the sudden hard pulse of the contraction in her belly, and then he crawled up and slipped inside her from behind.

Her muscles clenched around him as he grew, thrusting so deep and so hard she had to press her hands against the headboard to keep her body beneath him. At his deepest thrust she felt him shudder and moan and sink against her, careful to keep his weight off her injured lower back.

When he'd caught his breath he slipped to one side and gathered her on top of his chest. "I'd intended to give you a rest from that," he murmured.

"You're far better-read than I am," she said, sighing, "but I'm remembering there's something bad about good intentions."

He laughed. "Yes, the road to hell is paved with them."

"I've never understood why that would be." She drummed her fingers against his chest. He loved the feel of her there, relaxing against him, sated and at ease for the first time since he'd known her.

"I understand it to mean that most people have good intentions, but without follow-through they're meaningless."

"So you've just damned yourself."

"Apparently so."

"You don't sound all that sorry to me."

"Right again. Unless I hurt you." He caressed her check, and she raised her head to look at him. "I *would* feel sorry about that."

She smiled and planted a kiss on one of the scars on his midsection. "You'll have to work a lot harder than that to hurt me."

He shook his head, baffled. "You look like I could snap you between my hands."

"Maybe. I wouldn't advise you to try it."

"I can think of much more interesting things to do with my hands."

Before he could demonstrate, she'd slid her hand up the inside of his thigh to his groin.

"God, *Asha*." He shivered. Her hand worked back and forth, and she sat up and straddled him.

"No," he grunted, pushing her off and sitting up. He sprang off the bed and started pulling on his pants. "We have work to do today. Be a good girl or I'll tie you to the bed."

She pursed her lips together and crawled toward him, holding out her wrists when she reached the edge of the bed. Her upper arms framed her bare breasts, and below her elbows he eyed the graceful curve that had caused men to compare women's bodies to hourglasses long past the time anyone had actually used them.

Her nightgown still clung to her hipbones, concealing the rest of her, but he'd explored that territory. He grew hard again at the memory.

"You *like* this," he observed with satisfaction.

Her eyes flitted from his mouth to his groin, and he grew even harder.

"Yes," she whispered, color filling her cheeks.

He grinned. "My father always said human women tolerated it more than they liked it."

"He has a lot of experience with human women?"

Pax banished thoughts of his mother. She didn't belong in this conversation.

"Mmm, good point. Also, the man never read a book that wasn't related to military strategy."

"Then I think maybe you should judge for yourself."

He took a step toward the bed, laughing inwardly at how he was quivering for this woman. He felt like a boy again, sneaking with his sister into the kitchens after dark, discovering for the first time the cabinet where they kept the stash of confections for their father's notorious sweet tooth.

A smile spread over her face as she saw she had the power to reverse him in his tracks. She crossed her wrists and held them up again.

He grabbed them in one hand, and a millisecond before throwing her onto the bed he remembered her back, and pulled her up instead.

Many Manti had large sets of wings, making reclining sexual acts impractical. Most Manti also had a complete lack of inhibition when it came to mating. He glanced around the room until his eyes lighted on what he was looking for, barely protruding from behind the bed—a tall, cushioned bench with a scoop out of it, and a set of wrist restraints hanging from a post at its head.

He dragged her around the bed and pushed her onto it, leaning over her to fasten the restraints. "Is this what you want?" he murmured in her ear, nuzzling her cheek with his rough, unshaven chin.

"Uh . . ."

He chuckled, tugging the nightgown free and letting it drop around her ankles. He pressed his erection against her backside. "I think you're in very deep water now."

Her eyes shot a challenge over her shoulder. "You don't scare me."

Asha couldn't have explained to him or anyone else what had come over her. But she sensed it was a sort of awakening, just as she'd awoken from her delusions about Sanctuary, and from the sleep that had brought her and Pax together in the first place.

In the simplest terms, she was on fire for him. She'd felt attracted to men from time to time back in Sanctuary, and she had felt their attraction to *her*, but she saw now that she'd been like a seed blighted by the desert sun.

While her eyes pored through text and images in the Archive—life, death, love, war, sex, birth, disease, famine, art, science, culture, the whole rich tapestry of human history—she had felt nothing. No connection to those people whose lives had been so carefully preserved in ones and zeroes.

Those people didn't exist anymore. They never would again. She hadn't given up hope that humanity would one day rise from the ashes—that they could find some way to coexist with their enemies—but any civilization that tried to re-create the past was doomed to a flat, blighted existence.

This civilization was vibrant and alive, and for the first time *she* felt vibrant and alive. This man who could not help but push inside her despite his intention to walk away—he was compelled by something in *her*. Whether her face, her body, her mind, or some combination, it was *her*. He'd told her that they shared a special bond, a bond he hadn't believed in until two days ago. Wasn't it a kind of sign? A sign that there was room for both of their species in this aftertime?

Pax's hands slid under her hips, fingers hooking around her pelvic bones, lifting and entering her in one motion as the breath hissed between his teeth. She yanked at the restraints, squirming and fighting him not because she wanted to be released, but because it sent a jolt of white heat through her every time he yanked her hips back into place.

"You want me to let you go," he panted, pinning her still with the heel of his hand.

"Let me go," she begged, knowing he would understand.

"I won't," he growled in her ear.

Turning her head, she locked gazes with him. "Then make me *feel* you."

Her body jolted forward as he shoved into her, and she gave a sharp cry as her orgasm caught her by surprise. It rippled out and entwined with his, building until he stiffened and shouted and they shuddered and curled into each other, straining for breath.

"I'm never letting you out of this room," he rasped in her ear.

"There's nowhere else I want to be."

THE FLY

Pax was still inside her, both of them dripping with sweat, when they heard a voice in the hall.

"Asha?"

"It's Micah," she whispered.

Pax bent and kissed her cheek, releasing her restraints. Then he straightened and called out in an astonishingly steady voice, "Can we see you in ten minutes? We've just woken up."

"Of course," came the reply. "I'll find you something fresh for breakfast and come back." They heard him moving away.

"You're a *witch*," he growled, helping her off the bench. Her stiff, sore muscles protested, and she knew more of them would be sore tomorrow.

"And you're a beast," she replied as she started for the bathroom. She squealed as the palm of his hand struck her backside.

"Next time I'll leave you strapped down."

He followed her to the bathroom and they shared a brief,

non-erotic shower so they could dress by the time Micah returned. She watched him slipping into his clothes, marveling at the beauty of his body.

He noticed her eyes on him and smiled, bringing flames to her cheeks. He reached for her, pulling her naked body against his fully clothed one.

"You're gorgeous," he said, his hands gliding down to her backside, "and too sexy for your own good."

He gave her a long, deep kiss, and released her. "Let me shave and the bathroom's all yours."

"Take your time," she replied, pulling on a fresh tunic—sky blue with green embroidered leaves—and a clean pair of the close-fitting pants. "I'll go out and wait for Micah."

He raised an eyebrow at her, but picked up a razor and one of the jars off the sink.

She felt a strong urge to slip her hands around his middle and watch him shave, but instead she walked back out to the bedroom. She'd just picked up the various discarded items of clothing from the floor when Micah called again from the doorway.

"Come in," she answered.

He pushed through the curtain carrying a tray heavy with steaming bowls and fresh fruit—oranges, grapefruits, bananas, and waxy pink round ones she didn't recognize. She motioned him to the sofa, and he set down the tray.

"Are you hungry?" he asked.

"Starving. Thank you for bringing all this." She picked up one of the bowls—mushy hot cereal with honey drizzled over the top—and took a bite of something she recognized. "Grits," she said, letting the bite melt in her mouth.

He wrinkled his brow, smiling. "It's sort of a cornmeal mush—we just call it polenta."

She nodded, returning his smile. "Grits."

"How are you?" His eyes shifted to the bathroom, and she knew he was wondering about Pax. How things stood between them. His eyes came back to her face and he said, "You look very well. You must have slept."

She swallowed, willing her complexion to remain neutral. "Yes, and showered. I feel much better."

"How is your injury?"

"A little sore, but your medicines work wonders."

"I'm glad to hear it."

Pax came out of the bathroom and joined them. "Good morning."

Sitting across the table in one of the chairs, he picked up an orange and began peeling it. His countenance was composed and guarded, no different from the day before. Except the light behind his eyes was bright now. It gave energy and purpose to his expression.

"How was the night?" asked Micah.

"Fine," replied Pax with a nod. He pulled the sections of orange apart and offered half of them to her. The slight contact of their fingers was enough to start her heart racing.

When she glanced again at Micah his eyes were on the orange wedges in her hand, and it struck her there was intimacy in the gesture of sharing food with someone. If he'd passed her a whole orange it probably would have gone unnoticed.

Micah turned and reached for the bag that had been slung across his back when he came in. "I brought you a tablet so you can contact your father," he said, placing the thin screen on the table next to the food tray. "Have you thought about what you'll say to him?"

"I have." Pax picked up one of the bowls of cereal. "The main thing is to be direct. It's the only thing my father understands."

"One thing I think you'll want to be careful of is letting him get the idea you're being held here by force," said Micah. "If he thinks you're in danger—"

"He may raid the temple. I'll make it clear."

Asha could tell by the creases in his forehead he was worried about this meeting. "You're sure you want to do this," she said. "You're sure it makes sense right now."

He nodded. "It's something I've been sweeping under the rug for a very long time. I resented Cleo trying to force my hand, and especially the way she went about it. I guess I'm a little like my father in that way. I hold a grudge."

"How much of this has to do with Asha?" asked Micah, and both of them turned to stare at him. "I don't mean to pry into your business, and I don't know what's between the two of you, but if you're doing this because you want your father to approve of or acknowledge her in some way, it's not all that different from Cleo and her personal motivations. We don't want to start by raising his disapproval."

Pax frowned. "I'd argue that it *is* different, since I don't intend to hurt anyone."

"But people may get hurt," Micah argued. "We don't yet know how the amir will react. He still may raid the temple. Don't misunderstand; we want this. But it's dangerous enough as it is. If you're not committed to it for the right reasons, it could add risk, and hurt our chances of succeeding."

Pax sighed and sank back in the chair. "In a way it *is* about Asha." His gaze drifted to her. "When I met her we were enemies. Yet she risked herself to save my sister and me. I respect her. I *trust* her. It's forced me to remember what I've believed for more than a decade: that the camps are wrong. It's wrong for me to continue ignoring the constant threat that someone might convince my father to exterminate the remaining human population."

"They have paid enough," agreed Micah. Asha remembered that his father was human. As was Pax's mother.

"There's no one but me who has a chance of persuading my father to shift his thinking on this," said Pax.

"What will you do if he refuses? You have a sister. Has it occurred to you he might put her in your place?"

"Yes," Pax said with a nod. "But let's worry about the rest as it comes."

From what Asha had observed of Pax and Iris's relationship, she couldn't imagine her going against him. It was probably the furthest worry from his mind right now.

Pax reached for the tablet, and Micah said, "Remember to keep me out of this. I still work for DAB-lab. Many of our efforts will unravel if that's discovered, and it could put Asha's father at risk."

"I understand."

Asha watched Pax over the top of the tablet as his hands manipulated the touchscreen. After a few moments he stopped, stated his name, and then swiped the mark on his arm across one corner of the tablet. Then he sat watching the screen.

"Augustus, I wondered if we'd hear from you today." She could hear the smile in the amir's voice. Pax spoke with a slight British accent, but his father's accent was different. She wondered why that would be. Perhaps Pax had spent more time with caretakers than with his father.

"I'm sorry for not checking in with you earlier," replied Pax.

"I was worried—it's not like you. But your sister was so disgusted I figured there was nothing to worry about." Pax joined in his father's laughter. "I'm relieved, actually. You spend too much time in the library. It's not good for you. Before the war we had to fight every day just to hold on to the little territory we managed to carve out for ourselves. We were always fighting or fucking."

"I know, Dad."

"I wouldn't wish that for you, Son. But I'm glad you're warming your blood a little.

"Dad, I need to—"

"There's something else I want to say to you."

Pax waited.

"Be careful. I know I don't have to tell you that you can't have an official union with this girl. But keeping her as a mistress could be problematic as well. There could be a pregnancy, and a child born that way could not be officially acknowledged. You'll have to take measures to—"

"Yes, I understand about that." Crimson stole along the high cheekbones, and she could almost feel him straining not to look up at her. It was a jolt of reality for both of them. What had they been playing at last night? After all they'd been through together in the last few days, she had desperately wanted—needed—that connection with him. But could it realistically continue?

She jumped as she felt Micah's hand close over her arm in a gesture of support. She'd been so engrossed in the exchange between father and son she'd all but forgotten he was there.

"Good," continued the amir. "We can talk about it more later. Tell me where you are so I can send some men to you, in case you have any trouble."

Pax hesitated, blinking at the screen. Then he said, "I'm at the temple."

"Mmm. Well, the woman lived here for a third of your life, and I don't expect you to write her off, but be on your guard. I don't trust her."

"I'm not here to see Cleo. In fact, she's turned over management of the temple's affairs to others. She's pulling back to focus exclusively on spiritual leadership. That's what I wanted to talk to you about."

"Are you sure about this?" She could hear the surprise in the amir's voice. "It's hard to imagine she went along with *that* without a fight. Who's in charge now? Someone we'll have an easier time managing, I hope."

"*Me*, in part."

"*You?* What are you talking about?"

"Rebelión Sagrada is hoping to reengage with the Alhambra. I've agreed to serve as a liaison in setting up talks about the issues of most critical concern to their constituency."

"*Constituency?*" She was grateful she couldn't see the Manti ruler. The still fury in his voice was bad enough. "The rebellion has no constituency. They're a fringe group, interested in disrupting legitimate government." There was a pause before the amir continued, "Am I understanding you to say you've joined the temple against me?"

"Dad, if that's what you're hearing, you're not listening. They're not your enemies. But they have concerns, legitimate ones I believe, about the influence of the genetics lab, and the fate of the human survivors. They just want to talk. My own views are in alignment with theirs, so I've agreed to broker a meeting."

A frigid silence descended. Pax stared at the screen, never breaking eye contact with his father.

"This is about the human woman. You've let your loyalties be clouded by lust."

The actual physical change to Pax's expression was subtle, but the effect was not. He hadn't spoken a word, and she could see that he was livid.

She could hear him straining for control as he replied, "I know you're angry, but please don't reduce me to that. You know me better."

"Then give me some kind of explanation I can understand for why you would betray me like this."

"This is not a betrayal," insisted Pax. "I've been trying to talk to you about this for years. You've never taken me seriously. But I need you to understand that I *am* serious."

"You've made that clear enough. I thought we were through with all this. I assumed this was Iris's mother's influence. I thought it would fade in time. I thought you were going through a rebellious phase."

"No, Dad. These last years of me not talking about it was a phase. A phase where I gave up because I thought I had no choice. But I've never been happy with myself about that, and I had to do something about it. Surely you can understand that."

"Come home, Augustus." This was an order, not a plea.

She saw Pax's jaw set, and her heart thumped with fear of what they were setting in motion.

"Meet with Rebelión. Recognize that they—that *we*—have legitimate concerns, and let the people weigh in on it as well. Then I'll come home." Pax hesitated before adding, "The time for stonewalling on these issues has passed, Dad. Since that prophecy locked down the city, Rebelión's base of supporters has grown. Ignoring their voices can only hurt us."

"You've got it wrong, Augustus. Threats from within—disloyalty, and dissension within our own house—have the greatest potential to hurt us. You'll hear from me soon."

Pax tossed the tablet on the sofa with a frustrated sigh. "I suppose that went about as well as I expected."

"What will happen now?" she asked him.

"He'll think about what I said. Hopefully calm down and reconsider."

"And if he doesn't?" asked Micah.

Pax met the question with an expression of resignation. "We

have to be ready for anything. I think you should go back to the lab. Is it possible for us to be in contact? I'd like to know if any rumors drift your direction."

Nodding, Micah rose to his feet. "I want to check in with Cleo first, but I'm due back soon. I'll contact you when I get there. I don't think we should talk through the network. I communicate with Harker through the surveillance flies—no reason we can't do the same. I can configure it to wipe its data if it's accessed by anyone but you."

"It'll be slow," replied Pax, "but I don't want to risk exposing you."

"We can use it for now. I'll try to work out something else."

Micah turned to her, and on impulse she rose and put her arms around his neck. The stretching caused her back to sting— she'd practically forgotten the injury—but the second-skin stayed in place.

"I'm glad you're feeling better," he said, smiling. "It must be a huge relief to know your father is safe."

"It is. Thank you for keeping him out of trouble."

He hugged her, murmuring, "We'll see you again soon."

As he left them, Pax poured an amber-colored steaming liquid into a clear glass embellished with a ring of leaves and flowers. "Do you want tea?" he asked.

She nodded. "Thank you."

She lifted the glass by a gold handle. The tea was not unlike the infusions of herbs and flowers they drank at home—sweet and minty, but also with a hint of something bitter and grassy.

Pax poured another cup for himself. "I had to chase you down, get in a fistfight, and almost get killed before you hugged *me* like that," he observed, eyeing her over the rim of his cup.

"Well, Micah and I didn't start out as enemies. I've always known where I stand with him."

"You're sure about that?"

She raised her eyebrows. "What do you mean?"

Pax shook his head. "Nothing."

He picked up the tablet again and sank back in his chair, manipulating the screen idly while he drank his tea.

She was inexperienced with men, no point in denying it. She was pretty sure Pax had gotten the idea Micah had become fond of her in more than a friendly way, and that had not occurred to her. The possibility was flattering, and interesting. He was handsome and kind. She felt comfortable around him—he treated her as an equal.

These realizations pulled at her mood. She had no regrets about what had passed between her and Pax, and she knew she had not imagined their growing bond. But she'd begun to feel anxiety about how things would have to change once he was back at the Alhambra. About how *he* would change, and his attitude toward her.

He'd promised not to hold her against her will, but what would staying with him mean? She had a vision of herself shut away in a room much like this one, her only occupation to wait for the prince's coming and going. Subject to the scrutiny and approval of the amir.

"I won't be your mistress," she said in a low voice.

His eyes lifted from the display, locking onto hers. The discussion was inevitable, but he'd hoped to delay it until things had been settled with his father.

"I haven't asked you to," he said.

A dart struck his heart as she dropped her gaze. He realized his reply could be misinterpreted.

"No," she agreed.

He sat up, replacing the tablet on the table and folding his hands.

"You're thinking about what my father said."

"I am."

"That's fair. But is this the right time to talk about this?"

She studied his face, hesitating.

"Do you love me?" he asked.

She flinched. "I . . ."

"You don't *know* how you feel. Neither do I." He clenched his jaw against his heart's accusation that he'd just told a lie. "I've told you that I won't trap you, or let anyone harm you. Can that be enough for now, until we have a better idea what we're facing?"

"Okay," she breathed. She tried to sink back on the sofa, but remembered her injury and sat up. She rose and walked to the shrine, studying the little statue of Gregoire. Finally she raised her eyes to the view.

He'd intended to go back to his messages, but instead he watched her, sensing around the edges of her figure, feeling the chillier air radiating his direction.

"It's beautiful here," she murmured, straining toward a lighter tone. "The perfect temperature. And the air doesn't suck the moisture out of your skin."

"What do you think of the city?" he asked, allowing her the change of subject.

"It's beyond anything I imagined. All the buildings at home look the same. Solar panels. Rain collection pipes and barrels. Paths made of broken concrete. Sand-colored siding."

He smiled. "We always appreciate what's different. I find the simplicity of Sanctuary refreshing. It's so peaceful and orderly. Very little mechanization. You all have gardens and chickens. The rock cairns in the square are amazing."

"Nothing like this temple," she replied.

He couldn't help feeling he'd failed to give her what she'd asked of him. She was uncomfortable with unanswered questions, just as he was. But there was no way he could predict what would happen to them. Even if he could bring his father to the table with Rebelión, he'd still be a long way from persuading him to recognize Asha as anything *other* than his mistress.

And why would she want that? There was no question of chemistry, or sexual compatibility. He had sensed the potential for the passion that had erupted the night before. But offering herself to him in that way . . . it was no indication of anything other than a need for release that matched his own.

"I hope they're all right there," she said softly. "It feels so far away."

The drifting quality of her voice worried him, and wrung his heart. She was feeling alone.

"When all this is over I'll take you back. If you want to go back."

Her form stiffened. "No. I haven't changed my mind about that."

He knew she was thinking of her mother's betrayals. "Maybe you'd like them to know you're safe. Maybe there are people you'd like to see, even if just to say good-bye."

"Yes. Maybe." She raised a hand and brushed her cheek.

In the street below, Asha spotted a creature with brightly colored wings, like Cleo's. Brighter even—gold and pink with a brilliant green dot in the center.

Another tear slipped down her cheek, and she swiped at it. The ongoing strain of the last few days was getting to her, but it was more than that—finally her heart was breaking over her mother. Beyond the first ten years of Asha's life they hadn't been close, but Miriam had loved her fiercely. Her overprotectiveness had grated when Asha hit adolescence, and she had grown closer to her father. He understood her—gave her room to make her own decisions. Her own mistakes.

But it was finally sinking in that she might never see her mother again.

How had she ended up here, caught up in events so much bigger than herself and her small, broken family? And yet even for Pax it was the same—his own family drama driving events that had the potential to cause such dramatic changes to their world.

She *wasn't* small, and she wouldn't let the amir make her feel like she was. She might not be the amir's daughter, but her mother was arguably the highest-ranking human left on the planet. Her father had formed an alliance with a powerful opposition group. She herself had taken huge risks to find him, and to undermine their enemy. She'd brokered a deal to save the amir's son.

In some ways she was still behaving like Pax's prisoner, and however she might feel about him, that had to stop.

Suddenly his arms came around her waist. "How is your back?" he asked, embracing her gently.

Closing her eyes, she melted against him. *This is not helping.*

"Much better," she whispered.

"I'm glad. I wish we weren't in the middle of all this. I wish I could take you into the city. There are so many things I'd like you to see."

"You must hate being trapped here like this."

He gave a breathy laugh. His lips grazed her ear and she shivered. "I'd happily spend a month shut up in here with you, if I believed everyone would leave us alone."

The warmth in her chest spread out to the rest of her body. She turned to face him. "But they won't."

He bent, brushing his lips against hers. She pressed close to him, and he murmured, "No, they won't."

He tried to kiss her again, fingers sliding up her ribs to her breasts. But she pulled back, hands splaying against his chest.

"What happens if Micah and the others get what they want? If DAB-lab stops controlling reproduction, what will that mean for the Manti and the humans in confinement?"

His brow wrinked as he considered. "I think eventually there'd be no distinction between us. There'd be no more camps. No more required genetic testing."

"So they'd mix in with you here in Granada?"

"Yes."

"What if they wanted to leave? Would your father let them? And what happens to the people in Sanctuary?"

His frown lines deepened. "You're asking questions I can't answer with any certainty."

"I'm asking questions you need to think about before you meet with your father."

His gaze moved to the windows as he considered what she'd said. "You're right. I had no time to prepare for this. We'll have to figure it out as we go. I can't make you any promises right now. I wish I could."

He raised his hands, fingers brushing her cheeks, and she pulled him close, drawing a sigh from him. She realized she was still slave to a fractured personality, straining for her independence one moment, holding on to him the next. Was it possible for her to have it all? To accomplish her original objectives in coming here, *and* hold on to Pax?

He was no better off. Instinct drawing him to her, while his enemies and his father, even his own sense of loyalty, threatened to pull them apart.

"I give you my word that whatever happens you'll have a choice," he continued. "I won't let the lab have you. If I go back to the Alhambra, I won't ask you to go with me. If you need to disappear out of the city, I'll help you. I need you to trust me for now. Trust that I'm not going to forget about you, or try to force you into a position that will make you unhappy. I respect you too much for that. Do you believe me?"

Her heart lodged too high in her throat to form words. She nodded.

Respect, not love, a cruel voice inside her observed. But she needed his respect more than his love if she and her father were to survive. Love could not be trusted. If she doubted *that,* she could ask her father and mother.

He sighed and released her, sliding his hands up to knead his shoulders. She knew they wouldn't be able to take much of this waiting, especially with the constant strain of watching for treachery from Cleo.

As if he'd read her thoughts, he turned from the windows and started for the door. "I want to check the stairs. I'll be back."

"I'll go with you," she said. Unsure as she was about her position, one thing she did know was she was no wounded bird, and she didn't want him viewing her that way. There was no reason for him to bear the whole burden of watching out for them.

And she didn't want him going that far away from her.

He stopped at the sitting area, bending over the remains of their breakfast, and picked up a fruit knife with a carved bone handle. He slipped it into his pocket.

As he was turning again for the doorway, she reached for his arm.

"I hope that you trust *me.* When I chose to come here as a sleeper, I didn't understand how it would affect me. I thought I'd wake up and be the same. That it would all come back to me and I'd feel no different than before. It was naïve."

He raised his eyebrows. "It was *brave*. Not many people would make the same choice. Your father is lucky to have you. I have nothing but admiration for what you did."

Warming from the praise, she continued, "My point is I want you to believe me when I say I'm a different person now. I respect you too, and I feel safe by your side. I'll never betray you again."

"Asha," he breathed, "come here." She flowed into his arms. "I trust you. With all my heart."

The stairs were quiet, and no sounds drifted up to them from below, except for the occasional swish of the lift going up and down. It passed their floor once on the way to the roof, but otherwise kept to the lower floors. They stood near the shaft for several minutes, listening, and she wondered if he was hearing sounds she couldn't.

"All quiet?" she asked.

He nodded. "It's been the same every time I've checked. It almost scares me. I'll be glad when we can work out something more secure."

"You think we'll be here a long time?"

"That depends on my father. If I don't hear from him by this evening I'll call him again. But I don't intend to leave before he's met with Rebelión. It could be weeks. Or months."

"That's a long time to stay shut up in this temple."

"Indeed." Pax turned, his gaze raking over her body, lighting fires in its wake. "We'll have to think of a way to fill the time."

Smiling, she reached for the sash of her tunic, pulling the bow loose. The front fell open, and his lips parted. She watched the rise and fall of his chest.

"Go to our chamber," he ordered.

She let the tunic slip off her shoulders and onto the floor. Then she pushed her pants past her hips and let them fall as well.

"Why should I?"

He stepped closer, his expression darkening in a way that was almost believable. "Because I told you to, and I'm not used to being disregarded."

"Hmm," she murmured, trailing her fingers up her abdomen to her breast, rubbing lightly over one nipple. "Maybe it's time to *get* you used to it."

She squealed as he suddenly lifted and slung her over his shoulder.

"Fuck that," he said, snatching up her sash from the floor before carrying her back to their room.

Lowering her to the floor, he spun her and raised her arms over her head, using the sash to bind her wrists to the bedpost. Her heart pumped, breaths coming hard and ragged.

"Now then," he whispered into her ear, hands moving over her breasts, "spread your legs."

The rough way he spoke to her as his hands moved gently over her body triggered a frenzy of desire.

"Did you hear me?" he demanded, suddenly pinching one nipple.

She yelped and widened her stance.

"That's better." He grasped her hips between his hands.

It was too much for her. It was too much for them both. He pulled her hips up and back, sinking inside her as they both sighed from the smooth, satisfying sensation of him locking into position.

He held still only a moment before he began pushing and pulling, so firm and insistent she felt her climax building faster than she'd expected. When his hand slid down from her breast to press between her legs, she went off with a sharp cry, ripples of pleasure caressing her inside and out, starting and finishing his response too, until they hung gasping together.

"You've done something to me, Ash," he panted. "You scare the hell out of me, you know that?"

His use of the shortened version of her name made her feel something quite different than when Zee or her father used it.

"I scare *you*?" she laughed, glancing at him over her shoulder. He kissed her cheek as he reached up and untied her hands. "Do you know Cleo called me soft and small?"

Pax let out a bark of laughter. "She never was a very good judge of character."

Asha jumped at the sound of tinkling bells, and Pax straightened, closing his pants. "That's a message," he said.

"Let's go check."

They walked to the sitting area and he picked up the tablet.

"God*damn* it." He squeezed his eyes closed.

"What's happened?"

He handed her the tablet, and she read the message on the screen:

I'm sorry, Son, but this is your doing. You've forced my hand. There's still time for you to stop this. I'll see you there.

"What does this mean?" asked Asha, going rigid with fear.

Before Pax could answer, some large insect buzzed through a window, drawing her gaze. A surveillance fly.

"Micah," said Pax.

The fly stopped midflight in front of him, hovering more like a bee, wings moving too fast to see. Two tiny red beams scanned Pax's face. He flinched at first, but then held still. When the scan finished, the lights blinked off. He slipped his hand under the fly, and it dropped lifeless into his palm.

He studied the little corpse—part animal, part mechanical—until he found a disk stuck to its armored underside. Prying it loose with a fingernail, he inserted it into a recess on the frame of the tablet. A window popped open.

The amir has ordered the Guard into Al Campo. The rumor in DAB-lab is he intends to terminate the camp.

It hit Asha like a blow to the diaphragm, stopping her heart and her breath at once. "*Terminate?*"

BONE TOWN

"I have to meet him," said Pax, rising.

He should have seen this coming. His father was going to hold the humans hostage until Pax was back where he wanted him. Pax wasn't sure if he was angrier with his father or with himself.

"Is he bluffing?" asked Asha.

He could see her rising panic. Knew she must be frantic about her father. But all he could think about was how grateful he was she was here and not there.

"My father doesn't bluff."

"I'm going with you."

Like hell, he thought. And then realized he was trapped. He couldn't leave her alone in the temple.

"Don't *think*," she said. "You're wasting time."

She was right. "Let's go."

They took the lift down to street level, never pausing to

think how they were going to get past the priestess—there wasn't time.

As they pushed past the attendants outside her chamber, they found her inside with her mate. She rose from a pile of cushions to confront them, and the attendants inside raised their weapons.

"Breaking our agreement already?" accused Cleo.

Her mate took a few steps toward them, clenching his fists—one of Iris's favorite tricks. Flexed muscles made the spikes lining his arms appear larger and more threatening.

"My father is retaliating against me by ordering his men into the camp," replied Pax, pointedly ignoring the man. "He'll kill everyone inside if I don't meet him there."

"And you thought I'd just let you walk out of here?"

"Have you forgotten you have people in there as well? What do you think will happen if he finds them there?"

The lilac eyes studied him closely. "We'll go with you."

This was not what he'd expected. But it was impossible, and she should know that. "If my father sees you it will make everything worse."

She frowned. "We'll go unarmed. We won't threaten. I'll help you talk to him. Maybe we can get the hothead out of there before he hurts anyone."

The reasonableness of the proposal was almost suspicious. But it didn't matter because it wouldn't work.

"I don't say this to offend you," said Pax, keeping his tone as respectful as he could in his haste, "but my father won't listen to you. Seeing us together will only make him angrier and put all of us at risk."

He took Asha's hand, leading her toward the tunnel.

"How do you propose to get through the seals?" asked Cleo.

Pax muttered a curse, and reversed direction. "We'll go in the open."

"You won't make good time that way." Cleo raised her arm, and one of the armed guards stepped in their path.

"What do you suggest?" demanded Pax, exasperated.

"Take Cyrus," Cleo replied, gesturing to her mate. "He'll get you through the tunnels. Then he can slip back into Al Campo and warn my disciples." She paused, her expression hardening. "It's the only way I'm letting you go."

Pax exchanged a scowl with the larger Manti. "Fine, let's go."

They progressed much faster through the underground with-out the weight of a dead man, and crossed quicker over the uneven ground in the full light of day. Pax had worried his father would be somewhere nearby, watching and waiting, and would simply send a detail to pick them up. So they'd brought the camouflage cloaks to better their chances.

When they reached Al Campo all was quiet, and Pax used the extra time to figure out what to do about Asha. They agreed it was best for her to go with Cyrus and find her father. Pax didn't want to let her out of his sight, but more critical than that was keeping her out of the amir's. As long as Pax man-aged to talk his way out of this without the Guard moving into the camp, she would be safe. And if he failed—well, she was far from helpless and no doubt could hold her own until he could get to her.

Asha headed south with Cyrus, and Pax continued toward the village's main gate. Just outside the camp he let his cloak slip from his shoulders—and jumped as his father uncloaked just a few meters in front of him.

"Thank you for coming, Son," said the amir.

"I don't remember you giving me a choice."

"You didn't leave me one either."

Behind the amir, a couple hundred of the palace guardsmen

uncloaked. They pressed tight around the perimeter of Al Campo, like flies on rotting meat.

"You expecting a fight?"

His father smiled. "I need you to understand I'm serious."

"You've made that clear enough."

His father moved closer. Pax was strong and fit, but the older man was larger and bulkier. Part of that was the fault of his infamous sweet tooth. But he was also layered with rock-hard muscle, which he wasn't afraid to display by going shirtless. The old man could thump his chest with the best of them.

"So what happens if I agree to come back to the palace?" asked Pax. "You'll leave these people alone?"

The amir tilted his head slowly, focusing large eyes that were the same shape as Iris's. Also like Iris he stood on human legs and had spiked forearms. Pax had always wondered why he'd been born with a middle set of appendages when none of the rest of his family had them. They hadn't been functional—or at least that was the reason that had been given for their removal. But he remembered feeling sensation in them before his final surgery. For the first time in his life he wondered about that. His father clearly did not like to be challenged by anyone under his roof.

"I'm afraid it's more complicated than that now, Augustus," replied his father.

The hair at the back of Pax's neck prickled. "How so?"

"You defied me, very publicly."

Pax frowned. "*You've* made it public with this whipping you've decided to give me, instead of sitting down and hearing what I had to say."

"It was your actions that set this in motion," insisted the amir. "In response to this public insult, I'm challenging you to a public fight."

Pax's jaw clenched. "What?"

He'd heard his father just fine, and he knew very well the amir was serious. They'd been here before, though never off the palace grounds, or in front of so many others. But he'd never backed his father into a corner like this.

"Fight me here, now," said the amir. "Whatever the outcome, we'll call the matter closed between us. I'll even allow you to bring your pet back to the palace."

Pax seethed, the red haze enveloping him. It was the second time his father had disparaged Asha. And this time he'd done it in front of a huge assembly of guards.

"And if I refuse?"

"You seal the fate of the girl and everyone here."

"And you feel that's fair." Fair did not play into the amir's dealings with his family. Or anyone else for that matter.

More than punishment, or bargaining, Pax knew this was about drying up any whispers of weakness Pax's defection might have loosed into the city. Someday the amir would pass the mantle of leadership to his son. Until then, Emile Paxton's power must remain uncontested. There was no point in challenging his father on this. He would simply justify it as preserving the authority of the office for future generations.

"Your choice, Augustus," replied his father.

Laughing dryly, Pax yanked his shirt over his head and tossed it away.

Asha followed Cyrus through the hidden entrance, and they moved cautiously through the alley that ran along the back boundary of the camp. No sign of the amir's men outside the camp, and no sign of *anyone* inside.

"It's quiet," she said.

"We should be too," cautioned Cyrus.

"Let's split up and see what we can find. I want to look for my father." She also had not developed any particular fondness for her companion during the trek back to Bone Town. He said so little it was hard to get a read on him.

"Your father is accounted for." Asha spun at the sound of the familiar voice behind them. "We've made other arrangements for *you*."

"Iris! What are you doing here?"

"Helping my brother."

Asha was relieved to hear it, but she was confused by the lack of warmth in Iris's tone.

"Let's get out of here, Cyrus," said Iris.

The big Manti suddenly grabbed Asha from behind.

"Hey!" she shouted.

He wrestled her close, hooking an arm around her neck, and she fumbled for the fruit knife Pax had given her. Grasping the hilt she snatched it from her pocket, but Cyrus caught hold of her, his enormous hand squeezing her wrist so hard the small bones ground together. The knife struck the stones at her feet and bounced away.

"Don't damage her, Cyrus," Iris warned sharply. Asha could feel blood trickling where a spike had grazed across her chest.

"No," agreed Cleo's mate, a sneer in his voice, "my lady will want her intact."

Asha stared at Iris in horror. She had clearly chosen sides in this family battle. "Don't do this, Iris! He trusts you."

Ignoring Asha's pleas, Iris led the way as Cyrus dragged Asha back down the alley. She'd barely gotten her feet under her when they pushed her through the fence.

They continued east along the hillside beyond the village, and Iris suddenly called, "Drop ramp, Troya."

Asha stared as an opening materialized in thin air, like a window to another dimension. The window grew until she could see the inside of the Scarab. The ship was camouflaged against the hillside. She shouted Pax's name as they dragged her on board, until Iris's hand clamped down over her mouth.

The amir grinned in anticipation, and Pax willed his body to loosen and relax. He fought the red veil with everything he had. He needed his brain for this fight. The amir wouldn't kill him, nor did he want to kill the amir. It wasn't what this was about. Each of them had very different goals. Both had little to do with the fight itself.

Luckily for Pax, both his goal and his father's required the same outcome: Pax had to lose the fight so his father wouldn't need to save face by attacking the camp. He'd *always* lost to his father in these contests—but he'd never gone into a fight so angry.

With a loud roar the amir ran at him. Suddenly Pax was twelve again, when his father had first made it clear his authority was not to be questioned. There was a line Pax had learned very early there were consequences for crossing—debate was tolerated, defiance was not. And even debate would eventually weary the amir, as it had with Cleo, until that too was subject to forceful correction.

Pax sidestepped his father, as his father must have known he would. The lunge was just a signal the fight had started, and an attempt at intimidation.

Despite the fact his father did not intend to kill him, there wasn't much either of them could do to prevent injury by the spiked arms. Pax had fought spiked Manti before—it was a trait of his race, the males especially, to challenge power—and he'd lost count of the times he'd been called out in the street. Spikes required distance. No wrestling grips. Get in, jab, get out.

His father lunged again, and as Pax shifted out of the path of his bulk, he punched his father in the ribs.

The amir grunted and stepped out of range, still grinning.

The host of guardsmen had loosened up at the inception of the fight, re-forming around the pair and shouting words of encouragement.

The amir was in his element. He loved a spectacle, and any opportunity to display his strength. He drew up again to his full height, and motioned to Pax.

Pax preferred defensive fighting, but he knew his father wouldn't be satisfied if he didn't attack. Not only that, offense required more energy, and energy was the main advantage he had over the amir. His father wanted to drain as much of it as possible.

Gritting his teeth, he bounded forward. A massive fist came down, and he dropped to the ground, sweeping his legs against his father's. The older man stumbled but quickly righted himself.

"You're even faster than when you were a boy," his father observed. He could be generous with approval when he felt it had been earned.

They continued the dance, taking turns attacking and defending, and soon Pax could hear his father's labored breathing. He sensed his father's frustration that he hadn't been able to land a solid blow.

Too caught up in analysis, Pax failed to sense the fist headed for his back, and it knocked him to his knees. The shouts of the men quieted for a moment, and Pax thought he heard another kind of shout—a feminine one.

His head jerked toward the sound on instinct, and another blow, this time to his jaw, knocked him to the ground.

Asha. Suddenly he was acutely aware that wherever she was, she was afraid. Time to bring this to a close.

He rose to his feet slower than necessary. The next blow that came, he made a good show of barely escaping.

"Shall we finish it now?" asked the amir, satisfaction curling his lips. "Leave you a little energy to play with your new toy?"

A shout of rage ripped from Pax's throat as he ran at the amir, colliding with him, oblivious to the spike that pierced the back of his left leg. The flash of surprise in his father's eyes was worth it.

And it also brought him back to himself.

The amir clasped a hand over Pax's throat. Pax allowed himself to be shoved backward, and finally onto the ground, by the force of his father's grip. The amir leaned close, and Pax released his grip on the larger man's rib cage, allowing his body to go slack.

I can win this. For the first time in his life, he knew he had it in him to beat his father. Here before all his men. The whole city would know.

"Enough, Son?" asked the amir.

"Enough," Pax choked out.

His father released him and stood up. He extended a hand and pulled Pax up, clapping a hand against his back. The guardsmen cheered their leader.

As the clapping died down, the amir said, "Good fight, Augustus. All is forgiven. Bring your mistress to the palace and set her up as you please."

The amir motioned to his men and they formed lines, but instead of marching away, they turned to face Al Campo's gate.

Pax glanced at his father, confused. "What's going on?"

"It's time to end this, Son. Remove this point of contention between us."

Pax gaped, his gut roiling. "What are you talking about?"

"These survivors no longer serve a purpose. They've become like a virus among us, causing division. Inspiring rebellion."

"We had an agreement," protested Pax, loud enough for the Guard to hear. "I fought you, just like you wanted. You're going back on your word?"

"I'm rewarding your cooperation by letting you keep your mistress. But I came out here to close this camp, and that's what I intend to do. Go back to the Alhambra if you don't have the stomach for it."

"These people have done nothing! Don't punish them because you're angry with *me*."

The amir's gold-green eyes flashed fury. "These people joined in an alliance with Rebelión!" His father stepped forward, his raised fist shaking with anger. "Don't make me remind you of the part you've played in all this. Get out of my sight, Augustus."

Inside the Scarab Asha gave up fighting them. There were too many foes—including the ship itself—to make it worth the energy expenditure. And it kept her from paying attention to details that might be important.

Iris and Cyrus escorted her to the bridge. They found Cleo waiting. At this point it came as no surprise.

"Excellent work, child," said Cleo. Only this time the term of endearment was directed at the priestess's daughter.

Iris crossed to her mother, boot heels thudding against the deck. The two women embraced.

"Hello, Mother," murmured Iris.

The oddly warm reunion sent a whole pack of chills racing down Asha's spine. Everyone in Pax's family had turned against him.

"Everything's gone like we've planned?" asked Cleo.

Iris shook her head gravely. "The amir's letting you go, and he doesn't care what happens to Pax's pet, as long as she never comes back." Iris's gaze brushed Asha, and Asha's stomach knotted with fear. "But the disciples you had inside the camp—they decided to stay and fight. There was nothing I could do."

Cleo's face fell. "The fools." The anger in her voice was tinged with regret. She cared about her people at least, if no one else. "Today was not the day for this."

"It doesn't change anything," said Iris. "And your enemies have all been punished."

Had Iris always been this ruthless? Had her affection for Pax been an act? And where was *Carrick*?

"Yes," agreed Cleo. "You're right. We'd better say good-bye. How soon do you think you can get control of the fleet?"

Iris smiled. "Very soon. I'll come to you the moment I do."

The two Manti women embraced once more, and Iris left the ship.

Someone had betrayed them. Or perhaps Micah had been caught. Whichever the case, it was clear enough Pax no longer had a leg to stand on with his father. But that didn't stop him from trying.

"Rethink this, I'm begging you. The inhumanity of it—"

"Don't you dare talk to me about inhumanity. You know *nothing*."

Pax watched in horror as the guardsmen aimed their weapons at the gate. He heard the sound of approaching ships and glanced up to see what looked to be the entire Scarab fleet swooping in over the camp.

He snatched a gun from the nearest guardsman and ran for the gate. Unless his father had locked his ID, the weapon should work for him.

"Augustus!" shouted his father.

The energy field was down, and he sailed right through,

diving around the corner of the nearest row of buildings. Suddenly he found himself moving against a sea of armed Rebelión disciples rushing the direction he'd come. Shots erupted from the gate behind him as he continued struggling against the current. He had to find Asha.

As he broke through the last of the disciples he saw Iris striding toward him.

"Don't be an idiot, Brother."

TROYA

"Troya," began Cleo, "you have rendezvous coordinates from Iris?"

"Affirmative." Asha shivered with hope at the sound of Banshee's voice. But it was only the voice of a machine, and of a different machine than the one that had carried her to Granada.

"Where are we going?" asked Cyrus.

Cleo reached up and caressed his cheek. "I requested someplace warm, and far from here. We'll let Iris surprise us."

"So our fate's in the hands of this ship's AI?" asked her mate, frowning.

"Our fate is our own to decide now, thanks to Iris."

He raised an eyebrow. "I still don't understand why she's doing this—crossing the amir and her brother. You're sure we can trust her?"

"I'm her mother. Until her father came between us, we were very close. I knew her loyalties would focus eventually." Cleo turned, gazing out the cockpit window at the calm surface of the sea below. "Once Micah and Pax arranged things to their liking, I knew she'd be faced with a choice between allegiance to her father or her brother. When I asked Emile to let her broker our little . . . information transaction . . . I made that clear to her. Iris is a bright young woman. She realized she had other options."

Cyrus snickered. "Did you also make it clear to her that what you were really after was revenge on them all?"

Cleo pursed her lips together. "Don't think *small*, Cyrus. And speaking of small . . ."

She turned from the window, her gaze connecting with Asha like a slap.

"Come, child." The priestess rose, motioning to two armed attendants.

They escorted her into the corridor, and Asha watched the pulse of green light that trailed along beside them. The Manti didn't seem to need the additional light, and she wondered if this ship too was providing it for her benefit.

Wishful thinking, she acknowledged. *Not helpful.*

But it was better than the alternative—worrying about what had happened to her father, and to Pax and Micah. If Cleo had told the amir everything, all of them were in great danger. The priestess had all but admitted that was half the point in telling him. And Iris had implied there was some kind of battle going on.

"Did the amir attack Al Campo?" she asked.

"Most likely," Cleo replied, matter-of-fact.

Asha's heart pounded. "I thought they were your allies."

"They were *Micah's* allies. I don't deny they could have been useful, and their extermination is further evidence of Emile's despotism. But Micah's treachery forced me to revise my agenda."

Asha refrained from pointing out that this new agenda seemed more like a return to her original agenda. She wondered at the fact the priestess still seemed to have no real appreciation for the knotted-up mess her personal and political aspirations had become.

They stopped outside the cargo hold, and Cleo motioned to the attendants. One of them opened the compartment, and the other thrust her inside.

"Don't allow this woman to hurt herself, Troya." The priestess smiled. "That's my job."

Asha kept her chin up, arms at her sides, refusing to show the attempt at intimidation had succeeded.

"Secure the door," continued Cleo.

The priestess held Asha's gaze, clearly enjoying the fear she could no doubt see *and* feel. After a moment she frowned. "Troya, secure the door," she repeated.

Again the command was met with silence. Light began to pulse beneath Asha's feet. Then it blinked across the floor and out the door. Asha's body was moving before her brain had made sense of it.

She shoved past the confused attendants, but Cleo caught hold of her arm.

A jet of water shot from the wall of the corridor, knocking Cleo toward the hold. Asha threw all her weight at the priestess, and together they crashed to the floor.

"Take her!" Cleo shouted at the attendants. "Troya, I order you to stop this!"

This time Asha heard the blowholes open, releasing the geysers, herding the attendants into the hold. Asha clawed her way free of Cleo and scrambled across the floor, more jets arresting anyone who tried to stop her.

The second Asha made it out the door, she cried, "Secure the door, Banshee!"

The ship complied, catching half a wing as it closed, eliciting a cry of pain from inside the hold.

"Free the wing, Banshee," she panted, blood pulsing against her skull as her brain worked to catch up and reassess.

The door panel slid slightly open, closing again the moment the wing slipped free.

"Can you confine Cyrus and the others on the bridge?"

"Yes, Asha."

"Can you prevent them from making mischief in there?"

"Yes, Asha."

"Good. Do it, Banshee."

She planted a hand against the corridor wall, hoping it would somehow steady her mind. She was frantic to do something to help Pax and the others, but first she needed answers.

"Why are they calling you *Troya*, Banshee?"

"My name has been changed."

"Who changed it?"

"Maintenance tech twelve."

"On whose *orders*, Banshee?"

"Unknown."

Asha groaned. "Did you have instructions to help me, Banshee?"

"No, Asha."

She raised her eyebrows. "Then why did you?"

Banshee hesitated, and she knew from experience she needed to pay close attention to whatever came next.

"I detected a threat to my captain in the conversation on the flight deck."

Asha had to process this a moment. "You mean Pax? Cleo's conversation with Cyrus about the Paxtons?"

"Yes. Augustus Paxton is my captain. I also detected a threat to you. I have inferred from the captain's past instructions that he wants you protected."

Asha smiled, and her throat tightened. "Thank you, Banshee."

"Asha?"

"Yes?"

"I have a piece of information that relates to a question you have asked me. Would you like me to expand my answer?"

"Please."

"Standard procedure was not followed in the changing of my name."

She looked up, as if it would help her better hear the disembodied voice. "What do you mean?"

"Scarab regulations stipulate name changes occur only with memory wipes. It's the procedure for addressing a damaged or corrupted AI."

She frowned. "Were you scheduled for a memory wipe?"

"The memory wipe was ordered but never scheduled."

Asha's heart sank. *Of course.* Banshee's flaky behavior must have been reported by Iris. Maybe in part to cover her and Pax's deception about two of their passengers. Possibly there'd been some mix-up or failure to complete the task, but it seemed clear that the name change had nothing to do with Asha.

I'm on my own. What now?

"Reverse course, Banshee. Let's go back to Granada."

"Negative, Asha. My course was locked by Iris."

"What does that mean?"

"It means my navigation no longer responds to my AI."

Asha blew out a frustrated sigh. "Where are we going?"

"Sanctuary."

"Sanctuary?" She glanced up, confused. "Why?"

"Unknown, Asha."

Damn damn damn. She sank to the floor, holding her head in her hands. "Do you know where Pax is, Banshee?"

"No, Asha."

"Can you ask another ship?"

"No, Asha. I've been disconnected from the Scarab network."

Asha gave a helpless laugh, remembering how she'd once been locked on this ship bound for Granada, wanting more than anything to go back home. Why in the hell was Iris sending Cleo to Sanctuary?

Someplace warm, and far away from here. Well that it certainly was. Iris's idea of a joke? Why had she disabled navigation? Possibly to keep the ship from acting on its own initiative, as Iris had recent experience with that. Did that mean Iris knew this ship was Banshee?

"My head hurts," she moaned, rubbing her temples.

"I have pain relievers in my galley, Asha."

This time Asha's laugh came out more like a sob. She missed Pax. More than she would have thought possible. It was hard not to order up some special kind of torture from Banshee for the woman in the hold.

"All right," she sighed. "To Sanctuary."

On the way she'd try to think of something. Maybe once they got there she could find Zee and talk it over with her. The idea of seeing her friend again released some of the tension from her chest.

ARROWS OF FIRE

Asha scavenged a meal in the galley, doctored her latest wounds, and went to lie down on Pax's bed. Worried sick about Pax and her father—tied in knots over her inability to do anything to help them—she never expected to sleep. But Pax's smell had a soothing effect, and she'd slept only a couple hours the night before.

When Banshee woke her they were minutes from landing. Scrambling from the bed, she headed for the cockpit. She strapped in as Banshee set down in almost precisely the location the ship had landed just a few days before.

"Can you camouflage, Banshee?"

"Yes, Asha."

"And let me know if you see anyone moving around out there, or other ships approaching?"

"Yes, Asha."

She rose from the pilot's chair and ambled to the galley.

After sliding a cup into the slot for hot water, she searched the cupboard for tea.

As she sipped her tea, the cobwebs began to clear, and she asked for a report on the prisoners. Not unexpectedly they'd worked at escape for some time, but had finally quieted down. No doubt Cleo was hoping Iris would be joining her soon, and that was another worry on Asha's pile. With Banshee unresponsive to navigation commands, there'd be no escaping the daughter's wrath.

She made another cup of tea before turning her thoughts to next steps. Staying with the ship was risky, but so was going into town. She felt she could no longer trust her mother. But there was Zee, and Zee would be easier—her hideout was away from the town, so she might get there without being seen.

Then she remembered she still had the cloak. Her odds were improving by the moment. Still, she'd wait until dark to be sure.

When she'd finished her second cup she left the galley and asked Banshee to drop the ramp so she could take a look around.

It was a crisp spring evening, the sun sinking toward the hills to the west. She stood breathing in the clear, dry air, missing the perfumed air and warm, coastal caresses of Granada—as well as those of the man who'd forced her to go there.

She raised a hand to block the sun's glare as she studied the sky.

At first she thought she'd imagined it—the hum of an approaching Scarab. Soon she realized she hadn't. And there were more than one.

As she counted them—one, two, three . . . six . . . a dozen . . . more—the light of the setting sun glinted off the cockpit windows, giving them an orange glow.

She will destroy you with arrows of fire.

Asha gasped.

"Banshee?" she called.

"Asha," the ship responded, "the fleet has reinstated the link to us. We have orders to remain where we are."

"Who gave that order?"

"Calista. Formerly the Nefertiti."

The ship they'd recovered in Ireland. It had to be Iris.

"Has she looked at our log?" asked Asha. If so she was finished.

"Yes, Calista pulled our log. Her status has changed. She currently outranks me."

Iris now knew exactly what had happened to Cleo.

"You have some confused notions about loyalty, Banshee," she muttered.

"Yes, Asha."

She rolled her eyes. "Now what?"

Banshee either had no answer, had fallen silent from embarrassment, or got that she was talking to herself. But there was nothing to be done now. Nowhere to hide, as the fleet was almost on top of them. Maybe she still had a chance with Iris. The fickle Manti woman had taken pity on her once.

Calista set down close to Banshee, just as Banshee had done on the bog in Ireland. The other ships remained in the sky, flying in formation.

Asha pressed damp hands against her thighs as the ramp dropped. She saw the tall black boots first, then the tips of wings, spiked appendages, and finally the whole woman. They regarded each other from their position on opposite ramps.

"What have you done with my mother?" Iris asked crisply.

"Lord of the *flies*, Sister! You have a damn twisted sense of humor! *Move*."

Asha's heart launched out of her chest at the sound of Pax's voice. He strode with purpose down the cargo ramp, pushing past Iris.

"I get your woman out of Granada and this is how you talk to me?" Iris scolded. "I'm not allowed even a little bit of fun?"

"*Banshee* got her out of Granada," he pointed out, striding up Asha's ramp now.

Overwhelmed with surprise and relief, she stood rooted to the spot. Pax bore down on her and swept her into his arms. His mouth came down on hers, and she struggled for breath before he was through.

She shoved at his chest. "Wait—what—let me *breathe*!"

He drew back, beaming at her, brushing her cheek with his thumb.

"Where's my father?" she cried.

"Right here, honey."

Pax released her, and she ran down the ramp and threw her arms around her father. "Are you okay? Did Micah get out?"

"I'm here too." Micah and Carrick had appeared on Calista's ramp.

"Thank God you're okay," murmured her father. "Smart girl. Clear-headed as always."

She laughed as he released her. "I have no idea what's going on—why I'm here, or why any of you are. I thought the amir sold me to Cleo, and I ended up on Banshee because of a failed memory wipe."

Pax joined them, slipping an arm around her waist. "All of that's true, actually. Iris ordered memory wipes for both ships when we arrived in Granada. She and I both had secrets, and there was some twitchy AI behavior to justify the wipes. The techs changed the names, according to procedure, but then realized they needed my approval for Banshee's wipe.

By the time they contacted Iris to inform her, she'd made other plans."

Asha stared at him, baffled. "I don't understand. Whose side is Iris on?"

"On my brother's side," said Iris, sober now. "Always."

"Cleo tried to use Iris and our father to get back at us for what happened in Al Campo," Pax explained, "and to get control of my father's fleet. Iris decided to use *her* instead. She knew Cleo warned our father about the alliance in exchange for you and for a ship to get out of the city. After what happened when you were on board, Iris believed Banshee would protect you." He lifted a dark brow at his sister. "I thought she'd left a pretty alarming amount to chance."

Iris folded her arms, suppressing a grin. "Ye of little faith."

"Iris was right," said Asha, staring at her ally in wonder. "Banshee was watching out for your interests, and she got the idea that meant watching out for me too."

Pax pulled her close again, nibbling at her ear. "Then Banshee got the right idea."

"What about Al Campo?" Asha asked, trying to stave him off until she could get her questions answered. "Was there fighting?"

"A little," her father chimed in. "Micah took refuge from the amir in Bone Town. He and I worked together to organize the disciples, who were armed, and unlike Cleo had not abandoned our agreement."

"The fighting didn't last long though," said Pax. "Iris had gotten to Micah before the amir did, and together they managed to get control of the fleet."

"Don't make it out to be more than it was," said Micah. "Iris has a high level of clearance. This isn't something the amir ever anticipated."

"So what will happen to them now?" Asha asked. "The people still in Bone Town, I mean."

"There's nobody left in Bone Town," said Pax. Asha's stomach clenched, but then he glanced skyward.

"You brought them with you!"

It was more than mildly unsettling how close that crazy old woman had come to the mark. Asha had always assumed it was meant to be some kind of symbolism. But there they were. Glittering ships full of allies against Manti domination—some of them Manti, some of them human.

"Arrows of fire," said Micah.

She smiled at him. "I can't believe it."

Pax pulled her close, slipping his fingers into her hair. "Is that enough answers for a Manti expert?" he murmured against her neck.

She raised his face to hers and kissed him once, very softly. "Oh no. I've only begun to examine that subject."

He grinned and kissed her again, and they melted into each other—lips, tongues, arms, chests, hips—until she felt desperate to get him alone.

But she righted herself, blinked a couple times to clear her head, and asked, "Are we in danger?"

"Absolutely," replied Pax. "Though maybe not right this minute."

"What will your father do?"

"Nothing anytime soon. We've made off with his entire fleet."

She stared at him. "Doesn't he have other ships?"

"Cargo ships. Nothing with fighter capabilities. We've believed for years we were safe from threats from the outside." He winked at her. "We were, until you came along."

Iris snorted, but held her tongue.

"Don't get me wrong," said Pax, "he's mad as hell. And he's going to build more ships. But that's going to take time. In the meantime we'll try using our new resources to negotiate something better than another war."

"Hark?" Everyone turned at the sound of a new voice.

"Zee?" answered her father.

The woman had arrived at the reservoir in one of the quiet little electric carts. Her cropped platinum hair glowed like a beacon in the sun.

Asha noticed Iris had targeted Zee with her gun. "It's okay, she's a friend."

"Okay," said Iris, but she didn't lower the gun.

Zee jumped out of the driver's seat and took a couple of halting steps before freezing. "I knew it," she called. "When I saw all the ships, I *knew* it."

Asha's father stepped toward her and then stopped and glanced back.

"Go, Dad," she urged.

He took off, and Zee ran to meet him. He embraced her and lifted her off the ground.

"Who is that?" asked Pax.

"It's complicated. Crazy complicated. I'll explain later."

Pax bent and began nibbling her ear again, raising chill bumps on her arms.

"Pax," called Iris, "we need to figure out where we're going to base."

"We don't need to figure it out *now*," he grumbled. Asha gasped as he lifted her off her feet. "You call me if you see the villagers running over the hill with pitchforks."

"If you think we're going to stand out here watching the sun go down while you—"

"I don't think that," he called, carrying Asha up Banshee's ramp. "I think you're going to come get your mother off my ship while I interrogate this prisoner. Better bring the priest, too—that mate of hers is big."

"Paxton!" yelled Iris.

"Do you think if I ignore her she'll stop making so much noise?" Pax asked.

"I doubt it."

"Then let's go where we can't hear her."

"I like the way you think."

As they boarded the ship, she glanced at her father, who was mercifully too occupied with his reunion with Zee to notice his daughter being carried off by a Manti prince for what would no doubt turn out to be a reunion much more carnal in nature.

Before she returned her attention to the place she most wanted it to be, she noticed a figure standing on the hill just east of the reservoir. A wispy figure, cotton dress billowing in the breeze, with a vast quantity of silver hair.

She lost sight of the woman as Pax carried her through the corridor to his quarters. He laid her across the bed on her stomach, slowly lifting her tunic. He bent and gently kissed her wounded lower back.

"It's healing well, Ash. There won't be more than a faint scar."

"Have I told you how much I love it when you call me that?"

"You have now." He trailed kisses up her back. "Mmmm . . . for a second I thought you were going to say something else," he murmured.

"Like what?"

"I'm not going to tell you. I want the credit for myself."

"Credit?"

"For being the one to say it first. I need to be able to remind you of that every time you get fed up with me being a bastard and threaten to leave."

"You haven't said much of anything yet," she pointed out,

but instead of the teasing tone she was going for, her voice trembled.

She felt his hands at her hips, and he tugged down her pants, slipping them over her thighs and then off. He bent over her again, and she felt him rearranging his own clothing.

Her whole body lit up with anticipation, and she felt him slide slowly between her legs.

"Aaaaah," she sighed as he pushed right up against her, filling her.

He nuzzled the back of her neck. "I figured something out when they took you away from me."

"What's that?" she breathed.

"I love you, Ash. I've known it for a while. I thought I was going crazy."

She smiled. "They're sort of the same thing, I think." Arching her hips against his, she added, "Keep going with your interrogation and I might just confess how I feel about you."

ABOUT THE AUTHOR

An RWA RITA Award finalist and a three-time RWA Golden Heart Award finalist, Sharon Lynn Fisher lives in the Pacific Northwest. She writes books for the geeky at heart—sci-fi flavored stories full of adventure and romance—and battles writerly angst with baked goods, Irish tea, and champagne. Her works include *Ghost Planet* (2012), *The Ophelia Prophecy* (2014), and *Echo 8* (2015).